FOR

CHI

BARBOUR
PUBLISHING

For more information about Christine Lynxwiler, please access the author's Web site at the following Internet address: www.christinelynxwiler.com

Cover Illustration: Donna Nelson

Published by Barbour Publishing, Inc., P.O. Box 719, Uhrichsville, Ohio 44683, www.barbourbooks.com

Our mission is to publish and distribute inspirational products offering exceptional value and biblical encouragement to the masses.

 Member of the
Evangelical Christian
Publishers Association

Printed in the United States of America.

DEDICATION/ACKNOWLEDGMENT

To Kevin—If you could somehow see directly into my heart,
only then would you understand the depth of my love for you.
Thank you for your unwavering love and support.
You're an amazing husband and an incredible daddy.
You're God's man for me and I'm grateful.

A HUGE DEBT OF THANKS TO:

My daughters—Girls, you might think your thoughtful acts
and sacrifices go unnoticed when I'm on deadline, but they don't.
Thank you, thank you, thank you. I'm so proud of both of you.

Susan, for everything.

Jan, Sandy, Annalisa, Georgia Anne, Rach, Suz, Trace, and Candice.
How does someone write a book without critique partners?
I don't want to find out.

Becky, for allowing me the freedom to write the story I needed to write.

Aaron, for your input and encouragement.

Ellen, for sharing your incredible eye for detail with me.

And as always, most of all, the One from whom all blessings flow.
Without You I would be nothing.

CHAPTER 1

Besides Jesus, I've had three real loves in my life. I married the first one, the winter we turned ten, in a Christmas wedding at the top of Snowy Mountain. In exchange for my heart, the sweet, green-eyed boy gave me a pop-top ring. But the sun came out, the snowman preacher melted, and I lost the ring in the slush. After that, my heart remained unscathed for thirteen years, a record I blew when I fell madly in love with a starving artist during my second year in law school. The ring he gave me wasn't made from a pop-top, but it might as well have been when I caught him kissing his old girlfriend the night before our wedding.

Other than a whirlwind summer romance with my best friend's brother—can you say rebound relationship?—I've never even been tempted to risk it all again. Well, technically I guess I risked it all again this year when I ditched law school and inherited a new hometown, my *true* true earthly love—Jingle Bells, Arkansas. Which works perfectly, because how can a town break your heart?

So at twenty-six, I'm done with runaway-bride excitement and planning my life to suit other people. I'm content to live out my days in my favorite place in the world, where the spirit of Christmas lives in our hearts all year long. Yes, that's straight off the Jingle Bells welcome sign out on the main highway. And it's corny. But true.

It's especially true here in my shop—aptly named Forever Christmas. The front is the store section, about fifteen hundred square feet of all things Christmas. But in the back, I have my workshop—just call me Santa—where I paint, sculpt a little, and make ornaments. And upstairs is the three-bedroom apartment, where my grandmother babysat me during most of my childhood. Now it's mine and filled to overflowing with happy memories. Other than wishing I could pay the bills the postman brings every day about this time, who could ask for anything more?

I sift through the mail. Everyone around here still sends out Christmas cards, so this time of year the cards tend to outnumber the bills, which is nice. Today, though, nestled amid the bright colors, a white business envelope catches my eye. It's addressed not to the shop but to me—Kristianna Harrington, Town Council Member—and the return address is Mayor Augustus Harding, City Hall.

In Jingle Bells, we conduct town business with meetings and phone calls, or even a holler down the street, but the United States Postal Service isn't normally involved. Few things are important enough to warrant a stamp. Wouldn't it be nice if Uncle Gus were officially confirming the rumor going around about a new business buying the old Benning Building out on Crystal Lake? The economy has gone downhill since the distribution center closed. Maybe this is the news we've been waiting for.

Propping my hip against the counter, I snag a snowman letter opener from my pen-and-pencil cup and rip open the letter.

Dear Town Council Members:

As you all know, Jingle Bells has been steadily losing tourist trade and employment opportunities since the distribution center closed a year ago. A new opportunity. . .blah, blah, blah. . .Online company Summer Valley Outdoors is interested in acquiring the empty Benning Building and opening their first brick-and-mortar store in our fair town.

Yep. I called that one, didn't I? An early Christmas present for Jingle Bells. "Investor surveys". . .blah, blah, blah. . . His letters are just like his speeches—a lot of words to say a little.

We would do well to set aside sentimentality for the sake of the people we represent and consider their petition to change the name of Jingle Bells to Summer Valley.

Change the name of Jingle Bells?

I sink to the stool at my workbench and stare blindly at the words.

Please let this be an elaborate practical joke.

7

Another examination of the envelope reveals the mayor's official seal beside his name. No one would dare to forge that.

"Kristianna."

I spin the stool around, the letter clutched against my paint smock.

My best friend, Ami Manchester, stands in the doorway of my workshop, holding two steaming coffees. "Girl, you look terrible."

"Thanks," I mutter.

She hurries over to me. "Bad news?"

"The mail came while you were gone." I trade her the letter for one of the coffees, grateful to inhale the calming aroma.

She reads the paper, then looks up at me, her hazel eyes puzzled but reflecting none of the panic currently twisting through me. "Change the name of the town? Has Uncle Gus lost his mind? Why would he even consider such a thing?"

Mayor Augustus Harding isn't blood kin to either of us, but like most Jingle Bells natives, he might as well be. I sigh. Just like with real relatives, I know his weak spot. "Easy enough. He owns that empty building. He probably had a hard time typing this letter for the dollar signs in his eyes." *Can't fight city hall.* The old phrase flits through my mind and hits me like a punch.

"Well, he'll have to sell the building without changing the town name. People won't go along with a crazy plan like this." Ami calmly spoons sugar into her coffee, then holds another spoonful over my cup until I nod for her to dump it in.

"Not if I have anything to say about it." I pick up my phone, run my finger down the ragged list Scotch-taped to the wall, and punch in the number for city hall.

While it rings, Ami retrieves the half-and-half from my tiny fridge and pours creamer in our drinks, then stirs them. I'm amazed by how unrattled she is. I'm a Jingle Bells resident by way of inheritance and love. But she was *born* here. Where's her outrage?

She passes me my doctored coffee. "There's no way people will go for this."

I appreciate her confidence, but as the daughter of two hardball lawyers, I'm also a realist. Money talks. Jingle Bells *has* been hard hit by losing the Benning Distribution Center. Our unemployment rate is atrocious. People are vulnerable.

"Open Monday through Friday," I growl the message aloud and push the OFF button. "Why did I think he'd be there on a Saturday?"

I give the list on the wall another quick scan. Next to the city hall number, I find the words *Augustus Mobile* with a local cell number scribbled beside them in Gran's handwriting. With any luck, he still has the same number. Things change slowly around here.

Usually.

I glance at the hateful letter lying on top of some half-finished Christmas ornaments. The call goes to voice mail, and I slam the phone down. "Let's go."

"Where?"

"To deal with Uncle Gus."

"You going to make him an offer he can't refuse?" Ami says in her best raspy mobster voice.

"Hey, if the concrete shoe fits. . ." I reach for my coat. "Seriously, come on."

"Kristianna, wait." Her voice is soft, but I spin around. "You know this whole name-change thing isn't going to come to anything. Why don't you just wait until Monday? We've got some wedding favors to finish."

"I'll get the favors done. But we have to take care of this." Tears prick my eyelids, but if I've learned one thing from my parents, it's that crying is a weakness. I blink hard. "Now."

She shakes her head. "This is Jingle Bells. It's always been Jingle Bells. It's always going to be Jingle Bells."

When she says that, I feel so stupid. Surely she's right. I raise my shoulders and relax them to try to stop the jitters that are coursing through me. "Maybe so."

"Definitely so." She pushes my cup toward me. "You're just in a no-caffeine haze."

I offer a wobbly grin and take a sip of my coffee. Definitely the best part of waking up today. "Okay, for now the ornaments. Later, Uncle Gus is going down." I sigh and retrieve a snowpeople bride-and-groom ornament from the counter. "What do you think?"

Ami grins, a perfect white smile. A bride smile. "I think you're going to a lot of trouble for me. They're beautiful."

"You know I love doing it. Passing out ornaments to all your wedding guests is such a cool idea." With my paintbrush, I start shading in the details, determined to ignore the uneasiness inside me.

"Way cooler since you're hand making them. Everyone in town will show up for the ceremony just to get a Kristianna original. Especially since you'll be in the wedding party. . ."

Is that doubt I hear? Just because I can't make it down the aisle for my own weddings doesn't mean I'll do something stupid at hers. Does it? "You don't have to butter me up. I already told you I'd make as many as you need." I pause and meet her gaze. "And you know I'll be there."

"Yeah, I know. So what's up with the mistletoe back here?" Ami points toward the little green sprig above the counter.

I laugh. "It's not Christmas without mistletoe, but since no one ever comes back here, I figure I'm pretty safe."

She smiles. "I should have known. You and your relationship safety nets." She ducks her head and touches the back of her hair in a way I recognize.

Something in her tone makes me set the ornament on the work counter. "Yeah?"

"Are you sure you're okay with being my maid of honor?" Her eyes bore through me with the penetrating power of Superman's X-ray vision.

How many more times will we go over this? "Yep." I retrieve the ornament and start painting again.

She snatches a stool from the counter and perches beside me. "You still having. . .the Dream?"

Sigh. So much for her taking the hint. Ever since I caught my first fiancé kissing his ex-girlfriend at the wedding rehearsal, I've had the Dream at least once a month. It didn't go away even when I was engaged briefly to Ami's older brother, Nathan. And it's been more frequent since we mutually broke off our obvious—to everyone but us—rebound engagement. One day, in a weak moment, I told Ami about the Dream—how everything seems perfect until I get halfway to the front of the church; then I turn and sprint back down the aisle. I always wake up out of breath and shaking. And I just had it again a couple of nights ago. "Why yes, Dr. Phil, I am. But I'm ignoring it."

She gives me her best Dr. Phil grin. "And how's that working for you?"

I pretend to spill my coffee on her, but she doesn't even move. "Fine. It's working just fine for me."

She holds up her hands. "Okay, subject dropped. Other than worrying about the Dream, do you really want to be in the wedding?"

"Who else is going to be your maid of honor? Garrett?" The three of us have been best friends since early childhood. But I picture six-foot-two, former-football-player Garrett holding a bouquet and smiling. "Mark's already claimed him as the best man. Besides, he'd look pretty funny in that gorgeous green dress. It would match his eyes perfectly, wouldn't it?"

She gives me the look—the one she uses on her third graders when she wants the truth and she wants it now.

Am I dreading standing by my best friend as she marries the man she loves? No way. Does my crazy recurring dream have me a little paranoid about messing up Ami's wedding? Um, yeah. Is there a small part of me that wishes I was the bride walking down the holly-lined aisle, without reservation, to meet my perfect guy? Oh, come on, I'm human.

But Ami is way more important than silly jealousy or irrational fear. "Are you kidding? We're Lucy and Ethel, Monica and Rachel, Thelma and Louise." When will I ever learn to stop the analogies while I'm ahead? "Okay, forget Thelma and Louise. But do you really think I'd let you get married without me by your side?"

Ami drains her coffee. "*You've* always wanted a Christmas wedding, though. I could have waited until June."

I carefully place the snowcouple on the counter and look at her sparkling eyes. "Yeah, right. The wedding's just a week away, and with every breath you're wishing you were married already."

Her cheeks turn pink. "It's that obvious?"

Only if you're not blind. "Maybe just a little. I've had my chance, Ami. This is your moment."

"You know, now that Garrett's moved back, the two of you might—"

I put my finger to her lips. "Shh. Every few years, you come up with this crazy theory."

"You did marry him once." Ami raises her chin stubbornly.

"We were ten. I hardly think that qualifies for a successful trip down the aisle. Besides, Garrett and I are best friends. Just like you and me. I'm not desperate." Well, not desperate to get married, anyway. If people saw my bank account, they might see why I'm a little desperate about the whole town issue. "If you don't drop this subject, I'll paint a mustache on every snowbride and Garrett can be your maid of honor."

"I just think—"

I raise my paintbrush toward the ornament, and Ami fakes a flinch, then sighs. "Look at the bright side, when you do find the perfect man, you already have a dress."

My wince is not fake. "Two dresses, if we're counting." Although as soon as Garrett shows me how to do more than just buy on eBay, I plan to rectify that. "With my track record, I'd better quit while I'm ahead. Two broken engagements make me quirky. Three would cross over to pathetic." Some things in life I can't do anything about. But in spite of what Ami says, I intend to fix the things I can. I push to my feet and yank off my paint smock. "Let's go."

"Huh?"

I wave to the ornaments. "I'll work around the clock on these, but I have to get this settled today. Right now. Please go with me."

She looks like she wants to argue, but I guess she sees something in my expression that convinces her it's hopeless.

She sighs. "Okay, I'm in. We're off to beard the lion in his den."

I give her a quick hug. "Thanks." I grab my jacket off its hook and toss Ami's to her. "He's not in the office. But that doesn't mean he's untouchable."

"You're going to his house?"

"*We're* going to his house." I push against the double doors that open from my workshop into the store and holler toward the back corner. "Sarah!"

"Yes?" In her midforties, Sarah's a quietly serious woman who has an amazing talent with fabric. Gran rented a corner of Forever Christmas to Sarah for her quilting years ago, and since I'm not an idiot who wants to change things that don't need changing, I kept the arrangement when I became the new proprietor. When she's out, I sell her quilts for her. When I need to be gone, she minds the store for me. It works for both of us.

"I need to go out for a while. Will you watch the store?"

"Is it going to do tricks?"

"Was that a joke?" I mouth to Ami.

"I think so," she mouths back.

"That was a joke," Sarah calls in a wry voice. "I'm a little rusty but thought I'd give it a try."

I laugh. "I like it!"

"I'll be glad to mind the store."

"Thanks."

I drag Ami out of the shop and into the cold air. Gray clouds hang low in the sky today, matching my mood perfectly.

As we walk down the sidewalk, I point at the shop we're passing. "Just think, Blizzard Barbecue would probably have to change to Sandcastle Sandwiches."

Ami gives me a puzzled look.

"If this stupid name change goes through. What do you think

15

they'd call Reindeer Games and Toy Store?" I shake my head. "That's such a cool name."

She sighs.

"Wouldn't you hate for it to become Fun in the Sun Toys?"

"That would be awful."

"Are you being sarcastic? Look over there. I don't even want to think about what Snow Place Like Home Pet Boarding would be renamed. But I bet it wouldn't be pretty."

Ami smiles. "Actually I've always wondered about that name. Doesn't it kind of indicate that you should keep your dog at home instead of leaving it in their kennel?"

I shake my head. "You're missing the principle."

"Because I really don't see this as a possibility."

"Just the idea of it should terrify you."

She doesn't look terrified, but I keep up a running commentary, unable to stop imagining the horrors that would come with the name *Summer Valley*.

I don't shut up until we stand in front of the huge white manor. Each of the four columns is as big around as a good-sized tree. Beautifully filigreed lattice borders the second-story balcony. It feels like we've been transported back to the days of hoopskirts and lemonade on the porch.

"Does the town own this place, or is it personal property?" Ami whispers.

"I'm not really sure. Uncle Gus has been the mayor ever since I can remember. And his daddy was the mayor before him."

"Your drawl seems thicker here."

I nod. "Yours, too."

"I never noticed how huge the house is," Ami says, still whispering. "Remember those watercolor paintings you did of the mansion and the grounds when you were first learning to paint?"

I nod. I still have them in the back of my closet, to be honest.

"You used to want to be married here."

"I had good taste." A new flare of anger raises my voice to normal and gets me back in the real world. "And Uncle Gus should be ashamed. Willing to sell out his heritage—our heritage." I grab her arm. "C'mon."

At the front door, I bypass the doorbell button and grab the handle on the lion's head door knocker, happy to bang it against the door several times. Somehow the loud, hollow knocking suits my mood more than a delicate chime.

Inside the house, we hear a familiar male voice yell, "Where's my jacket?"

"The lion is in his den," I murmur.

A minute later, Mrs. Harding opens the door. "Can I help you?" For every ounce that Uncle Gus is "good ol' boy," Mrs. Harding is "high society." I always thought the phrase "looking down her nose" was just an expression, but she really does it, her beady eyes glinting.

I give her my own glare. "We need to see the mayor."

"I'm sorry, but he's not here," she says, beginning to close the door.

CHAPTER 2

With half of my jean-clad leg uninvited in the mayor's house, I think of my mother and all the lectures she's given me about proper manners. Even in a criminal case, when she goes in with guns blazing—figuratively, of course—she's always polite, however thin the veneer.

I gently push against the door and try to sound courteous but firm. "It's urgent that I see him right now."

Mrs. Harding pulls the door open a little farther, probably to tell me again how he's not home or so I can get my leg out, but I slide my body into the foyer; Ami follows me. I try not to gawk at the vaulted ceiling and spiral oak staircase behind the lady of the manor. I was raised with money, but it's new money, spent on modern art pieces and sleek design. This is the Southern opulence of old money. I can almost smell the jasmine and honeysuckle.

Mrs. Harding's mouth opens and closes, and she narrows her eyes. "I believe I told you he's not home."

Yes, and I never did like to be lied to. "I know better. So unless you want me to—"

"What's going on here?" Uncle Gus's voice booms from behind his wife.

I look up in time to see him recognize me. A variety of emotions flit across his face—surprise, annoyance, the need to appease, and maybe just a little bit of fear. Of course, my sudden Rambo impersonation might have made me imagine that last one.

"Kristianna, what a surprise." No matter how many times I see him, I'm always startled by the mayor's resemblance to Colonel Sanders.

"I bet it is." I wave the letter. "What is this?"

Mrs. Hardy clicks the front door shut, then exits the room without a word, leaving the three of us facing one another.

Uncle Gus folds his arms across his ample stomach and smiles. "Now, kitten, calm down. I think it's fairly self-explanatory, don't you?"

I inhale and feel like a blowfish about to explode. No one but my grandmother has called me "kitten" since I was old enough to wear big girl panties. "Well, Mayor Harding,"—he hates to be called anything but Uncle Gus by the townspeople, I'm convinced, because he thinks the nickname makes him seem trustworthy and kind—"please explain it to me anyway. Exactly who is the Summer Valley corporation?"

"What do you mean?"

"Who owns it? Why do they want Jingle Bells?"

"I have met only a couple of the investors. They're not from around here." He strokes his white goatee. "If the sale goes through, though, there was mention of a nondisclosure agreement."

"Is it someone famous?" Ami asks, speaking for the first time since I pushed our way into the house.

The mayor's face reddens. "I have no idea. But I do know this company is talking about investing millions." When he says "millions," his face scrunches up dramatically. "This is exactly what Jingle Bells needs. Our saving grace."

I snort. "How can it be our saving grace if it destroys us? If this happens, Jingle Bells won't even exist anymore."

"Haven't you ever heard, 'That which we call a rose by any other name would smell as sweet?'"

I glance at Ami. Am I the only one who thinks it's ludicrous that Colonel Sanders is quoting Shakespeare to me? "You're kidding, right?"

He frowns. "I'll have you know I'm quite a fan of the Bard."

"Yes, me, too, but if you'll remember, *Romeo and Juliet* ended tragically." I slip my stocking cap off and stuff it in my jacket pocket. I'm hotheaded enough now as it is. "What if Bill Gates wanted to rename Seattle? Think the residents would be just as happy to live in Gatesville? Somehow I doubt it."

"You really should reconsider going back to law school." He raises his wrist and looks at his Rolex. "Would you look at the time? I have an appointment." He steps to the front door and opens it. "Thanks for stopping by, Kristianna, Ami. We'll see you at the town meeting."

"We'll be there." We walk out the door, but as we reach the gate, I turn back to where he is standing on the porch. "But this name change will never happen."

"Remember, sometimes, 'The needs of the many outweigh the needs of the few.'" He slips back in the house and closes the door.

"*Star Trek II: The Wrath of Khan*," I mutter. "From Shakespeare to Spock in one conversation. He has eclectic tastes, I'll give him that."

"Look who's talking," Ami jokes as we huddle together and walk into the bitter wind. "You recognized the quotes."

"Hey, whose side are you on?"

She tucks her arm in mine. "Always yours. Never doubt it."

Just as we approach the store, Ami pulls me behind the live Christmas tree, the pine branches brushing my jacket. "There's Mark's car. He's probably waiting in your shop."

Is that panic in her eyes? Our very town is threatened, and she's calm; her fiancé comes to visit, and she freaks out. I'm having trouble connecting the dots.

A pine needle pricks my face. "Ouch. And we're hiding behind a tree why?"

"Sorry. One of his friends is with him. I forgot to tell you I told him we'd eat lunch with them."

No doubt, visions of matchmaking dance in Ami's head even as we speak, but after the morning's fiasco, I'm too exhausted to care. "Okay. His roommate from college, right?"

"Yes. But I need to tell you something before you meet him."

I brace myself. "What? Is he five feet tall?" I laugh, but she doesn't. In fact, her face gets redder, so I backtrack. "Not that I would care. . . . It's just that I always seem to end up being escorted by guys who are shorter than I am. Guess that's what I get for being five foot eight." I sigh. "C'mon, Ami, I'm dying here. Cut me some slack. You know I'm not really prejudiced against short guys. It was a joke!"

"I know. It's not that. He's normal height."

"Then what?"

She looks at the Christmas tree branches, then over my shoulder, avoiding my eyes as if she's a doctor trying to figure out how to break the news that I have six weeks left to live.

I gasp. "He's a lawyer? Why didn't you tell me?"

She holds up her hand and stares at me in mock horror. "Don't be mad. You've been on this lawyer rampage for six months. And your case is settled now. You won. Maybe it's time to move on."

Two days after Gran's funeral, I was served with a lawsuit. A tourist claimed she'd tripped on the way out of the store and deserved thousands in pain and suffering. The woman's lawyer, who also happened to be her husband, went for my jugular. I give Ami something I hope resembles a smile. "What is this? Shock therapy for my attorney aversion?"

She shrugs. "Maybe. Your parents are lawyers."

Yes, they are. First and foremost. But even though he didn't understand why I wouldn't let the insurance company pay the fraudulent claim, my father had reluctantly represented me in court.

I give him points for that. My mother, on the other hand. . . Well, it's hard to give her points for much of anything these days. "Wow. All these years and I didn't know."

"Atticus Finch was a lawyer, and you loved him."

I laugh. "Fictional characters don't count." Although the only time I ever really liked the idea of the path my parents had chosen for me was when I read *To Kill a Mockingbird*.

She looks up at the sky, apparently beseeching help from above. "I couldn't tell Mark we needed to choose another groomsman because of this one's profession." Her weak grin says, "How silly is that?"

I can't wait to meet him. I know lawyers. Stuffed shirt, expensive shoes, big mouth. "Good thing he's not the best man."

"So you won't have to walk down the aisle with him? Yeah, that's what I thought."

I shoot her a grin. "Nah, it just wouldn't work. Best man/lawyer—talk about an oxymoron."

"Be nice, Kristianna. He's a Christian. Plus, you'll have to be around him a lot at the wedding. I need you to get along with him."

She's right. After the wedding, I'll never have to see him again. . . unless Ami and Mark renew their vows in fifty years. In which case, maybe I'll have mellowed. "No worries."

"While you're in a 'no worries' mood, you need to think about forgiving your mom, too."

"Don't push it."

She glances at me. "I know the things she said were awful, but when someone apologizes, you have to forgive them. Funerals are an emotional time."

Everything is so black-and-white for Ami. *She* would be a good lawyer. As a Christian, I agree with her theology. But with my mother, it's different. "She didn't mean the apology."

Ami gives an exasperated sigh and pushes ahead toward the door. This verbal ground is almost as familiar as the physical ground we're walking on. I follow more slowly. I can't remember ever being less in the mood for having my match made.

A siren wails in the distance as I walk into the shop to find Sarah and Mark talking to a gorgeous guy in jeans and a button-up flannel shirt.

Ami rushes past me to Mark's waiting arms, and the two steal a fairly discreet kiss.

"Thanks," I say to Sarah.

"If you need to go out again, that's fine. I'm going to be here all day." She retreats to her quilting corner, leaving me to stare at the man in front of me.

Ami turns around, still in Mark's embrace. "Shawn, this is Kristianna Harrington, my best friend and maid of honor."

I nod and give him my best maid of honor smile.

"Kristianna, meet Shawn Webber, Mark's college roommate."

I extend my hand, and he takes it in a firm handshake. "Nice to meet you."

His short dark brown hair stands on end, in a style that looks amazingly unplanned but equally just right. "You, too. Cool weathered look on your storefront sign."

Ami laughs. "Forever Christmas has been around since long before Kristianna was born."

I nod. "I inherited it from my grandmother."

"I see." His gaze flickers over the ornaments and knickknacks, then back to me. "Interesting place."

Does he think I don't know "interesting" is code for: "I can't think of anything nice to say?" I suppress a grin. "How interesting that you think so."

Mark clears his throat. "You ladies want to get some lunch?"

Ami gives me a pleading look. "That sounds good. Okay with you, Kristianna?"

The siren grows louder outside.

"Sure. But it'll have to be the North Pole so we can walk."

"North Pole?" Shawn asks.

Ah, the fun we can have with a nonnative in our midst. "Yes, it's a short walk to the North Pole from here. The North Pole Café, that is."

"I should have known."

Is that a grimace? I shoot Mark a look to let him know what I think about his friend, but he's too busy staring soulfully into Ami's eyes. I cut my gaze back to Shawn. "Ever tried a polar bear burrito?"

"No, but I've been craving some fried penguin tenders. Lead the way."

Mark snorts, and I'm pretty sure Benedict Ami giggles.

Sigh. So, he's not an easy target. "Anyway, the fire engines will make it hard to drive."

"There's a fire?" Shawn steps toward the window. The red fire trucks are parked around Mark's car and mine, effectively blocking us in.

"Mr. Pletka owns the laundry and dry cleaners. When he lived in Czechoslovakia, his apartment burned. He smells smoke occasionally."

"And sees it sometimes, too," Ami adds.

Mark glances out the window at the commotion. "At least once a week."

"And the fire trucks come every time?" Shawn's tone indicates he thinks we're playing some elaborate practical joke on him, that maybe the whole polar bear–burrito thing was just a lead-in.

We nod.

"Doesn't that seem a little ridiculous?"

I bristle, but Mark and Ami just laugh. "Welcome to Jingle Bells, man," Mark says and claps his friend on the back as they head for the door.

I double back to make sure Sarah really doesn't mind watching the store. When I get outside, they're ahead of me on the sidewalk, discussing the fire department's priorities. I clutch my coat against the wind and throw a wave to where Mr. Pletka and the firemen are sniffing the air, then jog to catch up with the others.

"Candy-cane parking meters?" Shawn is saying as I join them.

"So?" After the letter, I feel defensive of Jingle Bells. "Tourists love them. And the revenue helps pay for the town upkeep."

"Yeah." Ami's eyes are dancing, and I know what's coming. Conveniently, she doesn't notice the "cut" motion I'm making with my hand across my neck. "Kristianna is a big fan of the parking meters. She doesn't bother actually putting coins in them, though. She's a bit of a collector."

"Collector?" Shawn looks at me curiously. I hope he thinks my red face is from the wind. "You collect parking meters?"

Mark guffaws. "Not exactly."

Ami laughs, too. "Parking tickets. She gets them every day. Stuffs them in an envelope and just sends a check at the end of the month."

Great! I've gone from living in a town full of eccentric characters to being one of them. "My apartment is above the shop. And there's no other place to park. I'm trying to work out a deal with the town council. . . ."

"Which shouldn't be so hard since you're a council member," Ami chimes in again.

Where did her loyalty go? She's airing our dirty laundry—okay, *my* dirty laundry—in front of this. . .lawyer. Would Ethel do that to Lucy? I don't think so.

She and Mark have forgotten the whole thing and are walking arm in arm in their own little world. I sneak a sideways glance at Shawn. He's smiling. As a matter of fact, I'm almost positive that's a chuckle.

I cross my arms in front of me and hurry past him into the

North Pole Café. The smell of french fries and cheeseburgers mellows me, until Shawn speaks again.

"Where's the fire?" he murmurs.

"Didn't you hear? False alarm." I skid to a stop inside the busy restaurant. No empty tables—just one cozy booth in the corner.

"What about that booth?" Ami offers from behind me.

I ignore her. "Look. Four empty stools at the counter." I nod toward where Rosemary, her Santa hat askew, is ringing up orders.

"Come on," Ami grabs my arm and heads toward the booth. If she thinks I'm cozying up to—

Before I can complete that thought, she drags me into one side of the booth beside her, making up for the whole parking-ticket betrayal. Mark and Shawn slide into the seat across from us and grab menus.

"What's good?" Shawn asks the table in general.

"Everything," Ami and I chorus.

Mark shrugs. "When they're right, they're right. Nobody beats Geraldine's cooking."

After we order, Ami gasps and bounces up and down. "I just remembered. Tell Mark about the letter."

"Oh." I'm strangely more reluctant to air our town's dirty laundry in front of Shawn than I was my own. I thoughtfully examine the green wreath that's been painted on the window. "It was nothing."

"Nothing?" Ami does indignant really well. "Some crazy company wants to change the name of Jingle Bells to Summer. . .something."

Mark spews tea from his mouth.

Ami leans across the table and beats him on the back. "I know. I couldn't believe it, either."

Shawn looks at us like we're Larry, Moe, and Curly.

"Never gonna happen." I stand up to get some lemon for my tea, effectively ending the floor show.

An hour later, we've finished our lunch and had some good conversation, mostly about the wedding, and Shawn's been really nice.

Ami and Mark excuse themselves to speak to the florist at the table next to us. And I'm left alone with a silent Shawn—probably afraid to say anything in case I take offense. Guilt settles uncomfortably in my stomach.

Gran would be ashamed of me. She would have never judged someone based on his or her profession.

"So, what's your specialty?" *I'm trying, Gran.*

A smile flickers across his face. That rascal knows how hard this is for me. I bet Mark warned him how I feel about lawyers. "I just graduated from U of A. I'm doing some temp work right now until I pass the bar and find a position."

Okay, so there's hope for him. Maybe he won't pass the bar. Who knows? Something that on the surface would seem bad could be good and lead him down a whole different path. A much less litigious one.

"Mark said—," he says.

Just as I say, "Ami mentioned—"

We laugh. I motion him to go ahead.

"Mark said you went to law school."

"Yes, well, not by choice. My parents are lawyers. I found it hard to get off that particular speeding train."

"Why quit in your third year, though? You were so close. And I'm sure your grades were good."

At his words, I remember the day after Christmas last year when Gran told me she was dying. I'd never even considered going back to law school. Not as long as she needed me. Then after. . .I counted my blessings to have escaped. But I'm not going to share that with this man, no matter how interested he seems. I shrug. "It wasn't what I wanted to do. So, Ami said you're living in Little Rock?"

He stares out the window. "Actually, I'm in the middle of relocating here."

No way. "Here? To Jingle Bells?"

He raises an eyebrow. "Is this the part where you tell me this town isn't big enough for the both of us?"

I laugh. I can't help it. "Are you sure you can tolerate the fire trucks and the candy-cane parking meters?"

He fiddles with the sugar packets, then flashes me a grin. "It's amazing what you can put up with when you cut your cost of living by 75 percent."

That's logical, but there's more. I can feel it. And eventually I'll figure it out. In the meantime, never let it be said that I can't be gracious when the need arises. "Well then, let me be the first to say, 'Welcome to Jingle Bells.'"

CHAPTER 3

Hanging out at places like Candy Cane Lanes is one of the joys of living in Jingle Bells. Where else can you roll a shiny red bowling ball and knock down red and white striped pins? Unless you're me. Then you can just watch your shiny red bowling ball plop into the nondescript gutter over and over. Funny thing about gutters—they look the same everywhere.

"Kristianna, you're up." I have no idea how I got talked into this whole bowling team misadventure. One night a few months ago, right after Garrett moved back to Jingle Bells, the three of us were discussing all the things we could do with all of us living in town. Since we love Candy Cane Lanes, one item on the list was we could be in a bowling club together. I can't remember which one of them had the idea. Probably Garrett, since he loves bowling. Both of them know that even though I like it I'm a terrible bowler, so either way, it was ridiculous. But here I am.

Step, step, step. Release.

My ball starts out straight, but about halfway down the lane, it veers to the right. Same as always. Amazing how my bowling mimics my life. Everything seemed to be looking up with rumors of a big business coming to town. I was on the straight path to making the store successful again and not having to worry about being forced back into law school. But then, at the last minute, the gutter.

I immediately squeeze my eyes shut, but the groans behind me confirm this is not one of those rare lucky times when I knock down two or three peppermint-stick pins.

By the time I turn around, they've all composed their faces.

"You'll get 'em this time." This laid-back encouragement came from Mark, who is so competitive he'd challenge Michael Jordan to a free throw match.

I retrieve my ball and give it another try. Step, step, step. Release. Gutter. Repeat.

"Sorry, guys." I slump down in the chair between Ami and Garrett and lean my head against the half wall behind me. Some seventies rock song I can't identify blasts from the speakers above.

Garrett hands me a water bottle, and a grin spreads across his face. "Not that you worked up a sweat."

I accept the drink and shoot him a mock glare. It's amazing the way we've picked up our easy friendship again. When his mother remarried and moved away while Garrett was in college, we lost touch. He found out through the grapevine about Gran's death, and we started e-mailing. Nobody was more excited than Ami and me when he decided to move back to Jingle Bells shortly afterward.

"C'mon, sport, you know I'm kidding."

"And you know who got me into this." I deepen my voice. " 'C'mon, sport, it's just a bowling club, not a league. Nobody cares how well you bowl. It'll be fun.' "

He shrugs, but his easy grin never leaves. "What can I say? I love to bowl."

So it was he who suggested the bowling team. Figures. "I love oil painting, too, but I didn't sign us up to be on a team together."

His brow furrows with mock seriousness. "They have oil painting teams?"

"You know what I mean."

"You're mad because I'm not on your painting team?"

I don't want to, but I laugh.

Just a small laugh, a chuckle really, but enough that he makes an imaginary tally in the air. "One for me."

I don't even remember how many years ago we started trying to make each other laugh at odd times. Another thing we picked up easily with his return. Unfortunately, like bowling, he's much better at it than I am. He has a smile that makes everything seem like it's going to be okay. The other team is a group of retired elementary teachers in navy blue bowling shirts with ABC and 123 appliquéd on them. Their weakest bowler, who also looks to be the longest retired, takes down four pins, and her teammates excitedly congratulate her.

Mark picks up a spare, and we cheer.

"Not bad for an accountant!" Garrett calls.

Everyone laughs. The blaring rock song has been replaced by Jim Croce's "Time in a Bottle," and for a minute, I remember why I went along with this harebrained idea. Even with the uncertainty of the future, I feel safe and content with these people.

Ami isn't as strong a bowler as the guys, but she manages to add seven to her score.

"Wish me luck," Garrett says as he pushes to his feet.

"Like you need it," I mutter.

He just grins and bowls another perfect strike. Mark and Ami go wild. I make a "rah, rah" motion with my hand.

Thanks to me, we lose, but true to what Garrett said, nobody seems to care.

By the time we move to a round table in the snack bar above the lanes for our customary nachos and root beer, Ami is scrutinizing Garrett's hair.

"You are going to get that mop cut in time for the wedding, aren't you?" Ami asks.

He reaches back and grabs his blondish brown curls.

I take a sip of my root beer and smirk. "Afraid she's got shears in her purse?"

"With her, you never know."

"She does like to micromanage, doesn't she?" I turn to Garrett like Ami isn't here. "You should have heard her at the North Pole the other day, harassing poor Barry Stewart about the flowers."

"I was not harassing—Hey! No fair ganging up on me." Ami

puts her hand on Mark's arm. "Mark, you're not going to let them talk about me like that, are you?"

He laughs. "No way I'd get between you three."

"Wise man." I relax in my chair. "I think we'll keep you." For a second, fear clutches my stomach. What if I can't keep him? What if I can't keep any of them? When Gran decided to leave me the store, she knew it wasn't breaking even, but we'd both counted on this rumored new business coming to make that happen. Now, the new business is the enemy instead of the savior, and it feels like I'm rolling one gutter ball after another.

Garrett looks over at me, apparently reading my expression correctly. "Hey, sport. Things not going any better at the store?"

I shake my head. "Nope. Christmas rush? More like a Christmas plod at my place." I shrug when I see the concern on their faces. "But right now I have to think about keeping the town."

Garrett frowns. "Maybe—"

A deep voice behind us interrupts. "Is this a private party, or can anybody join?"

I turn to see Shawn Webber.

Mark jumps to his feet. "Glad you made it, man." To us, he says, "I told Shawn to drop by and check out the lanes." He waves an arm at the bowling lanes. "What do you think?"

Shawn looks over at the candy-cane motif. "Jingle all the way," he intones dryly.

Surely he's not standing in a perfectly adorable bowling alley with two Jingle Bells natives and two happy transplants and being sarcastic about our town. Is he?

Maybe I'm overreacting, because Garrett has apparently already met Shawn and seems genuinely glad to see him. They chat for a minute; then Shawn takes the only empty seat. Beside me.

For a few seconds, the table is quiet.

"Shawn's moving here," I announce. Not sure why. I always have an urge to fill in silence. Maybe because when I was growing up, there was so much silence to fill at my house. Jared and Emily Harrington communicated on a need-to-know basis, and I rarely ever reached that level.

Garrett smiles at Shawn. "Do you bowl?"

"Looking to replace me?" I growl under my breath.

"Why in the world would you think that?" His green eyes widen with mock innocence. "I was just curious."

"Sure."

"Actually I do bowl," Shawn volunteers.

Short of snapping, "Who cares?" which would undoubtedly prove that I do, I have nothing to say.

But Garrett does. He starts talking bowling with Shawn. After a minute, I consider offering either to trade seats with one of them or allow myself to be decapitated so that they can quit leaning around me. Mark and Ami have slipped back into couples' world, and I figure Garrett knows exactly how I feel about lawyers, so he's doing me a favor. I scoot my chair back and silently prepare my argument for the town meeting. I need to be passionate but not fanatical. Persuasive but not with the emotion all polished out.

When I zone back in, Ami is saying, "Shawn, if you really want to see Jingle Bells the way it's meant to be seen, you have to get Kristianna to show you around."

I blink at Ami. Have I wandered into Stepford Wives' world? *I thought you were my friend.*

"Sounds great." Shawn smiles at me, and the dimple in his chin deepens. At least he didn't hem and haw and stammer around. "You busy Friday night?"

Danger, Will Robinson, Danger. Friday night is too much like a date. "Actually if you want to see the town, it's better to do that in the daytime."

"Yes, I did notice the crank handles sticking up from the sidewalks."

He is so not being sarcastic about my town again. I open my mouth to tell him to forget it.

But he speaks first. "Saturday afternoon, then. I'll be there when you close at four."

He knows my store hours. How? Why? I shoot a pleading look at my best friends. "Y'all want to come?"

"Can't," Ami says, entwining her fingers with Mark's. "We're spending the day with Mark's parents."

"I'm gonna have to pass, sport." Garrett slaps me on the shoulder as if I were a football buddy. "I'm setting up an online bookstore for Scott, and I promised I'd have a dummy ready for him to look at by Saturday afternoon."

I consider waving my arms in the air. Want a dummy for him to look at? I'm the obvious choice. I should have cut and run as soon as Shawn showed up.

"FRUITCAKE FIVE AND DIME—WHERE EVERYTHING'S A DOLLAR?" Shawn reads the sign aloud, then turns to stare at me. "This makes sense to you?"

"Perfect sense." I knew this tour was a bad idea. "It used to be the Five and Dime, but who could sell at those prices these days?"

"So why not just change the name?"

What is it with people thinking names are just expendable? I cross my arms in front of my chest. "It wouldn't be the Five and Dime if they change the name, now would it?"

He shrugs. "Whatever you say." He points over to Rudolf's. "Want to get a bite to eat?"

"I don't know. Are you going to make fun of the big red nose on top of the cash register?"

"Probably." His dimple flashes. "But my brother's a chef, so I always check out the local food when I go somewhere new."

An hour later, we've hit most of the food joints in town. Sounds fun, I know. But I'm like the royal taster out of control. I try it all—of course—in order to recommend the best culinary delights for our guest. And he nibbles daintily at those. Good thing we're not a couple. A few dates and we could give Jack Sprat and his wife a run for their money.

By the time the funnel cake is half gone, I've forgotten that I didn't want to show Shawn around town. I pass the flimsy paper plate to him. "I can't eat another bite."

"Are you quite sure?" He pinches the plate between his forefinger and thumb as if it were a particularly nasty Exhibit A.

I consider holding my stomach and moaning, but I just nod. "Positive."

I think my expression gives me away, because Shawn frowns. "Does the phrase 'trans fat' mean anything to you?"

I check out my reflection in the Deck the Halls Home Decor window and dust the powdered sugar off my short green jacket. "You're not going to sue Santa's Snack Shack for using the wrong oil, are you?"

Shawn meets my gaze in the glass. "I sense some latent lawyer animosity here."

"Shawn, you're so wrong." I can't hold back the grin. "There's nothing latent here."

He turns to look at me, then laughs.

At least he can take a joke. Sort of a joke, anyway. I nod toward the plate in his hand. "You didn't try the funnel cake."

"You didn't save me any powdered sugar."

Oops. "Powdered sugar is way overrated."

He raises an eyebrow. I think he's onto me.

"I'm serious. Real men eat it plain."

He pinches off a bit and pops it in his mouth. "Not terrible." He smiles. "It'd be better with sugar, though."

I motion toward Santa's Snack Shop. "Want me to go—"

"No. There will be other sweet things."

Yeah, maybe, but by now, I'm looking for any place that doesn't have food. "Want to go in Deck the Halls?" I ask, veering toward the front door.

"Okay. You're the guide." Shawn drops the paper plate in the Santa hat trash can and follows me through the doorway into the warm shop. It's divided into two halves. One side features room displays with tastefully arranged furniture and accessories. The other side contains several aisles of household items—towels, sheets, rugs, dishes, and kitchen gadgets—and of course, a huge section of Christmas decorations.

There are maybe five other shoppers in the whole store, but less than thirty seconds after we enter, a loud siren goes off, and then a creepy-sounding Santa voice blasts out from behind us, "Ho, ho, ho. Ho, ho, ho." I jump even though I knew it was coming. A red and white light flashes one aisle over. "Attention shoppers, it's time for your Deck the Halls five-minute special on our stainless steel teakettles."

I tug on Shawn's sleeve. "C'mon, let's go."

He follows me to the next aisle and glances around. "You've got to be kidding. Is there a hidden camera?"

"You don't like it?" I can't stop grinning. The five-minute special always does that to me.

Shawn shrugs. "It's a little offbeat, but that's what I expected when I decided to move here, I guess." He picks up the display kettle and runs his hand over it thoughtfully. "I lose points for not liking the ho-ho-ho surprise, don't I?"

It's going to take some time to get used to him, but I'm having fun. And it's kind of cool that he cares about "losing points" with me. "Who's keeping score? I'm just showing you around town." I snag a box and tuck it under my arm. "And getting a good deal at the same time." As we approach the cash register, I glance at him over my shoulder. "Besides, if I were keeping score, you'd gain points for being so honest."

I feel an honest lawyer joke coming on, but I force it down. A few minutes later, I even invite him to the Come One, Come All Christmas Dinner at my house. If *I'm* honest, I'm not thinking of him as a "lawyer" anymore.

CHAPTER 4

So how did it go with Shawn?" Ami asks as we walk toward city hall.

"Fine."

"Fine fine? Or just fine?"

I pull my hood up. "Ames, you're the only person I know who can get so much meaning out of one word."

"Stop stalling and answer the question." Ami waves at Mrs. Bright as we pass her house.

"Yes, Your Honor. Hi, Mrs. Bright," I call. When we're out of earshot, I say, "Hey, have you ever noticed that Mrs. Bright sits out on her porch year-round?"

Ami pulls my hood back and peers at me. "Ohh, it must have gone really well. You've moved beyond stalling to distraction."

She knows me too well. "It was fun."

"That's a nice variation on 'fine.' You got along well?"

"I think we might be getting together again. Oh, and I invited him to the Christmas Dinner."

"You invited him to the Island of Misfit Toys? Hmm. . .sounds promising."

"The more, the merrier. Especially if people have nowhere else to go." City hall is straight ahead. I put my hand to my stomach. "Butterflies."

Ami jerks her head to look at me. "Oh. About the meeting—do you have a speech?"

"No. I was going for impromptu but impassioned." My stomach clenches. The butterflies are rioting. "Not preparing a speech seemed like a good idea at the time."

"I don't think you're going to have to worry too much. Who's going to want to change the town name?"

"Good point." But I can name ten families who are still suffering from the distribution center closing. And those are just the ones I know very well. What will they be willing to sacrifice for a paycheck?

As soon as we are in the door, Mark and Garrett motion from the back row, and Ami gives my arm a squeeze. "Knock 'em dead." She hurries over to sit between her fiancé and Garrett.

I start up the aisle, and the first person I notice is Jack Feeney. As an "ace reporter"—his words, not mine, trust me—he thinks himself above the monthly arguments about zoning issues and fences erected too close to boundary lines. But the press does always have to be notified of our meeting agenda, so I'm not surprised to see him here tonight. At twenty-five, Jack thinks his journalism degree from the local community college and his tell-all reporting style are going to get him world acclaim.

I tap the bill of Jack's baseball cap as I pass where he's slumped in a red plastic chair, chewing on his pen. "What's wrong, Jack? Couldn't find a runaway-bride story to keep you busy today?" After a year, at least I can finally joke about his break-into-journalism piece. No small feat since I was the subject.

He straightens and shoots me a rueful grin. "Believe it or not, I didn't want to miss the excitement."

Right after Gran died last June and I moved into the apartment over the shop, I allowed my sentimental nostalgic self to be suckered in to filling the town council position my grandmother had left vacant. The other council members made many promises to me, and though excitement was one of them, "exciting" still hasn't put in an appearance.

I have a feeling that's going to change today. I glance over the larger-than-average crowd. There must be at least a hundred people packed into the folding chairs.

I nod to Jack and move on down the aisle, greeting the regulars. "Sergeant Montrose, Birdie."

Our favorite policeman gives me an almost stern nod. He takes his job very seriously.

Next to him, his wife's sweet face lights up. "Honey, I haven't seen you in a while. I have to get downtown next week and pick up a few things, though, so I'll drop by."

"Okay, Birdie. I'll be watching for you." Truer words were

never spoken. I love her, but Birdie Montrose has a terrible habit of forgetting to pay for the things she "picks up." We merchants have a special phone tree we activate when she's downtown so we can all hide the valuables. I'd hate to think of what it would be like to have to call Sergeant Monty to come arrest his wife for shoplifting.

When I near the front row, my gaze falls on three middle-aged men in suits sitting in the center, with a flip chart balanced between them. Summer Valley Outdoors has come prepared. I should have written a speech.

"You planning to join us today, Kristianna?" Uncle Gus hollers out from the front.

"I wouldn't miss it," I call, hoping he recognizes the challenge in my voice, and make my way to the stage, where the other town council members greet me.

Scott McAdams pushes his thick glasses up on his nose and leans toward me, clutching his book to his chest. "Did I hear Birdie say she was coming downtown next week?" he whispers.

I nod. Scott owns the Cricket on the Hearth Bookstore, two doors down from my Christmas shop. He's a bit of a hermit, but if we need him, we can usually find him hiding behind a bookshelf, reading.

"You'll call me when she leaves your place?"

I cross my heart with my finger. "I promise."

Dottie Wells, the town librarian and another council member, waggles her fingers at me. The fourth councilman, John Stone, nods.

My anxiety melts away. These people are not going to let anyone change the name of our town. We're a team, a family. Give it your best shot, mister. After five minutes of discussion, this topic will be shelved, and we can move on to more pressing topics—like how to boost our economy *without* selling out.

We start with old business, which consists of how much—or in this case, how little—money the fall festival made last month. When that's done, Uncle Gus stands and motions dramatically toward the audience with his cane. Funny, you never see him with that cane except at town meetings and public appearances. "Sometimes opportunity comes knocking when you least expect it." He reaches over and tap, tap, taps on the hardwood stage floor. "Such is the case with the matter on the table tonight. Jingle Bells has an unexpected opportunity for positive growth. A revival, if you will. Jobs for your family members and substantially increased tourist traffic for those of you who own your own shops in town. It's a win-win situation."

Leave it to Uncle Gus to make it sound like we're being offered the chance of a lifetime instead of having our heritage stripped away by a corporate bully. I clear my throat and glare at him.

He motions to the balding man in the middle. "Frank."

The man grabs the flip chart and saunters up to the stage.

Dottie and Scott frown. Two for my side. I try to read John's expression, but he keeps his attention focused on the newcomer, his face inscrutable.

Uncle Gus nods to the man beside him. "I'm going to turn the floor over to our visitor, Frank Johnson with Summer Valley Outdoors."

For the next fifteen minutes, Frank shows us graph after graph of his company's growth and projections. I'm fighting to keep my eyes open when he says, "With these figures from our online company in mind, we're proposing to buy the empty Benning Building on the outskirts of town. We'll use half of it as a warehouse and open our first brick-and-mortar store in the other half. Numerous employees will be hired in both areas."

He continues to talk, but the buzzing from the audience makes it difficult to hear him. So he raises his voice a notch. "Surveys have shown, though, that the store will be more profitable if it is located in a town that shares its name. And that, ladies and gentlemen of the city council and citizens of Jingle Bells, is the reason it would be beneficial to everyone to change the name of this lovely city to Summer Valley."

Hearing the words spoken aloud propels me to my feet. "Objection!"

"Kristianna, this isn't a courtroom." Uncle Gus sounds wryly amused. "But by all means, speak your mind."

"Um, well. . ." Why didn't I come up with a speech ahead of time? I was forewarned, but instead of being forearmed, I'm just scattered. "We've always been Jingle Bells. Everyone is used to the name. It's crazy to think about changing it." Wow. Good argument. After three years of law school, this is the best I can do? My parents should seriously quit trying to force me to go back.

"I hardly think 'what was good enough for our ancestors is good enough for us' is the progressive attitude your city wants." Frank's pompous retort actually clears the fog for me.

"You can't change the name of Jingle Bells for a business deal." I find my pleasant, but firm, voice. Finally. "This isn't a backward town against growth and progress. I'm sure we'd be fortunate to join forces with a company as successful as yours appears to be. But not if changing the name is a stipulation. We love our town, and that includes its name and all its eccentricities. We can work together." I hold up my hands as if framing a sign. "SUMMER VALLEY OUTDOORS—LOCATED IN THE CHARMING TOWN OF JINGLE BELLS." I cross my arms in front of me. "Or you can take your business elsewhere."

As I sit down, loud applause breaks out. My legs feel like noodles, but I'm proud of myself and, most of all, proud of my fellow townspeople.

Apparently unaffected by the negative response, Frank speaks again as soon as the noise dies down. "Our studies show that if the store is in an actual town named Summer Valley, it would be more appealing to the buying public. Therefore, I'm afraid my client doesn't see this point as negotiable." He waves his hand over the buzzing crowd like he's shushing a crying infant. "No one expects you to make the decision today. According to your town laws, we need a petition with a thousand signatures on it supporting the renaming process in order to get it on the ballot and get you on the road to a prosperous future. But remember, 'a rose by any other name. . .'"

I'm starting to hate Shakespeare.

"We have a hundred signatures so far."

People turn to look at their neighbors. I'm sure they're wondering who, exactly, were the traitors who signed that petition.

"One of your newest residents has agreed to come on board with us. He'll be collecting signatures, ready to answer any questions you have about the proposed name change. He told me earlier that he's already grown to care about this town just in the short time he's been here, so if he approaches you, hear him out, please." He motions to someone halfway back on the left side.

My mouth drops open as the man stands and nods.

"Ladies and gentlemen, I'd like to introduce you to your new neighbor and Summer Valley Outdoors' first local employee, attorney Shawn Webber."

CHAPTER 5

As soon as the meeting is adjourned, I blindly push my way through the angry mob gathered around Uncle Gus and rush to the back of the room to confront Mark.

Ami beats me to it, though. Her hazel eyes glitter with anger. "How could you not tell me?" she demands, hands on her hips.

Mark takes a step back and winces. "I'm sorry. I wanted to. But this whole thing..." He glances at me, then quickly over at Garrett. "It's complicated."

"Ames, cut him some slack. Maybe he just didn't want y'all to hate his friend before you had a chance to get to know him," Garrett says softly.

I narrow my eyes at Garrett. "So Ami and I are that quick to judge people?"

Garrett snorts. "You didn't even want to speak to Shawn because he was a lawyer and you've had a bad year with attorneys. What if you'd known about this?"

"I . . ." There's nothing I can say to that. I stare at Mark's white face. He can't stand to fight with Ami, and we all know it. I touch Ami's arm. "Garrett's right, hon. Mark was in a terrible situation. Shawn's an old friend."

Mark reaches for Ami's hand. "I'm sorry."

A smile teases the corner of her mouth. "Forgiven. But no more secrets." She hugs him tightly.

Garrett winks at me over their embrace. "Good job," he mouths.

Mark turns to me with his arm tucked around Ami. "We okay?"

I nod. "I'm going to fight to save our town, but I don't plan on losing any friends in the process."

"So you'll be civil to Shawn?" Mark asks, looking across the room to where Shawn smiles tentatively in our direction.

"At least until after the wedding."

Thankfully, I haven't seen Shawn in the two days since the meeting, or I don't know if I would have been able to keep my promise to Mark. The more I think about the town-name fiasco, the madder I get.

I glance at the notepad beside the cash register where I've been writing the words *Summer Valley*, then marking it out over and over. Who is Summer Valley Outdoors to come into a place they know nothing about and try to rename us?

My obsession with this is overshadowing my excitement about Ami's wedding. Even my love of all things Christmas can't keep my mind off the town meeting. If only I had customers, maybe that would do it. But other than a browsing honeymoon couple, there's been no one all morning.

The door chime rings, and I look up with a smile. Talk about the power of positive thinking. A teenage boy stands there, a big cellophane-wrapped basket in his hands. "Kristianna Harrington?"

I nod.

"This is for you."

"For me?" I take the wicker basket and set it on the counter by the cash register. "Who from?"

He shrugs. "I just got paid to deliver it." He's gone before I can press him.

The crackle of the yellow cellophane drowns out the background Christmas music that plays year-round in my shop. I drop the plastic to the floor and sink to a stool to examine my surprise. A plush, vibrant-colored beach towel is rolled up beside a pair of flip-flops and a huge bottle of suntan lotion. A very weird early Christmas present? I fumble for the envelope hanging from the handle and pull out a typewritten note.

Kristianna,

If Jingle Bells dies with its name intact, is that a victory? Sometimes our hearts can't see clearly what is right before us. If you could open your mind to change, you might be amazed by the view.

No signature, of course. But it couldn't have been any plainer if it said, "Summer Valley Outdoors a.k.a. Shawn Webber." My heart pounds as I fold the letter and put it back in the envelope.

I hate to admit that Jingle Bells needs Summer Valley Outdoors, but the truth is, tourist trade gets less every year. We need something to turn the tide. *I* need something. But I have to think, too. If Jingle Bells lives and loses the name, is that acceptable? I guess my mind is closed, thank you very much, because considering our whole tourist trade is based on Christmas, I don't see how that will work.

Still thinking about the words of the note, I absently lift a corner of the beach towel. Two paperbacks, both titles I've been anxious to read, are nestled behind the towel. Shawn Webber has been doing his research. I need to tell him not to waste his time.

Ami rubs her mittened hands together and leans forward to look down the street. "I always thought that on the morning of the wedding the bride was supposed to soak in a hot tub, then have her hair and nails done. Maybe I should have asked Jill to be my maid of honor."

I step around a man holding his toddler on his shoulders and take my place beside her. "You know very well that we have eleven o'clock appointments at Angel Hair and Nails."

She blows out a visible breath—our shorthand for "see how cold it is"—and stamps her feet. "Nowhere in the bride's creed does it say anything about standing on a street corner in freezing temperatures waiting for a marching band."

"You must have been skimming. It has to be in there. Besides, you know you weren't going to skip the Christmas Parade after all these years of perfect attendance." Bad enough that she'll miss the festival next week. I guess it's only logical that a honeymoon takes precedence over hot cocoa, carolers, and a live nativity, but I'll still miss her.

"You've got a point. Oh"—her face lights up—"remember that year you, Garrett, and I had chicken pox, and your grandmother made a cozy place for us to watch the parade from her balcony? That was the best parade ever."

"How could I forget? She made Dad carry pillows and blankets out, and Mother kept muttering that Gran needed to get on meds quick to stave off the madness."

"But then your gran fixed beef fajitas for supper and everybody quit fighting."

I smile. "Mother loves fajitas. Gran always knew how to make everything all right."

"She'd hate what's going on between you and your mom now."

My smile fades. Ami has an amazing bond with her mother. She doesn't understand the twisty-curvy maze that is my maternal relationship. "I can't help that. To me, forgiving Mother would be a betrayal of everything Gran held dear." Even standing in the noisy, pushing parade crowd, I can hear Mother ranting at me about how hard they've worked to overcome Dad's past, to bring the Harrington name back to meaning something. I can see the fury in her eyes when she realizes I'm not going to sell the shop and apartment. And that I'm not going back to law school.

"If only you'd—" Ami's eyes widen. "Oh no. It's Mark." She

grabs me and turns us both in the opposite direction.

In spite of her bizarre behavior, I'm grateful for the distraction. "Since when does your beloved fiancé's presence instill sheer horror in you?"

"You know it's bad luck for him to see me the day of the wedding."

"God makes our luck."

She nods and bites her lip.

I understand tradition, so I grab the red ski mask out of my overcoat pocket.

"I know you're right, but still I'd rather—"

I slide the mask down over her face while she's still talking.

She gives a muffled laugh through the tiny mouth hole. "Perfect."

"I should have known you two would be here," Mark's voice booms from behind us.

"Two? Who two?" I turn with a playful grin that falters when I see Shawn with him, probably here to drum up signatures for his petition. "Mark, you know the groom isn't supposed to see the bride before the wedding." Wink, wink.

He stares at me, then at Ami's back. "Oh."

"So. . ." I drawl, "what would Ami be doing out here in broad daylight where you might see her?"

"Oh. In that case maybe you and your fascinating red-capped friend would like to keep us lonely bachelors company." Mark may be a little slow on the uptake sometimes, but when he catches on, he plays along real good.

Ami steps backward squarely on Mark's foot.

"Ouch!" He grabs his shoe. "Your friend has a mean streak."

"A mile wide, I'm afraid. But this is a public street corner, so if y'all want to watch the parade from here, you're welcome to." I concentrate on ignoring Shawn's incredulous look. Wonder if I could get away with stepping on *his* foot.

"I can't breathe in this," Ami hisses next to my ear.

"Take it off," I hiss back.

"No. We have to go."

Could I look any more idiotic? Well, maybe if I had a red ski mask on. So I turn to Mark again, ignoring Shawn. . .again. "On second thought, we have to get going. Say hello to the clowns for us." The other ones, I should have said.

"Are you sure? We can leave." The concern in Mark's voice makes my heart melt. He may not completely understand Ami. . . . Who am I kidding? I don't even completely understand Ami. But he wants to make her happy.

"No, we're good. Thanks, though."

I lead Ami away, but while we're still in earshot, I hear Shawn say the word "crazy." I'm not sure if he means Ami and me or the town, but either way, I'm offended.

As soon as we're out of sight, Ami yanks the ski mask off and gasps for air. "I never could stand these things." She takes a couple of more deep breaths. "That was our street corner, and the parade's about to start. Now what are we going to do?"

I glance around for a place where we can see but not be seen— then it hits me. "Come on, Juliet, our balcony awaits."

CHAPTER 6

Ten minutes later, we're tucked into my balcony chairs with warm blankets.

Ami raises her mug of hot chocolate toward me. "Here's to your brilliance. This is way better than the street corner."

I look down at the marching band. "Yeah, we should have made this a tradition a long time ago."

"Plus we can see Mark from here. And Shawn."

I lean forward. She's right. "Yep, and they'll never notice us up here."

"What do you think about Shawn?"

"The lawyer?"

She rolls her eyes. "No, the other Shawn, the candlestick maker."

I hit her with a pillow. "Stop it. This man is after everything we hold dear. Besides that, he thinks he can buy me with a beach towel and a couple of paperbacks." At the thought of the anonymous gift, my face grows hot in spite of the cold. Especially since I'm pretty sure I never mentioned those books in front of him. Considering he's Mark's friend, it's not hard to guess who he's pumping for information about me. Maybe I should have Mark sign a nondisclosure agreement. But today isn't the day for that discussion. "Ames, what do you think I think about him? I'm trying to wait until after your wedding to declare war."

"Honestly, though. If you could ignore the fact that he's working for Summer Valley, would you think he's cute?"

I sigh. "Get real. His eyes are so blue I found myself humming 'Blue Christmas' over and over the other day at the North Pole. And that dimple in his chin? You could park a sleigh in it."

"So"—Ami shoots me a coy look—"his eyes are depressing and he has an abnormally large hole in his chin. I'll take that as a no."

If it wasn't her wedding day. . . "He's incredible looking. And you know it. But even if he weren't the enemy, he's still a lawyer." I almost scream the last word, then sit back because we may be twenty feet in the air, but sound carries. I'm not sure what kind of response yelling "lawyer" might cause in a crowd. I'd hate to cause mass panic and ruin the parade. "Just because you're in love doesn't mean I need to be," I whisper to make up for the scream.

"I know," she says as she makes her nest in the big armchair. "But it's so nice."

"I'm glad." And I really am. "You and Mark are made for each other."

"There's someone out there made for you, too, K-anna."

"Um-hum. . ." I pull my fleece blanket up around my cold

hands. It's too much trouble to disagree, but the truth is, I'm not so sure. I thought Jeff was the one, right up until the horrific scene the day before our wedding. And then came my disastrous rebound relationship with Nathan. He epitomized that elusive childhood crush, the best friend's older brother, whom you never speak to but worship from afar and write mushy diary entries about. After I was all grown up and had a broken heart that needed healing, his attention was a balm to my tattered ego. He was fresh from a breakup, too, so I'm sure I served the same purpose for him. We came to our senses just in time and realized we weren't in love with each other, but not before I officially became known around here as the bride who couldn't make it to the altar.

"Here come the horses," Ami says, jolting me from my memories. "And there's the youth group float."

Garrett's pulling our church youth group's float this year. He has his window down in spite of the cold temps, and his arm rests lazily on the door. Probably wants to be sure he can hear any extra commotion on that trailer packed with excited kids. "Conscientious" is his middle name.

"It'll drive him crazy, wondering why we're not on our corner with Mark."

As soon as she says that, he leans out his window and waves up at us.

I grin and wave.

Ami jerks back. "He saw us!"

I glance over at the corner. "It's okay. Mark's not looking.

Garrett's the only one who noticed us."

"Weird to be watching the parade without Garrett," Ami says as the tail end of his trailer goes over the hill.

"Everything's changing." Maybe that's why I've been so snappy lately. It just feels strange. Like the world is one beat out of sync.

"And I started it." Ami's voice cracks a little.

"Hey, don't do that." I can feel my own throat clog. "This is the happiest day of your life."

She grins, her eyes misty. "It is. But I'll miss you and Garrett. Us."

Reality slams into me like an avalanche. "We" are over. The terrific trio is no more. How much will Garrett and I hang out once Ami isn't here? Even I can see that will seem odd.

She reaches out for a hug, then buries her face in my shoulder. "What if I'm not good at being a wife?" This time, her voice is thick with tears, but I have no trouble recognizing cold feet.

I smooth down Ami's hair. "Mark is your future. He's God's man for you. And your marriage is going to be wonderful."

She mumbles something against my shoulder.

I release her. "What?"

She sniffs. "I said, do you think I have time for a bubble bath before our hair appointments?"

I push away the churning in my stomach and smile for the bride. "Definitely."

Amazing how much pressure it takes off when you're not actually the one getting married. I made it down the aisle just fine. Now I stare at the doorway, waiting for Ami and her father to appear, being careful to make the audience remain a blur. Being in front of crowds isn't my thing, and fainting might ruin Ami's moment. Although, she's so focused today that she'd probably just have a couple of the groomsmen pick me up and cart me out so the ceremony could continue.

This thought draws my eyes to the groomsmen. Bad mistake. Shawn is looking straight at me, and naturally, I avert my gaze. Then I think, *Hey, he was looking first. Why should I look away?* So I look back. By then, his attention is elsewhere, but Nathan nods at me. It's kind of weird to be standing up here with an ex-fiancé just across the aisle. We parted on good terms, but there's a tiny feeling of what might have been—if the fantasy of being in love had been reality. I jerk my gaze away. Some roads are better left untraveled.

My gaze flits to Garrett, and his warm smile calms me. I can't believe how freaked out I've been about Ami getting married. We'll still be the terrific trio. We're just adding a fourth. Okay, so technically that's not a trio, but we'll be the fearless foursome or something. We'll make it work.

Just as I'm thinking Garrett looks good in a tux, he gives me a discreet thumbs-up and "The Wedding March" begins. The crowd rises, and Ami, radiant in white, floats gracefully down the aisle on her dad's arm.

The ceremony goes off without a hitch. I almost cry a couple of times, but no sobbing aloud. So that's a good thing.

I am still a little teary, I guess, when it's time to take Garrett's elbow and walk out. He brings his other hand up and over mine, and I look up, startled. I'm undone by the compassion in my friend's green eyes.

"Walking down the aisle wasn't that hard, was it?" Geraldine hugs me and then keeps her hands on my shoulders. "Maybe you won't run away next time?"

"I didn't—"

She steps back and looks at me. "Now, now, I read Jack's piece. Good journalism."

Yellow journalism is more like it. I could have won a libel suit with no problem if I weren't so nice. The café owner is the fourth local today to mention my little foray into prewedding desertions. And of course, Shawn is on my left in the receiving line, taking this all in. To his credit, the lawyer-come-lately hasn't asked me what they're talking about, but who knows? Maybe he's read the back issues of *The Jingle Bells Journal*.

"That boy might make a good husband."

I jerk my attention back to Geraldine, terrified that she's fingered Shawn as "good husband" material. "Who?"

"Pay attention, girl," she says gruffly. "Jack Feeney. He's an up-and-coming star in the newspaper world."

Garrett reaches over from the right and gently touches my elbow. I hear his unspoken words, "Hang in there, sport."

Still looking at Geraldine, I nod. Message received. "You know, Geraldine, Shawn here is new to town. I was telling him about the amazing polar bear burrito you make at the North Pole. Rumor has it you use real bear meat."

She draws herself up to her full six feet, her purple satin dress stretched taut across the shoulders. "You know I don't use bear meat!"

"And I didn't run away." I smile to take the sting out. Since Gran was so well-known and I spent a lot of time here growing up, the townspeople think they helped raise me. "Honor thy father and mother" takes on a whole new meaning for me in Jingle Bells. It's a fine line.

Geraldine shakes her head and moves on to torment the rest of the wedding party.

I sag back against the wall, thankful for a lull, even though it's at Ami, Mark, and Garrett's expense. The Stewarts have the bride and groom cornered with a miniseminar on the subject of wedded bliss. Next to me, Mrs. Bloomfield is pinching Garrett's cheek over and over and telling him how she remembers when he used to collect aluminum cans for extra money. I'm considering how to rescue him. After all, he saved me from Geraldine.

"So you've got your eye on Jack Feeney?" Shawn studies me intently.

I tilt my face to the ceiling, then stare at him. "Are you kidding me?"

He grins. "Yes."

I shake my head. "Don't mess with the maid of honor."

Mrs. Bloomfield lets go of Garrett and skims quickly past Shawn and me. I guess since—even though I stayed with my grandmother a lot—I wasn't officially raised in Jingle Bells, I'm off the hook. She moves on down to Ami's younger sister, Amber, and Nathan. But here come the Stewarts. Who thought up this whole receiving line tradition anyway? A torture expert?

The Stewarts own the flower shop. Their son, Barry, actually runs the shop now, but the older couple spends most days there, telling anyone who wanders in how to have a romance like theirs after sixty years. This might not be a bad thing. . .if every third sentence weren't punctuated by a kiss. Sounds romantic but gets old after a while.

"Kristianna, Kristianna." Considering the length, you'd think Mr. Stewart wouldn't stick with his habit of saying everyone's name twice when it comes to me, but he always does. A matter of principle, probably.

"Hi, Mr. Stewart, Mrs. Stewart."

They kiss. In honor of my greeting, I guess.

"You're a good friend, sweetie, to forget your own heartbreak and stand beside Ami today," Mrs. Stewart says, wiggling her painted-on eyebrows and shifting her head toward Nathan. Shawn follows her body language directions, but I stare straight ahead. Just when you think it's safe to go back in the water. . .

"True love will come," this from Mr. Stewart. "Won't it, dear?" Kiss. Kiss.

I can stand up to Geraldine, but these love-struck octogenarians are beyond me. I'm helpless to protest.

Mrs. Stewart pulls her hand from her husband's clutch and pats mine. "Maybe we can help—"

Shawn clears his throat. "Did I hear someone say you all did the flowers? The orchids are particularly exquisite. And fragrant."

My hero.

The Stewarts talk to Shawn about flowers for a minute, then move on down the line quickly, beaming. I mouth a thank-you to him as soon as they're gone.

"You owe me," he murmurs, his grin still in place.

"That figures. Never expect a lawyer to help for free."

After Jim Johnson shakes our hands, I lean against the wall again. "I didn't ask you to rescue me, so I can't possibly owe you." I meet his gaze directly and lower my voice. "You might as well know that I made a commitment to get along with you today for Ami and Mark's sake, but come tomorrow, you're in for the fight of your life."

"Fair enough." His dimple flashes. "In that case, do you want to go out after the reception?"

A surge of adrenaline brings me upright. "With you?"

He nods but doesn't speak. Probably horrified that he asked out someone who doesn't have a high enough IQ to realize he's asking her out. But he didn't say, "with me"; he just said, "go out."

I instinctively glance at Garrett. I assumed we'd hang out after the wedding—commiserate about Ami getting married, check out the festival downtown. But he looks pretty cozy with Mark's coworker.

The long-legged redhead doesn't seem in any hurry to move on down the line, either. Garrett and I have the rest of forever to commiserate, and I don't feel like being alone this evening.

Shawn is still watching me.

"Okay." My mind revolts. Okay? What was wrong with "No, thank you," or even "Kind of you to offer, sir, but I'm cleaning the grout in my kitchen?" I think the orchid fumes are finally getting to me.

CHAPTER 7

So you're going out with Shawn after we leave?" Ami turns for me to unzip her white satin dress.

I shrug. "I don't think it's a date."

She glances over her shoulder at me. "I'm surprised you agreed to go."

"Yeah, me, too." I snag her going-away dress from the closet and pass it to her. "It looks like Garrett probably has plans, and I didn't want to go to the festival alone." Is that pathetic or what? But if you can't be honest with a friend, who can you be honest with? I plop down in the rocker while she changes.

"So you like him?"

I jerk my head up. "Who?"

She frowns. "Shawn. What's wrong with you?"

If only I knew. "Nothing. I have no idea how I feel about Shawn. To be honest, what fascinates me the most is the basket. And especially the note."

"Have you asked him about that?"

I shake my head. "I'm planning on bringing it up tonight. There's nothing to lose. I've already let him know that tomorrow the battle begins."

"And I thought your She-Ra years were over." She slips on her shoes and digs around in her purse. "I should have known you let that gorgeous blond hair grow back out for a reason."

"Hey, when you can have Princess of Power as your last name, why give it up?"

She laughs as she touches up her lipstick in the wall mirror. "I'll have to warn Garrett that you're revisiting that *He-Man and the Masters of the Universe* phase after all these years." She spins around. "What do you think?"

"I think you're a married woman." I take her hands in mine. "And it looks good on you."

"Thanks, Kristianna." She drops a kiss on my cheek and gives me a hug. "I'm glad you're here."

"Me, too."

"The ornaments were perfect. Did you hear everyone going on about them?"

I smile. "They really seemed to love them."

"Of course they did. Someday when you're famous, that will become the most valuable wedding favor in the history of mankind."

"In your dreams."

"We'll see." She tucks her arm in mine and leads me back toward the reception hall. "Let's go get you at the front of the line to catch the bouquet."

I try to pull away, but short of wrestling the bride to the ground, I don't see how to get loose. "Thanks, but no thanks."

As we reach the crowd, I lean toward her and lower my voice. "Why didn't you offer to let me go to the front of the line for the buffet? Then I'd have known you were really my best friend."

Naturally, I do catch the bouquet. Ami has her heart set on it, and for today, she gets her way.

As Ami and Mark run down the sidewalk, we pelt them with birdseed. She gives me a hug as they go by.

While they get into the car, I wave and grin until my cheeks hurt almost as much as my heart. I'm starting to wonder if I'm the type of person who doesn't handle change well.

An arm slips around my waist, and I glance up to find Garrett smiling down at me. How does he always manage to do that—know when I need him to be there?

"Thanks." I give him a one-armed hug and tap his boutonniere with my free hand. "A tux is a good look for you."

"That will come in handy if I ever decide to become a maître d'."

"Or be in a lot of weddings."

"Speaking of weddings. . .you going to let me be your best man?"

I'm startled, until I realize he's nodding toward Ami's bouquet in my hands.

"Oh." I toss him a saucy grin. "Sure. If you'll let me be your maid of honor."

"It's a deal. Want to run change and check out the festival?"

My smile freezes. Why had I been so sure he was with the redhead? We always used to go to the festivals together, especially this one. Even the early years we were in college, before Garrett's mom moved away, we all came home for the Christmas Festival. I feel like a worm. "Um. I told Shawn... I thought you were... That is, we were going to..."

Garrett just nods, his eyes unreadable. "No problem."

"Let's all go together. Shawn won't mind."

He raises an eyebrow. "Then he's more generous than most. I'll look for you. We'll see how it goes."

"Right."

He sprints down the sidewalk toward his truck. I stand there alone in the milling wedding crowd, feeling like I've lost my two best friends.

Shawn stares at me, then at the horses plodding around in a circle. "You're really going to go for a pony ride?"

I nod. "Really and truly. But they're horses, not ponies."

"Why?"

"Because they grew up?"

He frowns. "You know what I mean. Why ride these horses? They go around in a circle. Slowly."

I smile. "I've done it every Christmas since I was a little girl. No year ever seemed like the year to stop doing it."

"Maybe this is the year?"

I put my finger to my cheek as if I'm considering it. "Nope. I don't think so. You sound like my dad." My parents had decided—since I was going to be tied up with Ami's wedding—they'd wait until Christmas Eve to drive over. When I'd reminded them of our traditional weeklong holiday, Dad had suggested that with Gran gone maybe this was the year to be realistic about how much time off they could afford and cut that down to a couple of days. "It must be a lawyer thing."

"How did I know this would come back to my job?"

I pat the horse on the rear as it walks by. "Just a lucky guess?"

Sam steps deftly through the circle of horses and nods. A tobacco-stained smile lights up his weathered face. His eyes look bloodshot. Hopefully from staying up late with the festival. When I was younger, he'd often stagger over to take my money. But he did a stint in rehab not long after I moved here. As far as I know, he's been sober ever since. "Ready to ride, Miss Kristianna?"

"Yep." I hold out my money.

"No charge."

"Sam, how many times have I told you, you can't make a living like that?"

He takes my five dollars, tucks it in his overalls pocket, then gives me a lift up onto the palomino. "Merry Christmas."

"Merry Christmas, Sam. Good to see you again."

"You, too." He doffs his engineer cap to me.

"Thanks. I'm glad to be here."

The horse doesn't seem to notice that I'm on her back. I tilt my head back and close my eyes as she ambles along. I don't want this to go away—the festival, the closeness of the town, Jingle Bells. What would happen to Sam? I open my eyes and look out at the booths lined up side by side. There's Big Bob, the guess-your-age-and-weight man. He's so happy using his talent. And he always hands out a tract after he's guessed, explaining how no matter your age or your weight, in the end all that matters is your relationship with Jesus. What would he do? Go to work for the sporting goods store? Maybe he could guess how many baseballs are in a barrel, but what if they won't let him hand out his tracts?

The horse stops suddenly. I sit there for a few seconds and stare out at the twinkling lights. All good things must end. Is that true?

I walk back over to where Shawn is leaning against the fence.

"Have fun?"

I nod.

He smiles and shakes his head. "Then I don't have to understand it, do I?" He takes my elbow and guides me back onto the sidewalk. "You fit in really well here."

My heart lightens. I do, don't I? "At the festival?" I cock my head and grin. "Are you saying I should have run away and joined the circus like I wanted to when I was ten?"

He rolls his eyes. "You fit in here, in Jingle Bells."

I glance over at him. "That's a high compliment."

"Want me to win you a tiger?" Shawn motions to the basketball booth.

"Sure. A girl can never have too many tigers."

I spot a familiar figure swooshing the ball through the hoop as we approach.

Garrett looks up and waves. The tux is gone, of course, in favor of jeans and a polo shirt.

"Hey, man," Shawn says and swings his hand out for an easy handshake. "You win all the prizes?"

Garrett shakes his hand and nods to me. "I said they could keep them."

Shawn laughs, but I know, from previous experience, that it's true. Garrett can't miss at these games. I have a closet full of stuffed animals to prove it. Even after I gave at least half of them away to children's hospitals.

Shawn pulls me gently toward his side and glances at Garrett. He nods toward the sign: CHALLENGE A FRIEND—GUARANTEED WINNER. "Want to do a challenge?"

"Nah."

"You sure?" At least Shawn doesn't say, "You afraid?" or make clucking sounds, but the implication is there.

Garrett gives him a measured look, then smiles. "You might show me up."

"You know what?" I say brightly. "I'm getting a little old for stuffed animals. . . ."

Shawn does a double take. "Let me get this straight. Pony rides are still acceptable, but stuffed toys aren't?"

Garrett throws back his head and laughs. "You still trying to keep Old Sam in groceries, sport?"

My face grows hot. I was hoping Shawn wouldn't figure out why I insisted on riding. "I like riding the horses. There aren't as many kids around as there used to be." That slipped out, but it's true. Families left town in droves after the distribution center closed.

"You know," Shawn says softly, "that's partly why I'm here. To bring the kids back."

Something about that simple statement brings tears to my eyes. I blink them away and look up in time to see Garrett frown. He has yet to say how he feels about the name change. But even if he's on my side, I don't want to discuss it tonight.

"Shawn, I'm not signing the petition. So don't waste your courtroom drama on me." I soften my bluntness with a smile. "No shoptalk, okay?"

"Sure." He claps his hand on Garrett's shoulder. "Let's all go see what they've got to eat around here. Have you seen this girl's appetite? Where does she put it, anyway?"

"In her feet," Garrett says.

"In my feet," I say at the same exact time, and we laugh.

Shawn grimaces. "Old joke, huh?"

I nod and hold up my size-eight, tennis shoe–clad foot. "My feet have been this size since I was twelve. They always teased me that the second helping of everything went straight to my feet."

Shawn puts his hand at the small of my back, and I look up at him. Awfully friendly for someone who knows we're going to be doing battle tomorrow. He smiles at me. "We'd better check out the food, then, before you have to buy smaller shoes."

Garrett scuffs his tennis shoe against the sidewalk. "I'm still stuffed from the reception buffet. Think I'm going to call it a night."

"You sure?" Did I let him down tonight? His green eyes are dark, still impossible to read.

"Positive. I've got so much work to do I'll be up most of the night." We say good night, and he walks off into the darkness.

"What does he do?" Shawn asks as we head toward the Santa Snack Shack cart.

"Garrett? Computer consultation and Web site design." I shrug. "And who knows what else? If it can be done on a computer, he does it. Paid his way through college out in California buying and reselling on eBay, I think. He does my Web site for the store to try to help me pull in mail orders. You should check it out sometime."

"You love your store, don't you?" He takes my hand in his as we walk.

It feels nice. I don't want to pull away. "It's like a member of the family."

"As is this odd little town?"

I chuckle. "It does sound weird, I guess."

"I just bet your family reunions are crowded."

I toss him a grin. "But fun."

We grab a couple of corn dogs and settle down on a couple of hay bales by the live nativity scene to eat.

A cow close to us unconcernedly chews her cud and gives us a wide-eyed stare.

"Who would have thought the Savior of the world would come

from such humble beginnings?" Shawn says after a while.

I glance over at him, surprised. "Sometimes the simple things are the most powerful."

"Do y'all have this all year long?" Shawn asks suddenly. "That shed looks permanent."

I nod. "We have several festivals a year, and the live nativity is at each festival. We celebrate Christ's birth every day in Jingle Bells. Does that strike you as sacrilegious?"

"Not at all. That's how I've always done it myself. Only without the manger."

We sit in silence for a while; then I push to my feet. "Shawn, I'd better go." He takes our corn dog sticks and drops them in the trash can while I zip my coat and slip on my stocking cap.

"I'll walk you home." He fastens his coat.

"You don't have to."

He reaches for my hand and pulls me toward the sidewalk. "I want to."

We walk hand in hand across the town square lawn. Jingle Bells Avenue is almost deserted, but Shawn leads me to a crosswalk.

"Afraid I might jaywalk and get us in trouble?" I tease.

"Since I know about your parking ticket record, I'm taking no chances."

As we reach the front door of my shop, he stops and tugs on my hand, bringing me closer to him. He grins, and his dimple deepens. "I had a great time tonight."

I gaze up into his deep blue eyes. "Me, too."

If I stand here long enough, he's going to kiss me. Besides the fact that holding hands with someone I've only known a little while pushes my boundaries, I'm also going to fight this man's agenda with everything I have over the next few months. I pull my hand free of his and fumble in my purse for my key. "Thanks for a great time." I quickly unlock the door.

His brows knit together. "Too bad tomorrow has to come so soon."

No need to pretend I don't know what he's referring to. "May the best man—or woman—win." I salute him as I slide into the shop and shut the door.

Up in my apartment, the moon shines through the French doors. I throw my fleece blanket around me and step onto the balcony just as Shawn reaches the other side of the crosswalk. I watch him turn toward the church building to get his car and realize I didn't mention the basket and the note. I smile in the dim light. Maybe I'll just let the supposed mystery remain for a while.

The muted noises of people shutting down their festival booths drift up to me with the cold air. I shiver and pull the blanket tight around my shoulders. "G'night, Jingle Bells. Sleep well, old friend."

CHAPTER 8

One good thing about a slow day in the store is that it gives me time to be an artist. I push back and examine my painting with a critical eye. I've tried to infuse the house I grew up in with a warm glow, but Thomas Kincaid, I'm not. I do manage to sell several paintings, though, and frankly, that's all that keeps the store going. Well, that and the Christmas ornaments and sculptures I sell on the Web page Garrett helped me set up.

My grandmother, Sally Harrington, shared her love of art with me. But beyond that, she gave me a loving place to stay while Mother and Dad were busy bringing justice to the world. And when I was old enough to read, she presented me with my first Bible. She tried to live like Christ in every situation and encouraged me to do the same. I fall so short, but her memory inspires me to keep trying.

When she went home—as she called it—she left me Forever Christmas and the delightful, if drafty, apartment above it. I didn't hesitate to move permanently to the place that had always felt like home to me. And unless my parents manage to hatch and implement some diabolical plan to force me back into law school, I'm not planning on going anywhere.

Growing up, I celebrated most of my holidays, weekends, and summers in Jingle Bells. But my parents came to stay here only once a year. Every December about this time, they'd close their Little Rock law office. We'd make the forty-five-mile trek from our Sherwood manor to Gran's front door. For one week out of each year, she'd manage to turn my dysfunctional family into something akin to the Waltons.

I glance over at the calendar. If things were normal, my parents would be arriving today. But Dad called today to reiterate that they're just coming for Christmas Eve and Christmas this year. According to him, they look forward to seeing me then. Right. That's why they cut our normal weeklong visit down to two days. Because they are so looking forward to seeing me.

Still, like a slow day at the shop allows me to paint, Mother and Dad's absence will allow me to relax and enjoy my first Christmas in residence. And mourn my first Christmas without Gran.

The phone rings, and I jump. Sad when the shop is so quiet that a phone startles me. I pick up the cordless and push TALK. "Hello."

"Hey, stranger."

"Ami! How's married life?" I stand up and stretch my back.

She giggles, and I can imagine the mischief dancing in her eyes. "Even better than I thought it would be. I'm so happy that I couldn't wait one more second to call you."

"You sound it. I'm glad." And I am. Jealous? Probably. But glad that she's so happy.

"You okay?"

"Sure. Why wouldn't I be?"

"Dunno. Are you painting?"

I look over at the easel. "How can you tell?"

"Your voice is different when you paint. Thoughtful. Kind of melancholy. Besides, Tuesdays are Sarah's day to be closed, and you usually paint when you're alone."

"Yeah, well, I'm trying to get Mother and Dad's Christmas present finished."

She takes a deep breath. "Has the war started yet?"

I chuckle. "I've made some notes, but I'm waiting for my cohort to get home from her honeymoon to help me figure out a strategy. Have you been thinking about it?"

I hear Mark murmur something behind her. She giggles again. "Um, not really. But I will."

I smile. "You're hopeless."

"I know."

"How was the cruise?"

"Wonderful, but every time anyone sneezed, I cringed."

"Let me guess. Geraldine gave you her lecture about how the flu can run rampant on 'those big boats?'"

"Yep. I won't even tell you what she said about the food on the islands. Mark has to force me to eat every time we go out."

We talk for a few more minutes about the tropical paradise they're enjoying as honeymooners, and she hangs up with a promise to call Christmas Day.

Before I get back to my painting, Susie from Mistletoe Music phones to let me know that Birdie Montrose is in town.

I run to the back and snag my "Birdie" box. For the next ten minutes, I swap the valuable items on my low tables for inexpensive ones. Just as I finish and stash the box in my workshop, the door chime rings.

Since Sarah's not in today, I take off my paint smock and hurry to the front of the store to greet my somewhat kleptomaniac friend.

Instead, the teenage delivery boy once again stands inside the door, clutching a huge straw bag. He hands it to me wordlessly, then slips out the door.

"Thanks. I think." I hold up the beach bag. My name has been woven into the front. In red, my favorite color. A small envelope dangles from the handle. I sit down at the counter and peek inside my latest gift. A snorkel mask, also red, lies on top. I pull it out, and beneath it is an exquisite mother-of-pearl jewelry box. My hand trembles as I open the box. I smile at my silliness, but the smile freezes on my lips as the notes of "Love Me Tender" fill the room. I've loved that song for as long as I can remember.

Curiosity won't let me not explore every nook and cranny of the intricately designed box. The last drawer I open holds a perfect pair of pearl-and-diamond earrings. I'm no jeweler, but they look real to me. Summer Valley obviously has an expense account. But are they courting me because they see me as their primary opposition? I remember my hand in Shawn's the night of the wedding. Or is it more personal? Or both?

I open the envelope. The words swim on the page as tears blur my vision.

Kristianna,

    Praying for you to have a Jingle Bells Christmas filled with love, happiness, and especially peace. Relax. The battle can wait.

Talk about conflicted. I run my fingertip across the smooth finish of the jewelry box. On the one hand, I'm incredibly touched. If Shawn's words are as sincere as they sound, it means he realizes how hard this Christmas will be on me with Gran gone and the future of Jingle Bells at risk. Which brings me to the other hand. Am I being lulled into relaxing while he's out racking up signatures on his petition? Is this an elaborately staged ploy to bring me over to the dark side?

Another good thing about slow days—plenty of time to pray. I rest my head on my hands and let the tears flow down my cheeks unchecked.

I can't do this alone, Lord. Gran's gone. For now, Ami's gone. Things are weird with Garrett. I can't forget the hateful things Mother said, and I can't just act like it never happened. Probably thanks to that, both my parents are avoiding me. I don't want to lose Jingle Bells, too. Please give me strength, courage, and wisdom. The words of the beach bag note flit through my mind. *Oh, and peace would be so nice.*

This time when the bell rings, it *is* Birdie. I quickly shove the basket under the counter and go to hug her.

"Kristianna, you get prettier every time I see you."

"Right back at ya, Miss Birdie." I know my nose still has to be bright red from crying, so in addition to her issue with sticking things in her bag, she must be going blind.

When I first discovered her problem, I looked up kleptomania. I don't think she truly has it. As a matter of fact, I'm convinced that Birdie's "picking things up" without paying has more to do with forgetfulness than larceny. The other shopkeepers share my theory, but none of us want to find out what Sergeant Montrose would think.

"Are you almost ready for Christmas?"

She eyes the table nearest the door. "I think so. Just a few more things on my list." She digs in her bag. "If I could find the list." She digs deeper. "Where do all these things come from?"

I think I have a pretty good idea. But I'm able to stay close to her, which always works best, until my phone rings. Awfully busy for a slow day. I give Birdie a nod and step a few feet away to answer. Keeping her within visual range, of course. "Forever Christmas."

"Hello, sweetie. That man just left the flower shop." Mrs. Stewart's voice crackles like there's a bad reception, but I know there's not. "We can't decide what to do."

I move to see Birdie better. So far, so good. She's looking without touching. "What man?"

"That Shane or Shawn or something or other. The one who's getting signatures."

A groan comes from low in my throat. I should have known.

"He gave us a lot of good reasons to sign it. But the thought of Jingle Bells changing its name just breaks our hearts, so we asked for time to think about it."

"Good. We don't have to sign that, Mrs. Stewart. Jingle Bells will make it without being swallowed by Summer Valley."

"I hope so, sweetie, but he's sure working the street."

Fury pours through me as I remember his sweet note about me relaxing. "Now?" Miss Birdie looks at me in alarm, so I lower my voice. "On Jingle Bells Avenue?"

"He's in Angel Hair and Nails right this second."

"Thanks, Mrs. Stewart, I have to go." I hang up the phone and turn to Birdie, my heart pounding. "Miss Birdie, I'm going to have to run a quick errand." I motion toward the door. "Maybe you can drop back by after a while." I'll have to call Scott from my cell phone and warn him she's heading his way.

"Oh, that's fine, you just go right ahead. I'll be here when you get back."

"But—" How did this go from terrible to worse?

She points at the potbellied stove in the corner. "If I get tired, I'll sit over by the fire and drink some cocoa."

Is she in cahoots with Shawn? I slump. "Oh, it's okay. I guess my errand can wait."

"Now, now, don't be silly." She pulls my coat off the rack and shoves it into my arms. "If it was important a minute ago, it still is. I'll mind the store." She rubs her hands together, and her eyes crinkle at the corners. "It'll be fun."

Yes, fun like electrolysis.

Blind fury propels me down the sidewalk, and I barely even see the beautiful Christmas decorations in every storefront. I'm almost to Angel Hair and Nails when Shawn comes out. Smiling. I stride up to him. "What are you doing?"

His brows knit together. "My job?"

"I'm supposed to be relaxing and enjoying Christmas while you're out here murdering my town?"

CHAPTER 9

Murder?"

Oh, he looks so innocent. What's he going to do next? Tell me it was all a mistake and enter rehab?

"Who was murdered?" a trembling voice behind me asks.

I glance around to see the Campbell twins. Ninety-five if they're a day, but they still walk around Jingle Bells Avenue frequently. Ermyl looks frightened, but Elva's eyes sparkle with excitement.

"No one." I say quickly. "No one has been murdered." I shoot Shawn a glare. "Yet."

"Watch out, young man." Elva taps Shawn with her umbrella as she walks by. "I'd say you're in a spot of trouble. Come on, Ermyl. You know children nowadays and their figures of speech."

"Um, yes. We'll be seeing you Christmas Day, Kristianna."

"Yes, ma'am." I wave good-bye.

They look back and frown at me. The sisters insist I call them by their first names, but I refuse to forgo "ma'am."

"At least you're polite to someone."

I spin around to face Shawn again. "Do you know what you've done?" I should have only been gone a couple of minutes, but panic wells in me as I realize how much time has passed since I left the store. "What you made me do?"

He shakes his head slowly. "One thing I've already learned, I couldn't possibly make you do anything."

I've got to get back to my shop, and I have to have someone to help me. "Come with me."

He steps back and lowers his eyebrows. "With you?"

"Hurry." I stop short of grabbing his hand and turn the motion into a gesture to follow me. "You're going to help me repair the damage," I call over my shoulder to where he *is* following, though more out of curiosity than anything, I think.

When we get almost to my shop, I slow. "This is the plan. When you go in, I'll introduce you to Miss Birdie. I'm going to sit her by the fire, and you're going to talk to her until she gets warm enough to take off her coat and give it to me."

"Are you crazy?"

"Probably, but just listen. Then you're going to distract her while I look in her bag."

He nods. "Oh, I get it." His voice is laced with sarcasm. "I guess the Jingle Bells natives have never heard of walking barefoot together across hot coals or surviving in the mountains as a team. In order to bond, we're going to rob an old lady."

I glare over at him. "Bonding is so not the point here. Getting my merchandise back is. Just work with me. I'll explain later." I push open the door.

Birdie peers around a display in the back. "Oh, good. You're back." She clip-clops across the wooden floor to meet us. "Not one customer came in. Business must really be down."

Ouch.

She looks curiously at Shawn behind me. I'm not sure introducing him to another townsperson is a good idea, but I've already dragged him in here. Besides, I'm sure she remembers him from the town meeting. Might as well go through with my ridiculous plan.

I make the introductions and motion toward the stove. "Want to sit down and have that cup of cocoa now, Miss Birdie?"

"That sounds lovely."

Shawn guides her over to the armchair, carefully adjusting it a little closer to the fire right before she sits. Then he relaxes into the rocker beside her. I stand between them, keeping our chitchat going. By the time we've exhausted the weather and the upcoming holidays, she is shrugging out of her coat. I take it gratefully. "Let me go hang this up."

I excuse myself and circle around to the back, making a quick side trip through my workshop, where I clean out her pockets. Of my things, that is. Not a lot, considering she was given free rein. A few of my ornaments and a small snow globe. I need to get my hands on her bag, though, so I leave my finds on the workbench and take her coat to the front to hang on a peg. I can hear Shawn keeping up a running conversation as I walk back to them.

"Would you like to see the petition?" He pulls it out of his briefcase, and I stare, mesmerized by the paper that may hold our future. Forget sugarplums. Visions of snatching the petition from his hand and stuffing it in the stove dance through my head. He gives me a hard glance, though, and as I look at Miss Birdie, scooted forward intent on reading the signatures, I realize this is my distraction. Not what I had in mind, but maybe it will do.

I slip around behind her and squat, deftly removing two more snow globes, a soft nativity scene for babies, and a couple of spools of ribbon from her bulging bag. I stuff the other things on a low shelf and carry the ribbon and the nativity scene to the cash register. She won't be happy if she doesn't end up with something.

Five minutes later, she's bundled into her coat and is clutching her purchases, the ones she happily paid for. After she leaves, Shawn stares at me, obviously waiting for a serious explanation. I hold up one finger and quickly dial Scott's bookstore number. As I watch Shawn's eyebrows draw together, I consider saying something cryptic like, "Elvis has left the building," or "The Eagle has flown." Instead, I just say, "Scott, it's Kristianna. Birdie's heading your way."

He thanks me and hangs up quickly, no doubt to get his own Birdie box out. I turn to Shawn, who is frowning.

"Birdie's very forgetful. So she picks things up and forgets to pay for them."

He shakes his head. "This town is nuts."

I shrug. "Maybe. But that's just the way we like it." I turn my back and rearrange my Twelve Days of Christmas display.

A few seconds later, footsteps sound on the wood floor, and the door opens and closes. I turn around to watch him walk down the sidewalk, clutching his briefcase. I wonder if he got Miss Birdie's signature.

I pull my knee to my chest to tie my shoe and glance over at Garrett. It seems kind of odd to be bowling without Mark and Ami. "Did Mark tell you who was taking their places?"

Garrett shakes his head. "No. I just got a text message from him today reminding me to show up tonight and saying they'd gotten replacements."

"Weird. I got the same thing from Ami."

I look up as a vaguely familiar willowy redhead saunters in. She waves at us, or to be exact, she waves at Garrett. Oh yes, it's all coming back to me now. She's Mark's coworker, Lila. The one Garrett was talking to so much at the wedding.

Before I can comment, Shawn walks in behind her. This night just gets better and better.

Garrett leans toward me. "Don't look now, but I think we've been set up."

I groan. "Leave it to the honeymooners to think we need dates. What are we going to do?"

"Well, Shawn said he could bowl, and surely if Lila couldn't, Mark and Ami wouldn't have invited her."

"Oh yeah, because we wouldn't have anyone on our team who

couldn't bowl, would we?" I half laugh. "Besides, I'm not worried about winning."

"Good thing," Garrett says, grinning.

"Easy for you to joke." I nod at the cash register where our counterparts are paying for their shoes. "You're paired up with a beautiful accountant. I ended up with a man who's trying to destroy the town I love."

He shakes his head. "Come on. That's dramatic even for you."

Ha. If I were being dramatic, I would have mentioned that he's a lawyer, to boot. "What do you mean 'even' for me?"

"Oh, wait," he says, his tone overly apologetic. "Maybe that was someone else who didn't eat beef for six months after your class visited a cattle farm."

I blush. "I was only ten."

"But that didn't keep you from writing letters to your senators, encouraging them to stop condoning the senseless murder of helpless animals."

"Okay, so I know how to embrace a cause, but this is not the same thing," I murmur to Garrett as Shawn and Lila walk up.

Garrett shakes hands with Shawn and smiles at Lila. "Glad you two are here." He nods toward the next lane, where a raucous group of four men are warming up. Their rust-colored polyester shirts proudly proclaim GREASE MONKEYS. "We were feeling a little hopeless."

I do a double take. Hopeless? How did the fact that we were feeling hopeless escape me?

"Lila, have you met Kristianna?"

He sounds really happy to see her. And I'm not sure it has to do with bowling. Maybe I'm the only one not thrilled with this arrangement. I paste a smile on my apparently hopeless face and stick out my hand. "Thanks for coming to help us out. Did you drive all the way in from Little Rock to bowl?"

She shrugs gracefully. "Well, it's not a long trip, so it isn't a big deal. Mark said you guys needed a fourth, and I love to bowl." She maintains eye contact with Garrett while she answers my question. I'm guessing Mark didn't have to twist her arm.

I glance over at Shawn, who is quietly putting on his shoes. He's probably afraid to speak to me after the other day. I must have seemed crazy, and now that I've had time to think about it, I'm not sure how to act. Logically, I know he's just a temporary employee. But a part of me feels that he is Summer Valley.

I had the Dream last night. As usual, I couldn't see the groom's face. But I had the strangest feeling that Shawn Webber, his dimple flashing, stood patiently waiting for me at the front. Of course, as soon as I hit the halfway mark up the aisle, I ran for the door. But still, if it was him, maybe it's significant that he was there. Or maybe not.

I clap my hands. "Y'all ready to bowl?"

"Sure." Lila smoothly hoists her bag to the wooden shelf and unzips it.

Behind her back, Garrett nods toward her monogrammed bowling ball bag and winks at me.

I snatch a shiny red ball off the rack and barely manage to hold on to it as my arm extends, stretching almost to the point of no return. Oops. I use the other hand to heave the Mr. Universe special back up to where I got it and ignore Garrett's broad grin. After I massage some feeling back into my right arm, I carefully choose a lighter ball and set it on the revolving rack. "All ready," I proclaim to the world in general.

Ten minutes into the game, Lila's bowling, Garrett's keeping score, and Shawn comes back and sits beside me, without speaking.

"Hi, Shawn."

He nods. "Kristianna."

Lila bowls a strike. Naturally. Because how would it be fair otherwise? She and Garrett high-five, then chat for a minute while the pins reset.

I glance back at Shawn. "How's it going?"

He looks confused, like he wonders if I'm asking about the signature gathering or just conversing in a casual way. He should be confused. Even I don't know what I'm looking for.

"Fine."

Safe answer.

Lila's laughter rings out. While the other team bowls, Garrett is apparently regaling her with an amusing tale.

When I turn back to Shawn, he smiles at me. "Truce?" he asks.

Anything's better than this miserable, stilted conversation. I nod. "Why not? I came to bowl."

Garrett unfortunately overhears this last comment and raises an eyebrow. "Glad to hear it. Show us what you've got, sport."

I growl under my breath as I walk by him and take my shot.

To my amazement, my ball doesn't go all the way into the gutter. It kind of dribbles on the border and ends up knocking down two peppermint-striped pins.

"Woohoo!" Garrett jumps up like a crazy man with his hand in the air.

I stop and stare at him, so he lifts my palm up and slaps it. I smile.

But when I look at Lila, she's frowning. "You don't bowl?"

I open my eyes wide and nod. "Every Tuesday."

"Do you understand about the arrows on the lane?" She speaks very clearly like I'm really simple. "If you follow them with your ball. . . ?"

I hear Garrett snort, and I lose it.

Lila seems even more puzzled by my laughter.

Bless her heart.

Maybe if I explain. I straighten my face. "My ball has a mind of its own," I offer, without so much as a chuckle. "That's why I'm in a bowling club and not a league."

"Oh. Okay." She shrugs. "To each his own."

I hear my returning ball clunk into place behind me. "Oops. My turn again." I take careful aim once more and release. Straight down the arrow. At the very last second, it veers right and plops into the gutter.

"Unbelievable," Lila says from behind me.

I glance over at Shawn. Then back to her and Garrett.

That pretty much sums up my life these days.

CHAPTER 10

An hour later, I'm feeling like a Little Leaguer who wandered unawares into the World Series. Oh well, at least my team won. In spite of me. Thankfully, the hard part is over and it's time for my favorite part of the evening—nachos and root beer.

I switch my shoes and hear Garrett say, "You guys want to get a bite to eat in the snack bar?"

"Oh, not me," Lila pats her rock-hard abs through the red polyester shirt. "Way too high in fat." She glances at me, and I guess my open mouth makes her realize that was a bad answer. "I mean. . . I have to get home. Long drive."

"Okay, then, see you 'round," I call.

She nods to me, then loops her arm through Garrett's and smiles. "Ga-ar-rett. . ." The way she says it makes it sound like it has umpteen syllables. "I'm having some trouble with my laptop. Mark said if I brought it with me you might look at it when we got done."

"Oh, sure." Garrett's brow furrows. "You have it here?"

"It's in the car. I thought you might just walk out with me and look at it there." She smiles. "I have a good heater, so we won't freeze."

Garrett gives me a wide-eyed look that I try to read. Does he want to be rescued? Or excused from our weekly ritual? I don't say anything. He's a big boy. If he wants food, he'll have to just tell her. And if he'd rather go off with the redhead, that's his business.

"See y'all," he says and guides her out the door. Well, I guess that answers that.

I stare after them. Does being a good bowler make her think that she has the right to bat her eyes and take Garrett? Not that it's my business. I'm just saying.

"Sorry you got stuck with me."

I swing around to face Shawn. I forgot he was still here. "Oh, that's okay." Brilliant. I'm sure that made him feel better. I smile but do *not* bat my eyes. "Want to get something to eat?"

He nods and puts a hand on my elbow as we go up the steps to the snack bar and order our food.

When we're done, he guides me to a small table in the corner. Again with his hand on my elbow. A little proprietary, considering this isn't even a date. But maybe that's just my latent lawyer hostility showing. Or my not-so-latent town-name-change hostility.

He pulls a chair out for me. "Do you like to bowl?"

I sit. "Sometimes."

"You do it with gusto." He sits down across from me.

"That's not a phrase you hear every day."

He grimaces. "My dad used to say, 'Shawn, whatever you do, do it with gusto.'"

"So, are you gathering signatures with gusto?" I'm detached. Just asking a man about his job. Nothing more.

"It helps if you believe in the cause." He picks up the laminated menu and glances at it, then back at me. "In this case, I do, so yes."

"Do you realize how expensive it would be for us to change the names and themes of our shops? Yet, if we don't, we'll be left behind. Who will want to go to a Christmas-themed shop in Summer Valley?" My voice gets loud, and people around us turn and look.

He opens his mouth, and I hold up my hand. "Rhetorical question, Shawn. Don't bother answering." Tears sting my eyes. So much for detached.

"It's no bother." His voice is even, but I can see a flare of anger in his eyes. "This is just a temporary job for me. But it's one that makes sense. Every time I meet with the Summer Valley representative, he stresses that we're here to save the town. That's our number one goal."

I snort. "I'm getting pretty tired of hearing this 'saving the town' line. Don't you have anything new in your repertoire?" I glance toward the bowling alley door. How long does it take to "look" at a laptop? I need moral support.

A ponytailed blond shoves our nachos and drinks down on the table and hurries away.

"You're not the only one getting tired of something. I'm tired of being treated like Public Enemy Number One just for doing my job. Especially by you." He narrows his eyes. "I can't imagine why I keep seeking you out."

"Well, from now on, don't do me any favors."

Garrett appears beside me and pulls up a chair. "I'm starving. Mind sharing?" He takes a chip from my nachos without waiting for an answer.

Shawn pushes to his feet, his face still stormy. "You can have mine. I just lost my appetite." He leaves without even a backward glance.

Garrett raises an eyebrow. "Was it something I said?"

I close my eyes and rub my temples. "Not you, me. I hate his job."

"But not him?"

I glance toward the door Shawn just walked through. "No, he's a nice enough Christian guy. But I can't get past what he's doing to this town."

"What is he doing?"

I open my eyes and gaze at him. "Have you been living in an alternate reality lately? He's getting the signatures for the petition."

"The petition to get the name change on the ballot?"

I nod.

"But even then it has to go before the town for a vote."

"Right."

He shrugs. "Remember when you worked that one summer at the vet's office? You had to hold the animals still while the vet worked on them."

"So?" Garrett is one of the most intelligent people I've ever met, but sometimes his logic is harder to follow than a gas station attendant's directions.

"You didn't like to see the animals in pain from a shot or surgery, but it was your job."

"That was for their own good."

"Maybe—"

I jump up, suddenly terrified of what he's going to say. What if, for the first time ever, he's not on my side? "Garrett, I don't want to hear it tonight, okay? I couldn't take it if I had to argue with you, too."

I leave my nachos barely touched and hurry out into the winter night.

Winter should mean snow. Not rain. I rest my forehead against the window beside the cash register and stare out at the gray day. As droplets of rain splat against the glass, I peer at the round thermometer on the porch. Only a few degrees above freezing. I'd guess one-fourth of my Christmases have been white. But that doesn't stop me from hoping every year. But only for snow. Something inside me says my parents are hoping for an excuse not to come. Freezing rain would be that excuse in spades.

How many Christmases did Gran wait in this exact place for our car to pull up? She always met us at the curb by the time we rolled to a stop. Call me silly, but I want to do that for my parents. They probably won't appreciate it, but it feels right to me.

While I wait, I give the shop a second look. All the themed Christmas trees twinkle merrily, and every ornament is in its place. I've straightened the tables twice, and since the store isn't open, I know there's no point in checking them again.

A movement outside draws my attention. Right on time. My parents are so prompt that I sometimes wonder if they ever pull off the road and stare at their synchronized watches until they're sure they'll reach their destination at the appointed minute. The shiny black Mercedes glides to a stop behind my Jeep Wrangler. Both in the Chrysler family at least, if not closely related.

I snatch up my super-sized red umbrella, scoop a handful of change from the bowl under the counter, and run out the door.

My mother climbs out of the car, her auburn hair perfectly coifed. Her slate blue Liz Claiborne pantsuit doesn't have a wrinkle or crease, and she snaps open her color-coordinated umbrella with practiced ease.

"Hi, Mother." I lean toward her, and with the umbrella in one hand, she clutches my upper arms, her version of a hug, and kisses the air near my face.

"Kristianna." She reaches toward my hair and frowns. "Your hair has gone wild, I see."

Even though I know it's futile, I attempt to pat down my curly mess. "It's the same as always."

"A good stylist could do wonders for that, dear."

Speaking of futile... Number one rule of getting along with my mother—don't try to argue.

Dad retrieves their overnight bag from the trunk, then comes around to us, carrying a sleek black umbrella. His blond hair seems a little grayer at the temples than it was at Thanksgiving. But, at fifty, he's a striking figure in his well-cut black suit and light yellow shirt with a color-coordinated tie.

For as long as I can remember, his wardrobe has had only two kinds of clothes. Gym clothes for his daily workout and suit/tie combinations. He smiles absently as if he's surprised to see me. "Kristianna."

"Dad. Do you want me to get that bag for you?" I ask, even though I know he doesn't. Gran would have folded him into a hug and come away with the bag. Then she would have kept him so distracted with conversation that he wouldn't have noticed she was carrying it until she set it down in their room upstairs. I stand back as he walks past me toward the store. I'm not sure when we stopped hugging. But it's been long enough that I don't even consider doing it now.

Dad offers his arm to Mother, and she takes it. He has the overnight bag in his other hand, and she has her wrap draped across her arm. They face the store and square their shoulders as if bracing themselves.

I want to say, "It's only two days. You can stand to be around me that long." But instead I call, "I have to feed the meter. Be right in." It's one thing for me to get parking tickets, but my parents would have a fit if Doyle dared to slide one of those little green cardboard nasties under their windshield wiper. I don't want them

101

to declare war on Jingle Bells. We have enough enemies as it is. I funnel change into the candy-cane pole, then hurry to catch up.

They're almost to the top of the stairs when I come in. I give the Christmas wonderland one more glance and throw a switch to turn off the lights. Don't know why I thought they'd want to see what I'd done with the place.

I run up the stairs, my Birkenstocks slapping each step, and get to the apartment door just as they're about to go in. I lean against the top railing for a second, trying not to pant.

Mother looks back at me. "I'll never get used to going through a *store* to get to the living quarters." She says "store" like it's a dirty word.

I shrug and pull myself upright. "It's worth it to me."

She raises an eyebrow.

I meet her gaze, unflinching, because like it or not, that phrase is true of most things they don't understand about my life.

She turns away.

I catch my breath and follow them into the apartment.

My dad stands inside the door, staring at the tall tree in the corner.

The trees in the store are artificial and themed, but for my own apartment, Garrett and I cut an eight-footer from Mr. Pletka's Christmas Tree Farm. Every ornament I've ever had is crammed on its green branches, and multicolored lights glint off the shiny surfaces. As far as I'm concerned, it's perfect.

Mother just glances at it, then brushes past Dad. "Jared, why don't you put that bag in our room?"

He looks at her and nods. "Same place as always, Kristianna?"

"Yes, unless you'd rather have Gran's room." I immersed myself into Gran's life after she basically left it all to me, but I drew the line at moving into her room. I have my own spacious bedroom, always have had, and there's a nice-sized guest bedroom. I've kept Gran's room essentially the same. "I put fresh sheets on the bed this morning. And it has its own bathroom, you know."

"No, this will be fine," Dad calls from the guest room, where he's already stashing their things.

Mother narrows her eyes at me.

"What's wrong?" I ask. Last I heard, she wanted us to all just "get along."

Her expression smooths out immediately. "Wrong?"

I catch myself before I go ahead with the conversation. Rule number two—when my mother plays dumb, there's no point in trying to smoke out the truth. It comes out soon enough. Usually before I'm ready.

CHAPTER 11

Even though I've grumbled about them coming for only two days, the truth is, I have no idea what to do with my parents without Gran here. And when in doubt, I overschedule. Thankfully, the rain stopped, so a-caroling we will go. That will take care of a big chunk of tonight.

Mother is in front of the mirror. I told my parents to raid the front closet for warm coats, and somehow Emily Harrington managed to find a stylish ski suit I didn't even know I had, complete with matching gloves.

"It looks like it was made for you," I offer. I made a New Year's resolution early. I may not be able to forgive my mother for her tirade after Gran's funeral, but I don't have to make us all miserable. She glares at me. We can't seem to get our good intentions in the same time zone. When I'm nice, she's not, and vice versa.

Dad's inspecting the fireplace, and I do a double take at his outfit—jeans and a long-sleeved polo shirt. He didn't find that in my closet, so he must have brought it. My dad has gone casual.

"Y'all ready?"

"I really can't believe you signed us up without asking," Mother mutters, leaning in to check her lipstick in the mirror one more time.

"Come on, Emily. Maybe it will be fun." Dad picks up a down jacket from the back of the couch and puts on his hearty "meet the judge" smile. My heart sinks. He's dreading it worse than she is.

"There'll be hot chocolate after." What I don't say is, by then our hands may be too frozen to hold the cups. "We'll just do a few houses. Then if they keep going, we'll come home and I'll fix homemade cocoa."

Out in the frigid air, we walk to meet the others on the court square. We instinctively huddle together but don't really touch each other.

When we arrive at the square, Barry Stewart is organizing. Not only does he arrange flowers, apparently he arranges music. He immediately places Dad in the bass section and Mother with the altos.

"I paint," I say when he gives me a questioning look.

"What?"

"Never mind. Just put me anywhere." Singing isn't a talent of mine, but I love doing it. Especially caroling.

He stands me next to JoAnne Simmons, a teller from the bank. Thankfully, she has a beautiful soprano voice, strong enough that I don't get her off-key and loud enough to give me the luxury of singing out.

Thirty minutes later, we're on Sugarplum Street behind my store, singing "Jingle Bells"—what else?—for the twentieth time. I look over at my parents. Dad is belting out the tune; Mother has her lips pursed, but I can't tell if she's grimacing or singing. Either way, at least she's here. Maybe this wasn't such a bad idea, after all.

When we pause, a voice speaks up from the back. "I'd like to see them write a song about Summer Valley." We all turn to look, and Sam staggers forward.

Oh no. I can smell the alcohol all the way over here.

"At least Summer Valley wants to give us jobs," Fred Moore growls from beside Dad.

"Jobs? What about our self-respect?" Sam adjusts his engineer cap.

"Self-respect don't put food on the table," Fred fires back.

"Yeah," Billy Farmer chimes in. "I don't think my kids would be very happy with a package of self-respect under the Christmas tree."

I know what he means, but I also know his kids. A little self-respect wouldn't hurt them any.

Billy shakes his fist. "Go drink somewhere else. I signed that petition, and I'm proud of it."

Sam latches his left thumb in his overall strap and points his right finger at Billy. "Sally Harrington would turn over in her grave at the sorry lot of you, signing that petition like it's manna from heaven."

I can't help but agree with Sam's words, even though they're slurred, but I see Dad's face tense. And Mom pinches her lips together.

"If my mother were here," Dad says in his commanding courtroom voice, "she'd likely remind you gentlemen that Christmas Eve is no time to argue."

I give Barry a "hurry up and start a song" motion.

He jerks as if he forgot he was in charge. "Silent Night," he calls out, and the group obediently begins the song. Even Fred and Billy sing.

I watch Sam weave his way down the street and slowly out of sight. How do you help someone who has a heart of gold but can't seem to break free from that bondage? I stare after him and send up a silent prayer. For his safety. . .and for his release.

Before I can rejoin the song, a drop of rain hits my face, then another. The singing becomes disjointed and hesitant. Then the heavens open, like an unexpected spring shower, only freezing, pounding down on us. The carolers squeal and scatter.

"This way," I yell and motion to my parents. We run, with me leading the way, down the alley behind us to my back door. They crowd against the wall without speaking as I fumble with the key.

When we're in, I shiver and glance up at them. Mother's carefully applied makeup has melted, giving her a forlorn look. And Dad's nose is red enough to guide a sleigh tonight. "Mother, you take the hall bath, and Dad can use Gran's."

"What about you?" Dad says as they peel off their outerwear.

"I'll wrap a blanket around me and start the cocoa. Whoever gets out first can finish stirring it while I bathe."

Mother doesn't protest, and for a minute, I feel an odd pain. Gran would have insisted on me going first. But then, she enjoyed taking care of me.

Because she loved me.

Tears mix with the water on my face as I start upstairs. For the first time in my life, I'll be glad when Christmas is over.

The early ending to our caroling leaves me with a huge blank in my schedule. When we're all warm and dry, I glance over to where Dad is flipping through a *Canoe and Kayak* magazine. Since his only other choice was *Christian Woman*, I guess he decided to take the river. "Want to build a fire?"

Mother, ensconced in the glider chair with her reading glasses on and her sudoku book drawn up close to her face, glances up. "Do you think that's safe?"

"Gran always did it. I've just been nervous about building a fire without her here to help."

Dad slaps the magazine on the couch and stands. "Sounds good. Wood still out back?"

"Yes." He's two feet from the apartment door when I realize that when he's gone I'll be alone with Mother. "I'll go with you." I can almost always count on Dad to be the strong, silent type.

We tramp down the stairs and out the back door to my wood stacked next to the building. The rain is still pounding down on the alley, but now it's bouncing against the pavement in tiny balls. "Freezing," I mutter as I grab a couple of sticks of firewood.

"We need to get ready," Dad says and gathers an armload.

"Ready for what?" I make my way carefully back up the stairs with my burden.

Even with his arms full, Dad reaches around me and pushes open the apartment door. Who said chivalry was dead?

"Thanks," I grunt. "Ready for what?" I repeat.

Dad has dumped his wood. "Where are your candles?"

"Candles? For the fireplace?" I don't remember this step in starting a fire.

"What about flashlights? Do you have flashlights and batteries?" Dad walks away from me toward the dining room.

"Third drawer in the kitchen," I call after him. "Why?"

He sticks his head back in the door. "Ice is starting to build up on the electric lines. There's a good chance we'll lose power."

"Let's go to a hotel," Mother says from her chair.

"A hotel wouldn't have power, either, if we lost it here." Dad hurries through the apartment, divvying out the candles and flashlights to different spots in the house.

Mother rests her puzzle book on her knee. "We could go back to our house."

I give her an incredulous look. It's Christmas Eve. My parents decorate for Christmas entertaining. But we all know the maid packs those away as soon as their last party is over. A hotel would be more festive.

"We wouldn't make it to the interstate," Dad calls.

"Maybe we won't lose power." I lay the wood out in the fireplace the way Gran showed me last winter.

Dad kneels beside me and helps. "Might not, but we need to be ready. You have to think ahead."

As he strikes the fireplace match and holds it to the starter log, Mother walks over to watch. "My goodness, Jared. Obviously if she understood that, she'd be out making her own footprint in the world instead of living your mother's life here in the middle of nowhere, waiting to go out of business."

The wood bursts into flames. The muscles across my shoulders tighten, but I don't look up from the newborn fire. What she means is, I should be living the life they planned for me.

Dad glances at me, then at her. "It's Christmas Eve, Emily. There's plenty of time to talk about the future later." I notice he doesn't disagree with her. Just her timing. Jared Harrington is famous for his timing in the courtroom. He wouldn't dream of being any less perfect in his personal life.

The smoke makes my eyes water, so I push to my feet and squeeze Dad's arm. "Thanks for helping me. Now I think I can do it on my own."

Dad nods and clears his throat, obviously uncomfortable with my gratitude. "Yes, well, I need to go check on the weather."

He scoots out of the room before I can go with him.

Mother peers intently out the window. She doesn't look any happier to be alone with me than I am with her.

"At least we'll stay warm if the electricity goes off." I rearrange the couch pillow and sit down to watch the fire.

Mother purses her lips and nods. "That's one good thing."

"So, what did you get Dad for Christmas?"

She frowns as if I'm interrupting her favorite TV show. "You know what I always get him—a subscription to *The Wall Street Journal* and a new suit."

"No surprises this year?"

"No." She gives me a level gaze, her blue eyes hard to read. "We never want for surprises as long as you're our daughter."

"That's my job." My laugh is forced, but at least it's an attempt. "To keep your lives interesting."

Dad stomps in the door with a load of firewood. He dumps it beside the hearth and claps his hands together. "We're in for some interesting weather."

"What did I tell you?" I murmur, then blink. Did a smile just cross my mother's face? Probably just a shadow. I push to my feet. "Who wants to open presents tonight?"

Mother raises an eyebrow and purses her lips. "Are you sure that would be okay? Your grandmother always insisted we wait until Christmas morning."

She's right. I was so desperate to fill in this evening that I hadn't given it that much thought.

"I think we should do it," Dad says. "It's time the three of us start some traditions of our own."

I know he's right, but now that I've thought about it, it's hard to let the old ones go. "Mother?"

She shrugs. "It doesn't matter to me."

"Fine, then. I'll get Kristianna's packages." Dad goes down the hall and comes back with two professionally wrapped gifts. He hands them to me and pulls Mother down beside him on the couch.

"Thanks." I tear into the paper, unsure what to expect. Usually my parents don't seem to put any thought into my gift, but it never mattered because Gran always got me just the right thing. I pull out an attaché case and run my hand over the supple black leather. "It's beautiful." But what am I supposed to put in it? My painting supplies?

Mother leans forward and unbuckles a small pouch on the side. "There's even a place for your BlackBerry."

If I had one. Which I don't, because I don't need one at all. My simple cell phone works fine for me. I nod, though, and open the smaller present. Of course. A BlackBerry. "Wow. You shouldn't have." I look up to find my dad watching me intently. "Thanks," I say, a lump rising in my throat. Not because the gifts aren't things I wanted. But because they are gifts for an imaginary daughter. The one my parents wish they'd had.

"When you go back to law school, you'll use both of those," Mother says firmly.

For a minute, the room is quiet, except for the Christmas

music playing in the background and the crackling fire. I push to my feet and retrieve a large gift from under the tree and hand it to them. "Merry Christmas." *From the daughter you ended up with.*

"I wonder what this is," Dad says, his faked joviality almost worse than Mother's attitude.

He neatly pulls the paper apart at the tape seam and unfolds it carefully from around the painting of their house. When they turn it around, Mother's face relaxes for a minute, and she smiles. She likes it. And Dad does, too.

Relief floods through me, mixed with guilt that I didn't feel this way about the presents they gave me.

"It's very nice, Kristianna. Thank you," Mother says and runs her finger around the frame.

"This will be perfect over the fireplace." Dad smiles at me. "You inherited my mother's talent."

Mother mumbles something and shoves the wrapping paper from her lap as she stands. "Excuse me." She hurries down the hall, and I hear the guest bedroom door click shut.

CHAPTER 12

I'm startled. Usually Emily Harrington is the picture of composure. I've seen her face down hardened criminals without flinching. "Should I go check on her?" I ask, praying Dad will say no.

He shakes his head. "She'll be fine. Give her some time."

"Oh, here's one more gift for you." I find the tiny box for Dad and hand it to him.

He sets the painting against the couch and opens the gift, then gasps as he sees the harmonica lying there. "This is just like the one I had when I was young." He puts it to his lips and blows lightly.

"It *is* the one you had when you were young." Tears prick my eyes. "Gran and I found it in one of the boxes in the storage room, and she told me to give it to you this Christmas." I was eight when Gramps died and Gran converted the offices above the store into this apartment. She'd left many boxes untouched until we went through them together in the months before she died.

"There's a note." My dad's voice is thick, and I look away to give him privacy. He pulls a small paper from the box and reads aloud. "To my beloved son, Jared." His voice breaks, and he hands me the note.

The words swim before my eyes as I read silently. "I remember the boy who took pleasure in simple things. May you rediscover him."

Dad still has his head bowed when he speaks. "She said something similar to me before she died." He meets my gaze, and his eyes are moist. "I'm trying."

I nod and hand him the note back. That explains the blue jeans and his determination to give caroling a chance. Good for him.

He walks over to the fire and plays a soft tune on the harmonica.

"Sounds like you still remember how," I say as I join him.

"Some things you never forget."

I reach up and hug him, and his free arm comes around me, pulling me close. His Old Spice aftershave takes me back to my own childhood, and I smile. "Merry Christmas, Dad."

"Merry Christmas, Kristianna."

"I'm going to turn in. Gran left a gift for Mother, too." I motion toward a small package under the tree. "Will you give it to her and tell her I said good night?"

"Sure."

I walk down the hall and pause for a few seconds before the guest room door. I don't think Mother would welcome me with open arms. And I'd rather cherish the rare moment of closeness I just shared with Dad than end the night on a sour note.

In my room, I pick up my Bible and look at the clock. An hour until midnight.

A few verses into my daily reading, my mother's angry voice comes through the wall. "A Bible?"

Dad's deeper tone is quiet, and I can't hear his words.

"I don't care if I did carry it down the aisle. You know she had an ulterior motive, Jared. She never wanted you to marry me."

I reach over and turn on the radio. If there's more, I don't want to hear it. I still remember every hateful word she said after Gran's funeral. How glad she was that I could sell the store and apartment now and "move on." How they'd always tried to rise above this town and never could if I stayed in Jingle Bells. Acid rolls in my stomach as I play it over again in my mind.

I glance down at the Bible, open on my lap. Ironically, my verses tonight are about forgiveness and how God forgives us as we forgive others. I figure right now I need to just be really good, so I don't need as much. Ha. Like that will work.

I pray for a long time, then stare in the dark at the red numbers on my clock. We never lose power, but peace eludes me until I drift off to sleep.

"I really can't understand why you had to invite every stray person in Jingle Bells for lunch, Kristianna." Mother sips her iced tea at the table and watches me fly around the kitchen like a madwoman. I woke up this morning to three inches of fresh white snow. A white Christmas. And no time to go out and play.

"Like I told you, the guests are my friends. Besides, Gran did this for years and you never complained."

My dad, by the coffeepot, pauses in midpour. "Humph. Maybe never where you could hear it." He finishes pouring and lifts his coffee in a mock salute to Mother. "Your mother's never been comfortable socializing with the masses, dear."

I turn back to my broccoli casserole, unsure what to say to that. My parents don't profess to be Christians, but even besides that obvious difference, I occasionally wonder how we can share the same genes. Since Gran's gone, I feel so alone in this family sometimes. Like today. Gran and I would have talked things over after last night's drama. But my parents are pretending it never happened. And I guess I'm no better. I'm going along with their pretense.

When I turn, Mother is glaring at Dad, but she addresses her words to me. "Your Gran was an old woman. Gathering together a band of misfits around her table was just one of her many eccentricities. It seems funny for you to do it."

"Well, then everyone can get a good laugh while they're passing the rolls. Come on, Mother, help me make green bean bundles."

"What time will your. . .guests. . .be arriving?"

I glance up at the big clock on the wall. "Noon. We have an hour and a half to get it all done."

"I'll get out of y'all's hair," Dad says. "I think I'll take a turn around the town."

If I didn't know better, I'd think he's trying to leave us alone together. Today, I'm so busy I don't even care.

"Watch out for the riffraff," Mother calls to him. "Although

I suppose most of those will be showing up here shortly, anyway," she mutters, but I ignore it.

"Can you preheat the oven for me, please?" I ask pleasantly.

She moves to do it, and I'm grateful. My mother is used to servants, not serving. "Are you leaving the shop door unlocked like your grandmother always did when she was expecting guests?"

I nod.

She sighs. "I don't understand you."

Now there's the truest statement of the year, ladies and gentlemen. "I know."

"How many people are coming?" she asks as she refills her tea glass.

I do a mental count. "Anywhere from five to seven, besides the three of us."

"You mean some people didn't RSVP?" Horror fills her voice. You'd think failure to RSVP was a crime worthy of death.

"There are two I'm not sure about." One of those is Shawn. I invited him before the town meeting; considering all the events since then, I'm not expecting him, but who knows? Sam is the other one who didn't call, but unless he's embarrassed about last night, he'll be here. "We'll plan for ten."

"Well, if they didn't respond, I'd tell them they weren't welcome if they show up." She tears a pink packet open and pours it into her tea.

I stop with the freezer door open and stare at her. Surely there's a joke in there somewhere. "On Christmas Day?"

"Manners are manners"—she stirs the sweetener in with a long-handled spoon—"every day."

Gotcha. "Good. That means you'll be polite to all my guests." I unwrap the rolls.

"Don't seat me next to that drunken horseman," she says, her voice stern.

I don't even bother reminding her there's no seating chart.

When the door chime rings downstairs an hour later, I glance around the kitchen. Mother has retired to her room to rest before dinner. Too much strenuous tea drinking, I guess. Everything is ready. Garrett volunteered to bring the ham. Hopefully that's him. Or probably Dad back from his walk.

Sure enough, I hear steps on the stairs and Dad comes in, but he's escorting the Campbell twins. "Look, Kristianna. We got a man for Christmas," Elva calls.

"Elva, shame on you." Ermyl shakes her head. "You're going to embarrass Jared."

I laugh and hug them both. Sometimes I forget that Dad was raised in Jingle Bells.

Dad reaches out his arms, and I give him a hug, too. I smile. Talk about unexpected Christmas presents.

Dad graciously shows the twins to the living room, and the door chime rings again. This time, it's Garrett, bearing a beautiful honey-baked ham. He grins at me. "You're looking festive."

CHRISTINE LYNXWILER

I glance down at my red Mrs. Santa apron and laugh. "You know me—always in the Christmas spirit." I start to give him a high five. But he sets the ham down on the front table and pulls me into a hug. "Merry Christmas, sport," he says against my ear.

"Merry Christmas," I whisper. "I'm so glad to have you back."

And I'm glad he came. When he was nine, his dad left on Christmas Day, apparently tired of his wife and kids. I remember Garrett's mom called Gran, frantic. She couldn't find Garrett and was hoping he was with us. I led Gran straight to where I knew he'd be. I'll never forget him, huddled in our secret fort up on Snowy Mountain, tears leaving streaks down his dirty face. We didn't spend another Christmas apart, until college.

During the years we lost touch, there was a big hole in my life. I'm sure I would have adapted eventually, but it's incredibly nice not to have to.

He meets my gaze, his green eyes serious. "It's really good to be back."

There's something in his eyes that begs closer examination, but a peck on the door behind him stops me from pursuing it. "Oops. I didn't even hear the door chime downstairs."

"Me either." He picks up the ham. "I'll take this to the kitchen."

Dottie Wells sticks her head in. "Is this the party?"

I laugh. "This is the place. Come on in."

Dottie pulls Mr. Pletka into the room. "I found this old man loitering on the doorstep so I brought him, too."

"Old man, my feet," he says. Even after twenty years, he can't quite get American expressions right, but that doesn't stop him from trying. "You're no spring hen yourself."

"Well," Dottie says, "my birthday is coming up in a couple of weeks."

I hug her. "Celebrating the big 6-0, right?"

"You got it, sister."

Dottie's been having her "big 6-0" ever since I can remember, even though she's probably older than Mr. Pletka. But the town doesn't seem to mind. Last year, a couple of newcomers had the nerve to comment that she'd turned sixty both years they'd lived here, and they were never seen again. Rumor has it that tar and feathers were involved, but my guess is they realized what a nutty place they'd moved to and relocated voluntarily.

Dottie and Mr. Pletka gravitate to the living room, where everyone is laughing and talking. I step down the hall and tap on Mother's door.

"Come in." She's sitting in a chair in the corner, working on some papers.

"Merry Christmas." I smile. "You ready to face the crowd?"

She narrows her eyes. "Do I have a choice?"

"Not unless you want one of those women twice Dad's age to take him home with her."

She closes her portfolio and tilts her lips slightly upward. "I'd better rescue him."

She follows me back to the living room, and the door chime sounds again. "Must be Sam."

But when I open the door, Shawn smiles sheepishly, a large poinsettia plant in his hand. "For you," he says. "Thank you for inviting me."

"Thank you for coming," I mumble automatically and take the poinsettias. "These are my favorites."

"I figured." His dimple flashes. "I know we're wearing out the whole 'truce' thing, but think we could call a Christmas cease-fire?"

"I'm game if you are." But even as I say it, I wonder how many signatures he has. "Let's just relax and enjoy the day." I can't resist one little jab at his note.

He just smiles.

"Come on in." I guide him to the living room and introduce him to the group. The Campbell twins look puzzled, and Dottie frowns.

"Bear in dog's clothing, if you ask me," Mr. Pletka mutters.

Could be an interesting meal.

Garrett stands and shakes Shawn's hand, but even he looks uncomfortable.

Shawn seems unbothered by the hostility. I guess if you're a lawyer-to-be it goes with the territory.

The grandfather clock against the wall chimes twelve. Mother stands and looks at me expectantly.

My fault. I did say lunch at noon. "Why don't we get things going in the kitchen and give Sam a few more minutes," I say under my breath as conversation swirls around us. Dad and Shawn are debating the finer points of the best law schools while Dottie and the Campbell twins swap recipes. Garrett and Mr. Pletka seem to be taking it all in.

In the kitchen, I snag a vase from the china cabinet and put Shawn's flowers in it.

"Shawn seems very nice," Mother says.

I look up to see her eyes twinkling. I can count on one hand the number of times I've ever seen that particular look in her eyes. I groan inwardly. How did I miss this obvious complication? I've gotten so used to my parents barely tolerating my friends that I didn't consider how much Shawn would appeal to them. "He is nice. But he's not my type."

"What do you mean? He's an attorney."

"I've gotten over that."

"Honestly, Kristianna, is that supposed to be funny?"

Sometimes no answer is the best answer. Particularly with my mother. "Would you help me carry these hot dishes out to the table?" I hand her two potholders and nod toward the stove, then load up my own arms and push through the double doors to the dining room.

We work well together, to my amazement, and within minutes, the table is laid out in true holiday style. "Thanks for your help," I say as I ice the glasses.

She shrugs. "It's fine. Your grandmother never let me help with her dinners, so I assumed you'd be the same way."

I knock an ice cube onto a holiday napkin. As I reach to pick it up, I stop. Even though the cube is clear, the design of the napkin under it is distorted. Sometimes I think that's how Mother views the past. Particularly Gran's part in it.

A commotion in the other room saves me from having to reply. I hurry out of the kitchen. Sam, his hat askew, stands in the foyer with his fist clenched. Garrett stands between him and a red-faced Shawn.

CHAPTER 13

Guilt floods Sam's expression when he sees me. "I'm sorry, Miss Kristianna. Your grandmother was a gracious woman, but I don't think she'd have wanted this Judas in her house."

"Sam." I frown at him. "You know Gran would never insult a guest, no matter what his politics. Shawn has no family around, and I invited him for dinner."

He scoops his hat off and pinches it between his work-worn fingers. "I'm sorry." He nods at Shawn. "Sorry." He shakes his head. "I can't stay. Merry Christmas to you all." He turns and slips out the door. It clicks shut behind him.

My heart pounds against my ribs, but I turn to face my guests, all gathered in the foyer now. "I hope y'all are hungry. It's time to eat."

Shawn looks at me. "I don't have to stay."

"Don't be silly, young man," Dottie says. "If you don't stick around, how will you know the spirit of Christmas truly lives in Jingle Bells?"

"Dottie's right." I include everyone in my smile. "I'm sorry for not realizing this might happen. But we'll make sure Sam doesn't go hungry. So let's put this out of our minds for now, okay?"

In the dining room, I wait until everyone is seated; then I slide into the seat next to Garrett. "Will you offer thanks when we're ready?" I whisper.

He nods.

Across from me, Mother looks at Shawn next to her, then up at the ceiling. "Kristianna, I believe there's a draft over here. You know how susceptible I am to colds this time of year. May we trade seats?"

Could she be any more obvious? My cheeks burn, but before I can move, Garrett pushes to his feet. "I'll be glad to trade with you, Mrs. Harrington."

Her smile is cold enough to freeze a flame. "When you're seating people at a proper table, you can't exchange a man for a woman. It disturbs the balance."

Absolute hogwash, but as Garrett sinks back to his seat, I trade places with Mother quickly. Her determination apparently knows no limits.

Garrett meets my eyes across the table, and I think I see a small smile at the corner of his mouth. He knows about my relationship with my parents and no doubt saw through Mother's "draft situation" as easily as I did. But he didn't want to see me forced into anything. My spirits rise. It's nice to be understood.

As soon as I'm settled, Garrett says the blessing for the food, and then everyone is talking and eating cheerfully. Shawn at least pretends he's unaware of Mother's machinations, and the meal goes off without a hitch. While everyone is leaving, Garrett volunteers to take Sam a plate.

I grab a plastic divided platter. "Let's heap it up." I place another one beside it. "And here's one for dessert."

Garrett grins and piles ham on the first plate. "You don't have a soft spot for that old man, do you?"

I scoop a liberal serving of banana pudding onto the platter. "His politics agree with mine, if that's what you mean."

He frowns. "I wasn't referring to that."

"I know." I swat him on the shoulder, although my heart panics. What if Garrett agrees with Shawn and the others? What if my best friend is against me? At least for now, I'd rather not know. "I care about him. And feel sorry for him."

"Well, he won't go hungry tonight, that's for sure." He glances around the kitchen. "You want me to stay and help you clean up?"

More than anything. I'm too tired to wiggle. But I shake my head. "That would be great, but I'm worried about Sam. If you'll just take this and check on him, I'll be happy." I reach up and drop a kiss on his cheek.

His arm circles me in a hug. "I'll call you later so you can de-stress."

"Good." Especially with Ami gone, it will be good to pour out my troubles with my parents to a friend.

After he's gone and the others start to drift out one by one, Dad and Shawn are still engrossed in conversation, this time about golf.

Shawn apparently notices he's the last guest remaining. He stands. "I'd better go."

Mother sits down beside Dad on the couch. "Why don't you stay awhile?"

Shawn looks at me.

With all the enthusiasm I can muster, considering I'd like to go take a nap, I say, "Yes, why don't you?"

Dad asks him something about the golf courses around here, and Shawn sits again.

Mother retires to her room, and rather than follow her and ask her what she thinks she's doing with the obvious matchmaking, I go to the kitchen to face the after-meal disaster.

When the dishes are done, I wander back into the living room and sit down. Dad and Shawn have moved on to politics, a topic they apparently agree on. Mother's in the glider again, working a puzzle. Guess she thought I didn't want her in the kitchen.

My eyelids grow heavier. The couch cushion is so soft.

"You know, we might have a place in our firm for a young man as sharp as you are," Mother says.

I sit up straight.

Shawn is beaming. "Really?"

Dad smiles. "Come by and see us after you get your bar results."

"That would be a real honor, sir." Shawn nods to my mom. "Ma'am."

Okay, I'm wide awake now. What's wrong with this picture?

Who did Shawn come to see? Me or my parents? He probably meant to give my mother the flowers but just hated to say so.

He catches my eye and stands. "I'd better go."

I stand. Mother is behind him, smiling broadly. Pride shines in Dad's eyes. Why can't they look at me that way for who I am instead of who I'm with?

"Kristianna will see you to your car," Mother says.

I nod. Emily Harrington has spoken. I guess I'll see him to his car.

He shakes Dad's hand, and Mother gives him an elbow hug.

When we're on the stairs, I look back at him. "I guess you know you're almost a partner in the firm now, since Mother deigned to give you a hug."

His face turns red. "I wasn't being nice to your parents for a job."

I smile. "Oh, so you aren't interested in working with one of Little Rock's most prestigious law firms?"

We reach the bottom step, and he grins. "Just because I wasn't campaigning for a job doesn't mean I'm not interested."

"The truth comes out." We stand at the glass door and look out at the snow.

"Do you ever dream of going to sunny Florida on days like this?" he asks.

I shake my head and wipe the fog from the glass so I can look up at the solid white sky. "Nope." Not even when I get flip-flops and beach bags as gifts. "There's no place like Jingle Bells for Christmas." I smile. "Or any other day for that matter."

He scuffs at the concrete floor with his shoe. "You never quit, do you? You're a Jingle Bells supporter, 24-7."

"And proud of it."

"What about time to relax and think about more personal things? Don't you ever consider life more intimately than on the town level?" I recognize his tone. It's the lawyer gene kicking in.

"Sure I do. But the way I see it, my life, along with the rest of the town, is about to be obliterated if we don't win this battle. When someone's dropping a bomb on you, you don't sit around and explore your feelings."

As a matter of fact, if I'm going to talk to someone, I'd rather it be someone who's going to help me stop the Summer Valley madness. I need to be making lists of people to call and things to do. "It's been a long day, Shawn. I appreciate your coming. I know there were parts of it that were uncomfortable."

"No problem." He puts his hand on the doorknob, then turns back to look at me. "I have a feeling this is a hopeless case, anyway."

"Changing the name of Jingle Bells?" If he can see that, then maybe the battle won't be as difficult as I think.

"No. I was thinking aloud." He holds my gaze. "On a personal level."

Oh. "I'm sorry."

He runs his hand through his hair. "Yeah, me, too. Thanks for dinner."

He's really gorgeous. Even when he's dejected. And he's a nice Christian guy. I stand at the door and watch him walk to his car.

What am I thinking, letting him go? Unfortunately, my heart is doing the thinking these days.

Call me a coward. But I can't force myself to walk immediately up the stairs and face my parents. I kill some time in the store, getting things ready for the after-Christmas sale. Ten minutes later, I slip into my apartment.

My parents' bag is by the door, next to the painting I did for them. My dad turns from the window just as my mother comes down the hall. "That didn't take long," she says.

I'm not sure if she knows how short a time it really took, so I just nod. "I'm tired."

"Yes, well, so are we, so we'd better go."

"Thank you for coming." It seems to me that good-byes often reflect a magnified version of the relationship between the people who are being separated. With my parents, the ever-present awkward emotions swell to gigantic proportions when it's time to say good-bye.

"Yes, thank you for having us," Dad says. "And thank you for the gift. It's lovely."

Mother nods. "We'd like for you to come to dinner at our house after New Year's. What night would be best for you?"

Uh-oh. Family dinners planned in advance are always a bad sign. But putting it off will serve no purpose. "Friday night?" It's not like I have anywhere else to be on Friday nights. And I open the shop an hour later on Saturdays.

"Jared, are you free on the Friday night after New Year's?"

Dad frowns. "I can move racquetball to Tuesday, and that will be fine."

"Good." Her smile doesn't reach her eyes, and I'm suddenly sure they know how quickly my talk with Shawn ended.

They gather their things to leave, and once again, I tramp down the stairs, follow them to the front door, and lock up behind them. "Merry Christmas," I say softly and watch the glass fog up with my words.

Two hours later, I'm in my workshop painting when I hear a tapping sound on the window. I spin around in time to see a few pebbles hit the glass. I walk over to look out and see Garrett in the hazy twilight. He grins and holds up a big brightly wrapped box with a big red bow. A giggle slips from me as I run to the back door to let him in. My crazy friend.

"What are you doing?"

"Just spreading Christmas cheer." He hands me the box.

"You nut. You could have just called or even walked up to the window and knocked. It's street level."

"I know, but I've always wanted to throw pebbles at a window. It's so old movie-ish."

It is, isn't it? "Stay right here," I say. "I want to run up and get your gift." I didn't want to give it to him earlier in front of everyone, so I'd planned to ask him to get together, anyway, when he called tonight. He just beat me to it.

I take the stairs two at a time and am back in a flash. A little out of breath, but feeling more lighthearted already. "Here." I thrust the small package into his hand.

"Thanks." He motions toward the box on the counter. "You first."

I sink to a stool. He sits on the one beside me and watches as I tear the wrapping off. "Hey, didn't you want to save the paper?"

I stop, then see the teasing glint in his eyes. "Very funny." I use my snowman letter opener to cut the tape on the box and flip open the lid. I pull out a beautiful frame and stare at the photo of Ami and me sitting on the bottom step of the store stairs. Garrett is behind us in the middle, a hand on each of our heads.

I put my hand to my mouth. "Oh my. I remember the year of the camera." I look over at him. "You got that camera for Christmas, and we thought you'd never quit recording every second of our lives in photographs." I run my hand over the frame. We all have goofy grins, but you can tell we're really happy. "This is so cool."

"Your gran took that one for us." He motions toward the box. "There's another one."

The second photo has a matching frame, but the pic is one Garrett shot of Gran and me, the same year. "Oh, Garrett. I love it. I know exactly where I'm going to hang these." I hug him. "What a perfect gift."

He smiles. "Glad you like them."

Like them? This may be the best gift I've ever gotten. My mind jumps to the "anonymous" summer-themed surprises from Shawn.

Lately I've been receiving lots of presents. "Here." I scoot his gift from me over in front of him.

He rips it open with just as much enthusiasm as I did mine, and when he holds the ornament in his hand, he lifts it up to examine it. "Wow. This is amazing."

Last summer, right after he got back in town to stay, he and I took his dog, Shadow, kayaking. Big mistake. Thanks to the exuberant black Lab, we spent more time in the water than in the kayak. I worked hard to capture the boy and girl on each end of the kayak holding on for dear life, while the dog is up on the side with its front paws.

Garrett runs his finger over the details. "I can't imagine anything I'd rather have." He cups my face with his hand and drops a kiss on my forehead. "Thanks."

Before I can answer, he slides his hand around under my chin and tilts my face upward. I meet his gaze. His very close gaze. *What's he doing?* I open my mouth to ask him, and he touches his lips to mine. My hand instinctively tangles in his curls as I return his tender kiss.

Whoa. Double whoa. So that's what he was doing.

As I relax in the circle of his arms, my workshop fades away.

CHAPTER 14

After what seems like forever but is probably only seconds, Garrett sits back. His normally easy grin seems a little forced, but he points up above our heads. "Seemed a shame to waste that mistletoe."

I give a breathless laugh. "Yeah. A shame."

He pushes to his feet. "Want to go build a snowman? Then we can grab a bite to eat."

I hope he doesn't notice I'm still trying to shift back to reality. I shouldn't feel so jumbled inside. What's a little mistletoe between friends? "I don't know if anything's open."

He shrugs. "If not, we'll just have to make do with leftovers. C'mon, sport. Race ya to the park."

He turns for the door, and I touch my lips absently. What just happened? Whatever it was, he seems prepared to ignore it.

"You coming?"

I shrug into my coat and follow him out. He puts his arm around me loosely, shielding me from the cold wind. Ten minutes ago, I wouldn't have given that simple gesture a second thought. Now I can't stop analyzing.

We turn toward the park. For a few minutes, the only sound is our boots crunching in the snow.

"Look. There must have been a Christmas program today." He points at three kids in front of the two houses we're passing.

A girl in an angel costume is trying to build a snowman, while two shepherds are running and pelting each other with snowballs.

"Looks like fun," I say, hoping to get things back to normal. For me, that is. He seems totally unfazed by our mistletoe incident.

"It does, doesn't it?" He scoops up a handful of snow and starts to form it into a ball.

"Garrett, don't even think about it." Even as I protest, I know I actually welcome a return to the familiar teasing and camaraderie.

"Think about what?" he taunts, waving the snowball at me.

A motion from the yard catches our attention. We look over just in time to see one little shepherd grab the other by his brown gunnysack poncho and push him down. He comes up, swinging his fists. The snowball in Garrett's hand falls to the sidewalk as we stare at the boys while they roll over and over, throwing punches. The angel takes off for the smaller house.

Garrett wades into the fray and manages to come up with both wiggling shepherds held an arm's length apart. "Boys." His voice is commanding. "Cut it out."

They stop swinging and sullenly stare at each other. Garrett looks toward the house, then back at me.

I know. I thought the angel would have brought help by now, too. I shrug.

"You two were having fun a minute ago. What happened?" Garrett asks.

"He said our town is dumb." The boy's red hair stands straight out, and I promise you can almost see it tingle with indignation.

His white-haired counterpart crosses his arms in front of him. "Did not! I just told you my dad said we'll have to change the name to Summer Valley if we want more Christmas presents next year."

"You said, 'dumb ole Jingle Bells.' I heard you."

"Did not."

"Did so."

A man in a white T-shirt and stained jeans barrels out of the small house. "Hey, whatchoo doin'?" His tattooed arms look like Popeye's after spinach. "Let go of my kid," he growls as he gets closer.

Garrett releases the boys but stands his ground between them. "They were fighting."

The blond boy runs to the man's side and wipes at the blood trickling from his nose. "Daddy, Robbie said we have to change the name of Jingle Bells. Is that true?"

"Only if you want to eat and keep a roof over your head." We all turn to face a ruddy-faced man with hair the same fiery color as Robbie's. He has his hand on his son's shoulder and is giving Garrett the evil eye.

"Popeye" forgets about us and turns on his neighbor. "Garbage. I know how these big corporations are—full of worthless promises, hot air. My family's been from Jingle Bells forever. We're not moving." He flexes his muscle and spits on the ground. "And we're not living in Summer Valley."

Garrett walks back over to me. "I think they're too big for me to pull apart," he says under his breath.

I nod. "Yeah, they're liable to pull you apart. Let's go."

As we start to round the corner, I glance back at the two men, inches apart, yelling, while the angel and two shepherds look on.

Ami plunks the almost empty punch bowl onto the kitchen counter of the church fellowship hall. "You do realize that, technically, since I'm married, I'm a guest tonight, right?"

I wrinkle my nose at her. "Not this year, missy. We started plans for the party before you tied the knot. So grab that ginger ale and help me make more punch. Tonight you're a single."

She pours the soda into the bowl while I scoop vanilla ice cream in. As we finish, Mark walks through the door, Shawn behind him.

"Where's the punch?" Mark asks. "The natives are restless."

"You're just in time, honey," Ami says, with a saucy smile. "Kristianna just informed me I'm single tonight."

He wraps his arm around her waist. "I don't think so."

I hold my hands up. "Your wife was trying to shirk her hostess duties as part of the singles' group."

"Next year, sweetie," he says to Ami, "we'll be guests like the rest of the church." He picks up the full punch bowl, and Ami pushes the door open for him. They disappear into the fellowship hall's main room.

"Nice party," Shawn says. "Anything I can do?"

I start to say no, on general principles, but then I realize that this is the first real event our singles' group has had since Shawn came to town. Other than this annual party, we usually shut down over the holidays. Everyone from church brings a dish, but our group is responsible for entertainment and snacks before the meal. And any labor requires setting things up. As a Christian, I need to include him, in spite of what I think about his job choice. "Thanks. Why don't you help me grab some chips and dip from the counter, and we'll restock the appetizer table?"

"Sure."

We load up with chips and plastic containers of dip and head out the door with me leading the way. I immediately collide with someone and look up into familiar green eyes. Other than a glimpse across the auditorium at church, I haven't seen Garrett since the mistletoe incident, which will be a week tomorrow, so I'm curious how he'll act.

He looks from me to Shawn. "Hi." He nods to the kitchen. "Everything under control in there?"

I nod. "I think so."

"Good." He turns and walks away. So that's how he's going to act. Totally uninterested.

Shawn and I continue to the table, where we dump the dips and bags of chips. I look around for Garrett and finally spot him in the corner with Mark and Ami.

Okay, this may be weirder than I thought.

Shawn leads me over to Mark and Ami's table when we're done. I slide in by Garrett, and Shawn sits on my other side.

As soon as Brother Tom says the blessing for the food, people rush the potluck table, but in unspoken agreement, we wait for the crowd to thin.

"Look," Ami says, "Larry has his karaoke equipment all set up."

Thankfully, one of the guys in our group is a karaoke deejay and he does our New Year's Eve parties for free. "Good. I hope people will participate earlier than they did last year." Even the older people eventually warm up to it, but for a while, there are no takers.

"Come on. Let's get it started while people fill their plates. Pick a song." Ami grabs the laminated song list from the table and starts calling out titles. " 'I Will Always Love You' by Whitney Houston?"

"No way. You know I can't hit the high notes on that. Let's do something we can all do together. What do you guys want to sing?" If I'm going to do this, it *will* be with a group.

"How 'bout 'Achy Breaky Heart'? " I can hear the smile in Mark's voice even though his face is in the shadows.

"Oh yeah. Let's do it!" Ami is too excited. I roll my eyes at Garrett. "Come on, Garrett, you have to get up there with us."

"Sure, just call me Billy Ray." He swishes his nonexistent pony-tail with his hand.

"Shawn? Will you sing with us?" I ask.

He smiles and shakes his head. "Not my thing. I can't wait to laugh at y'all, though."

"That's the spirit," Mark says. "This is the only song I'm doing. Let me say that right now."

He knows Ami too well. Once she gets started on karaoke, it practically takes a power outage to stop her. She leads the way to the front, pulling Mark by the hand. Garrett and I lag behind, but eventually we're all under the lights.

I think everyone from church is here to ring in the New Year, and it looks like they brought a few friends. We giggle and sing our way through the old country music hit that we sang a million times during our teens.

The applause is deafening. I think everyone's just glad to see us in the spotlight instead of being up here themselves. We graciously refuse the shouts of "encore" from Dottie and talk her into taking the stage herself.

"We have to eat," Garrett calls and pats his stomach.

Mark calls to Shawn, who meets us in the buffet line, and I hear the opening chords of "Crazy." Dottie sings that every year. Which could be pitiful, but to be honest, she does a mean Patsy Cline. I hope she never quits.

"Lila, I'm glad you came." Ami's voice pulls my attention to the other side of the table a little farther back in the line, where Mark's redheaded coworker has a piece of celery and three wheat crackers on her plate.

I look down at my overflowing platter. That's why she wears a size two and I don't. We all make our choices. And on New Year's Eve, I choose to sample as much as I can from the great cooks in our congregation. I nod at Lila, but she ignores me.

"Hi, Garrett."

He waves with his free hand.

When we're settled back at our table in the corner, Lila appears almost immediately. "Can I pull up a chair?" As she asks, she plops her plate down between Garrett and me and snags a chair from the empty table next to us.

Sure. Be my guest.

When she sits, she turns her chair slightly toward Garrett, leaving me to look mostly at her back. A woman on a mission. And in spite of how irritated I am by her choice of target, I do admire her take-action attitude. I'm over here flopping around like a flounder on a butcher's block while she swims right to the fish she has her eye on.

We're almost done eating when Ami picks up the song title list again. "Let's do another one. Oh, look! Here's 'A Friend Like Me' from *Aladdin*." She looks at Garrett and me. "Remember when we used to sing that when we were kids?" She grabs Mark's hand. "Come on, y'all."

"Like I said, one's my limit. I'm going to have to pass." Mark puts a potato chip in his mouth.

Ami faux pouts, then smiles. "Lila, Shawn, how about it? Want to sing with us?"

"No thanks. Karaoke isn't really my thing." Lila has that same look she had when she saw me bowling. Bemusement, I guess you'd call it.

Shawn shakes his head. "I'd still rather be the audience."

Garrett clears his throat. "I need to check the food and make sure everything is okay."

Aren't we Mr. Conscientious?

Ami shrugs. "Let's go, Kristianna." She grabs my arm and pulls just as I hear Lila say, "Garrett, sweetie, will you get me another glass of punch?"

I grit my teeth and follow Ami into the limelight to sing about friends who stand by each other through thick and thin. Sometimes that's tougher than it sounds.

Two hours later, we've finally given up karaoke. Several lively games of Trivial Pursuit and charades are going on around the room, and as the hosts, we're circulating among the tables, making sure everyone is having fun.

Dottie and Elva and Ermyl Campbell are trying to show me how to play Mexican Train dominoes when the deejay taps the mike. "Okay, folks, just a few minutes till midnight. Time to gather close to your nearest and dearest so you can ring in the New Year together." The older ladies excuse themselves to go to the restroom so they "won't miss the countdown." And I'm alone in a crowd. I make my way back over to my table.

"Ready for a brand-new year?" I swing around to see Shawn smiling at me.

"Might as well be."

"Am I keeping you from someone?" he asks, and if I'm not

mistaken, there's a tad more than casual curiosity in his voice.

I involuntarily glance over to where Garrett is doing a bad job of acting out something in charades. Lila is stationed just a few feet away. Guarding her newfound territory. "No. I was just going to find Mark and Ami."

"Me, too. Okay with you if we find them together?"

"Sure."

Regardless of what Larry the deejay would like for us to believe, this isn't Times Square, so they're not hard to find. They've gravitated back to our original table. "Mind if we ring in the New Year with you?" Shawn asks.

"Be our guests." Ami beams. I'm sure she thinks her match-making is paying off.

We slide into chairs just as Larry begins the countdown. I can't keep from checking to see if Lila kisses Garrett. Instead, I see her standing alone near the other charades players, looking puzzled. I automatically scan the room, but Garrett's nowhere to be found.

"Happy New Year!" Larry yells over the microphone, and everyone cheers.

Shawn reaches out to hug me. "Happy New Year, Kristianna."

I echo his words and give him a hug, but I turn my head so his kiss lands on my hair. A nice Christian guy wants to ring in the New Year with me, and I'm wondering where Garrett is. Maybe my New Year's resolution should be not to look a gift horse in the mouth.

CHAPTER 15

"Welcome to the first meeting of the Committee to Save Jingle Bells." I smile at the crowd. "Dottie, thank you for keeping the library open late for us." She was really uncertain about doing it. But I begged, and she said yes.

Dottie nods. "Any time, Kristianna."

Oh, good. Maybe I won't have to beg next time we get together.

Ruby Lemmons waves her hand in the air.

"Ruby?"

"I was thinking we could call ourselves CARE"—she pronounces each letter very carefully—"C-A-R-E."

"What does that stand for?" I've tried for days to think of an acronym but haven't been able to find anything that works.

"Committee Against Renaming Everything." She smiles proudly.

A few people snort.

I glare at them. At least she's thinking about why we're here.

I'm pretty sure a few people came for the free refreshments. "That's original, but it may be a little broad for us. What if we focus on Jingle Bells? Even without a cute name, we can be a strong force in our community."

Ruby leans toward the woman beside her. "Maybe so, but I think we'd be a lot stronger *with* a cute name."

Great. Our first meeting, and mutiny's already brewing. I ignore her. "Did everyone get refreshments?" I point to the back of the room, and everyone turns. Ami waves from her post beside the hot chocolate and cookies. I asked Garrett to come, but he made a flimsy excuse. "Feel free to get some while we talk. This is going to be informal. Anyone have ideas about how we can save Jingle Bells?"

No one speaks.

I perch on the edge of the desk. "Does anyone know who else was planning on coming?"

"Where's David from Mistletoe Music?" Sarah asks quietly.

Scott shakes his head and pushes his glasses up on his nose. "Didn't you hear? David locked up."

We just stare at the bookstore owner. Sometimes he forgets to fill in the narrative.

He shrugs. "He quit. Out of business."

"I was hoping that wasn't true," I say under my breath. I heard it from Elva Campbell at lunch today, but sometimes she gets things mixed up. Apparently not this time.

In unspoken agreement, we observe a moment of silence for David's fate. All of us shopkeepers can feel the same doom breathing down our necks. This just brings it one door closer.

"My nephew would have been here tonight, but his wife's uncle offered him a job; he had to move the family down there," Ruby says.

The woman beside her nods. "They're dropping like flies."

This isn't how I envisioned the meeting. Whose side are we on, anyway? We sound more like we're giving reasons *for* the name change. I clear my throat. "Dottie? Where are the flyers you made?"

She weaves in and out of the rows, passing out the papers. "Look this over," she says. "And if you like it, I'll have plenty after the meeting you can pick up to post around town."

She hands me one, even though I saw it earlier. She's done them on paper with a candy-cane border. Underneath the heading "Vote Against Summer Valley," the words "Keep Jingle Bells Forever" are in bold black print. Then in smaller letters, "Where the Spirit of Christmas Lives in Our Hearts All Year Long." In very large black letters across the bottom, it proclaims, "Don't Sell Out!" The flyer won't win any awards for artistic creativity, but it gets the point across.

"This looks good," Scott says, and several people nod.

I look at the flyer again. "Yes, it does. We don't want to give the idea that we're against progress, though."

Ruby's friend sniffs. "Like we could afford to be."

"Kristianna has a point," Sarah speaks up timidly. "Do you think there's any way we can have Summer Valley Outdoors in town and still keep Jingle Bells like it is?" She gives a rueful grin. "Only thriving, of course."

"Wonder if we could split the town? Change the name of the part out there by the lake?" Ami says from beside the refreshment table.

I've wondered that, too. It sounds so simple, though. Surely Uncle Gus would have thought of it.

Woody Feezor stands. "Sounds good, but it won't work. If you split into two towns, we won't get any of the tax revenue from Summer Valley Outdoors. They'd have better streets, better services, better everything. In just a short while, Jingle Bells would die anyway." The insurance salesman shakes his head. "Sorry to be a killjoy." He sits down.

The outside door opens, and Jack Feeney walks in. "Is this the meeting of citizens against renaming Jingle Bells?"

"Hi, Jack. That's us. Come on in and join us." It'll be great to have the newspaper on our side.

"Just for the record," he says as he takes a cup of cocoa and a cookie from Ami, "I'll be reporting this meeting, but naturally, a reporter has to remain unbiased." He balances the cookie and drink with his notebook and pencil as he settles awkwardly into a back-row chair.

Naturally.

We talk for a while longer, tossing around ideas. "What about door knocking?" Ami says from the back.

"That actually sounds like a good idea," Scott says, smiling.

Ruby claps her hands together. "It does. They've got their lawyer going door-to-door. Why shouldn't we?"

Why indeed? "We could split into teams of two and meet every Saturday morning," I add. "It shouldn't take us more than four Saturdays to knock on every door. Or at least close to that." And maybe some more people will join our efforts by then. Especially if I buy bakery cookies for the next meeting instead of a generic brand from the grocery store.

"What would we say?" Dottie asks.

I hold up a flyer. "You can memorize your own little spiel encouraging people to protect our heritage, or if you're shy, you can just hand out a flyer." I turn to the group. "What do you think?"

Several people nod.

"At least we'd be doing something, right, hon?" Mr. Stewart says to his wife.

"Absolutely," she says. They kiss to celebrate their agreement.

"So everyone willing to knock on doors next Saturday, raise your hand."

Most people raise their hands. About twenty in all.

I'm encouraged. Not everyone is swept away by the promise of prosperity with Summer Valley.

"Does anyone know how many signatures that man has on his petition?" Mrs. Stewart asks.

No one says anything, and Jack clears his throat. "Well, now. I don't see what it will hurt for me to pass on this information. After all, passing on information is my job, isn't it?" He chortles, and his Adam's apple bobs. "Half. He has half of what he needs. And it's just the first week in January."

He sounds entirely too excited for an unbiased reporter, but I just nod. "Thank you, Jack, for sharing that information." I turn back to the group. "Now we know how hard we have to work, but remember, the signatures on this petition are just to get this issue on the ballot." Garrett reminded me of that the other day, and I'm holding on tightly to the thought. "So even a full petition isn't a victory. We'll beat this." I punch my fist in the air, but everyone just stares at me.

"I hope she's right," Ruby whispers loudly to the lady beside her. "I still think we'd do better with a name like CARE."

Meeting adjourned.

"Jingle Bells Water Company."

"Hi, Wilburta. It's Kristianna." I speak into my cell phone's mike on the dash as I cruise down the interstate. "I'm going to be a little late with the water bill so I was just calling to let you know."

"Oh, that's okay, sweetie. You just get it to us when you can."

I sigh inwardly. The joys of a small town. Of course, it would be awfully joyous if I could pay the bill on time, too. "Thanks. Your mama doing okay?"

"She sure is. She thinks assisted living is something God invented just so she could socialize."

I laugh. "Ah, that's so good. I know you were worried about her the last time we talked." Which was. . .let's see. . .three months ago. The last time I couldn't pay my bill.

"Thanks for asking, sweetie."

"Thanks for giving me some extra time." I always pay my bills. It's just a struggle to make my income flow match the deadlines.

"Don't you worry about it. What are you doing these days?"

I take a deep breath. Got to think like a politician and take every opportunity to spread the word. "Fighting the town name change. We'd love to have you come to one of our meetings."

"I got your flyer when I was over at the market. Looked interesting. I might just show up next time."

"You do that."

"I guess you're lonely since your gran passed on?"

I swallow the lump in my throat. People are right. Time helps. But even after six months, I miss her. "Yes, ma'am. But tonight, I'm going to dinner at my parents'."

"Do they live in town?"

Hardly. "No, they're in Sherwood." I glance up at the exit sign. And so am I. I ease off the interstate onto the ramp.

"Well, you have fun and give them a hug for me."

Yeah, right. I won't even do that for me, more than likely. "Thanks again, Wilburta." We say, " 'Bye," and I end the call.

Now that the friendly hometown call is over with, time to reach out and touch the corporate world. I press the 9 on my phone and hold it down. Pretty bad when you have the electric company on speed dial. I listen to the menu and speak the choices as commanded. Finally a voice says, "If you need an automatic short-term extension on your bill, press or say, 'One.'"

Um, that would be me. "One."

"Thank you. Your automatic short-term extension has been approved. Your confirmation number. . ." I end the call. I draw the line at writing down numbers while I'm driving. My electricity not getting shut off will be all the confirmation I need.

I pull into Dad and Mother's and punch in the security code. When the gate opens, I drive through and park in front of the huge house. Technically I grew up in this house, but it's never been home like Jingle Bells is. Maybe that's why my mother hates Jingle Bells so much. But that would indicate that she cared about where I gave my affections, and that's probably overestimating her emotions.

I ring the doorbell and pray. Visiting my parents is never easy, and this command invitation has all the earmarks of a showdown.

The maid who opens the door is not one I've seen before.

"I'm Kristianna."

"Come in," she says and takes my coat. "Your parents are in the living room."

When I walk in, Mother raises her martini glass. "Hello, Kristianna."

I nod. "Mother."

"Jared, fix Kristianna a drink."

"Kristianna, martini?" Dad holds up the ice tongs.

I can't hold back a wry smile. They know I don't drink. I guess that idea is so foreign to them they just can't wrap their minds around it, so they always offer. "Club soda will be great. Thanks."

I sit on the love seat across from Mother. Dad fills a glass with ice, pours in the fizzing liquid, and passes it to me. He comes around to sit in the chair beside me. "Did you have a nice drive over?"

The cell phone conversations about my bills flit through my mind. Nice drive? "It was fine."

The fake logs in the gas fireplace behind us hiss slightly. My ice shifts, clinking against the glass. Dad clears his throat and looks at Mother. She looks at me. My fingers squeeze around the glass. Here it comes.

"We might as well get straight to the point," Mother says.

Dad nods. "I always say if there's going to be unpleasantness, get it out of the way before the meal. That way we won't have any digestive problems."

"Don't be crass, Jared."

"Is there going to be unpleasantness?" I ask, praying my voice sounds calm.

"That depends on you." Mother's smile doesn't even come close to reaching her eyes. She sets her drink on the end table. "We're ready to get you back in law school where you belong."

This is such a familiar argument I can't muster up the enthusiasm for it anymore. I look down at my fingers, white around the glass. But I still react. I can't help that. "I don't belong in law school."

"You think you belong in that little hick town you're in?"

She wants a scene. And I'm not going to give her what she wants. I list the periodic table in my mind, like Meg from *A Wrinkle in Time*. Hydrogen. Helium. "Jingle Bells is the perfect place for me, actually."

"You think that simply because your grandmother ran away to there after your grandfather died. She didn't have to do that. The Harringtons would have been glad to take her in."

I barely remember my great-grandparents, but the thought of Gran living with those sour, stuffy people makes me shiver. Lithium. Beryllium. My memory of Madeleine L'Engle's wonderful story is fuzzy. Did this work for Meg when she was resisting IT?

"But no," Mother continues, "she took their only grandchild and moved to Jingle Bells to open a *store*."

Forget the periodic table. I think I'd do better with the twenty-third psalm. "You make it sound like she spirited Dad halfway across the world. She moved forty-five minutes away. And she made sure they saw him often."

Dad runs his finger around his shirt collar. He clears his throat. "Emily, we agreed earlier that this isn't about Mama. It's about us wanting what's best for our daughter."

"What's best for our daughter is a good dose of reality." She presses her palms to her temples, fingers splaying through her hair. "We agreed on that, too."

Maybe I can end this. Probably not, but it's worth a try. "Would it help if I tell you there's no way I'm going back to law school?"

Mother stands. She always stands for cross-examination. "What if you have to sell the store? Or worse, what if you can't? Then what?"

"Then I'll find a job. In Little Rock if I have to. And commute from Jingle Bells." I remember what Shawn told me the first day at North Pole Café. "It's 75 percent less in living expenses."

"What kind of a job?"

"Last time I was at Starbucks, I saw a HELP WANTED sign in the window." This is my life, isn't it? I'm twenty-six years old and have been making my own way totally for the last six months. Even in college and law school, I let them pay only the actual tuition. Against their protests, I worked a part-time job to pay the rest of my bills.

"Kristianna." Dad's disappointed tone still has the power to cut me like a knife. Who knew? "You'd throw your life away to spite us?"

"And this is what we're supposed to tell our friends?" Mother steps to the side like she's playing the part of a "friend." "What's your brilliant daughter doing these days, Emily?" She steps over to the other side. "Why, she's living in a dead little town north of here, driving into the city to work at a coffee shop." She shakes her head. "Even now, I don't know what to tell them."

I rest my head against the firm sofa back. Even their furniture isn't comfortable. My eyes scan the walls. "Where's the painting I did for you?"

They exchange a look I can't read. "We haven't decided where to hang it yet," Dad says softly.

"You should hang it over the fireplace. Then when people ask, you can say, 'Our daughter is an artist. And a good one.' That's what normal people would do."

The maid appears in the doorway. "Dinner is served."

Dad stands. "Shall we eat?"

I follow my parents into the dining room, where our salads await. Mother sits at one end of the long table and Dad's at the other.

I take my place on the side and say a silent blessing for my food. But I've barely finished before my mother starts again. So much for not wanting to cause digestive problems with "unpleasantness."

"If you're waiting around for us to start viewing your hobby as a career, you'll be waiting a long time." She takes a bite of her salad.

"Mother, I don't really care how you view my 'hobby,' as you put it. I *am* an artist, maybe not just like I've always dreamed of being, but I'm getting there. And I'm a storekeeper. I'm proud of what I do. But you don't have to be."

"You're a Harrington," she says, as if that automatically refutes what I've said.

"Yes, I am. And thanks to Gran, I'm proud to be a Harrington in Jingle Bells."

Mother looks at my dad. "Talk to her, Jared. Can't you make her see it's time for her to take her place in society and quit playing store?"

While my dad silently prepares his closing arguments, I take a quick inventory of the room we're in. Noritake china—worth more than I spent on my whole dining room suite. Real silver flatware—three years' electricity bills. Gold candlesticks—enough to feed five hundred hungry children in Africa for a year. Air—priceless, but conspicuously absent.

This house I lived in as a child has always felt like someone pulled up to the front door with a giant vacuum every day and sucked the life right out of it and its inhabitants. When I was young, I told Gran one day that my soul couldn't breathe here. But I didn't know why.

After I got older, I could plainly see the difference between this place and my grandmother's apartment, where she sang while she worked and read the Bible to me every night. She showed Jesus through her actions. I wish I could do that half as well as she did.

My dad still hasn't spoken when the maid shows up with our main dishes and takes my salad away untouched. It's the Emily Harrington diet, folks. Guaranteed results.

"Jared?" Mother says.

"I think she knows how we feel." He cuts his salmon.

"What about law school?" she prods.

He looks up at me. "You have one month to make up your mind about law school. At that time, we are withdrawing our offer to pay for the remainder of your schooling."

I blink at him. Do they think threatening not to pay for something I don't want is going to make me want it? "I've made up my mind, Dad. But thank you again for your generosity in paying for college and law school. I really appreciated it."

"You have a month." He pops a bite of asparagus into his mouth.

And I think even my mother gets the point that the matter is closed.

CHAPTER 16

So it was awful?" Ami asks.

I lift a cucumber from my eye and look over at her. "What?"

"Supper at your folks' house."

"Awful would have been a step up," I say.

"Ouch. I'm sorry."

"Yeah, me, too. Then, when I got home, I had two hand-delivered envelopes waiting for me. These gift certificates and the notice from Uncle Gus about the special city council meeting next Tuesday night."

"Oh no, you'll miss the last night of bowling."

"Yep. Sorry. You'll have to get someone to take my place."

"Bummer."

Yes, bummer. Because I have no doubt who they will get. And I don't want to even examine why the thought of Lila filling in for me makes me feel sick.

"Do you feel guilty about using the gift certificates?" Ami asks.

"Not one bit." After we spent the morning knocking on doors in our campaign to save Jingle Bells, it's poetic justice that Summer Valley Outdoors pays for an afternoon at the spa for the two of us.

She grins, her face stretching the shiny clear mask. "Good."

"I'm just glad the one business in Little Rock that remotely resembles something to do with summer is Sunny Day Spa." I put my cucumber back and close my eyes. "Wouldn't it have been awful if I'd gotten gift certificates to the Sun Street Hospital?"

"Or even worse, Summer Rest Funeral Home." Ami giggles; then I hear footsteps.

"You two making it okay over here?" Julie, our attendant, asks in her soft drawl.

I nod, and my cucumbers slip. I push them back up with my plastic-covered, paraffin-dipped hand. "Fine."

"I'll be back in a few minutes to get you ready for your massages."

Ami utters a low groan. "On our next honeymoon, I'm going to make Mark take me to a spa."

I prop up on my elbows and let the cuke slices fall where they may. "Do you think Shawn really thought a trip to the day spa for me and a friend—"

"I have to admit it was nice of him to include me." Still lying flat, Ami tries to scratch her face with her plastic-encased hand, but her finger sticks to the mask.

I smile. "He probably knew I wouldn't come without you. But do you really think he believes an afternoon of pampering will

159

change my mind about the name change?"

"I know it's hopeless. But I sure am glad he tried."

Enough to clue him in to my weakness for a relaxing massage? Before I can voice my thought, Julie reappears and escorts us to our massage rooms. All the stress of the past few months falls away. But when we meet back for the manicures and pedicures, I pick up where we left off.

"Ames?" I glance over at her. "Have you been telling Shawn things about me so he could do all these gifts?"

She jerks, and her manicurist frowns at me. "No!"

"Sorry." I knew she'd be a little hurt, but I had to ask. "Do you think Mark has?"

She shakes her head. "Definitely not."

I sigh. "It just feels like he knows me so well."

"Yes, but how could he go wrong giving you an afternoon here, especially with a friend along?"

"True. The other gifts, though. . . Oh, maybe I'm just paranoid."

"Maybe. He's certainly found a way to get your interest, hasn't he?"

I look over at her. "When we're together, the connection isn't really all that strong. But this whole anonymous gift thing. . . I don't know why that fascinates me so much."

"You like puzzles, and this is a puzzle," Ami says. "Have you ever asked him about the gifts?"

"No. For some reason, I don't want to." I want to keep them to myself. The thrill. Even the irritation. It is like a puzzle. Or a challenge. And I'm flattered that he cares enough about my opinion to single me out for gifts. Unless he's sending them to Dottie and Scott, too. That would be just plain creepy.

My manicurist, Ginny, lifts my left hand from the soaking dish and wipes it on a cloth. "Every woman loves the idea of a secret admirer."

I open my mouth to tell her that this is a secret admirer with a not-so-hidden agenda, but she's right. "True."

"As long as he's not a stalker," Ami's manicurist says.

Ginny launches into a story about her last boyfriend. She keeps us entertained until Julie comes by and frowns. "We're not supposed to talk to clients about our personal lives," Ginny whispers and finishes my nails quickly.

The spa day ends all too quickly, and after changing clothes, Ami and I head for my car.

"What was your favorite part?" Ami asks on the way home.

I shrug. "The rain-shower massage?"

She laughs. "I loved it all." She hits the dash. "I meant to talk to you. Now that you have a secret admirer, we've got to find somebody for Garrett. He and Lila seemed to get along okay at the New Year's Eve party. What do you think?"

I glance over at her, then lock my gaze on the highway. How can I explain to her how irritated I feel when I think of Garrett with Lila? I can't. Especially considering I didn't even tell her about the kiss. I've wanted to ever since she got back from her honeymoon a few days ago, but I couldn't find the words. Now it feels like I'm making a big deal out of the simple kiss by putting off telling her.

"Kristianna?"

"Huh?"

"I asked you what you think about Lila."

"Oh." I clench my hands on the steering wheel. "She's a good bowler."

"Yeah. Hey, we could get her to fill in for you Tuesday night. How did they get along when she filled in for me before?"

I shrug. "Fine."

She sighs. "You're a lot of help."

I just keep my eyes on the road. For some reason, the idea of fixing Garrett up with someone doesn't appeal to me right now.

"As members of the city leadership, it's imperative that we work together in our efforts to grow our fair town. Remember, 'united we stand, divided we fall.'"

One thing I can say for Uncle Gus: He usually comes up with off-the-wall quotes. But tonight, he's resorting to the tried and true.

He drones on. "Summer Valley will mean more money and more jobs."

My mind wanders to the bowling alley. Is Lila there with Garrett? Images of them laughing with their heads close together keep popping up in my mind. I shake my head slightly and force my attention back to Uncle Gus.

"Scott, think of all the new customers you'd have if Summer Valley comes in."

"I don't think customers would make up for losing my self-respect by caving in to pressure from you, Gus." Go Scott!

Uncle Gus frowns. "You need to think long and hard about that." He turns to me. "Kristianna, I know you like to think you're above the pursuit of the almighty dollar, but you'd be much busier, too. Plus, we'd be able to spend more money on the arts. Maybe even open a small art museum. Surely you can recognize the merit in that."

What I recognize is a line of garbage when I hear it. I give a ladylike snort.

He quickly switches his focus to Dottie. "And the library. We could add a children's wing. And bring back story hour. We'd have to hire an assistant for you, Dottie, and make sure you had all the help you need."

Oh, that's a low blow. How can he tempt little old ladies like that and still sleep at night?

I glance at the remaining council member, John. The Little Rock businessman who comes home to Jingle Bells every night is strangely silent. Or rather, Uncle Gus is strangely silent to him. No specially chosen persuasions for Councilman Stone? Why not?

The answer comes to me clearly. Because he's already in the bag. I look over at Jack Feeney, who is scribbling furiously in his notebook a few feet away. I think I'll at least give the "impartial press" something to report.

"Mayor Harding,"—calling the man "Uncle Gus" these days seems to give genuine uncles everywhere a bad name, and tonight

I can't do it—"you own the building that Summer Valley wants to purchase, is that right?"

He tucks his hand between the middle two buttons of his vest. "That's right."

"But the sale of that building is contingent on the name change, is that correct?"

"If I'm being cross-examined, I think I have the right to call an attorney," he says jovially, then looks around the room. "And I don't see a judge here, either."

"John, what about you?"

John's going to need a visit to the chiropractor, considering how fast he snaps his neck turning his head to look at me. "What about me?"

"Were you a potential investor for Summer Valley Outdoors before you became a city council member?"

His eyes widen. "No."

"So you were already a council member when you decided to invest in Summer Valley Outdoors?"

"Ye—"

"Kristianna! This is unacceptable." Uncle Gus has lost his jovial attitude. He slaps his notebook shut and looks at all of us. "As representatives of the constituents of Jingle Bells, it is your responsibility to encourage everyone to vote for the name change. There is no question as to whether it will be on the ballot." Uncle Gus clears his throat. "Unless. . ."

Something sounds so ominous about that word.

"Unless what?" I ask.

"I was looking through the town statutes last week and found an interesting law from several years ago. I have an attorney looking at it, but he believes, and so do I, that a unanimous town council vote on anything pertaining to the town is sufficient for a change."

I'm furious, but at the same time relieved. As long as I'm on the city council, there's no chance of that happening.

"What this means"—his tone is so condescending, like he's proud of himself for breaking it down to simple terms for the little people—"is that if you can vote unanimously to change the town name, we won't even have to put it on the ballot."

"And if we have a sudden heat wave tonight, we won't have to put on our coats when we go outside. I'd say that's more likely than his scenario," I mutter to Dottie, but she looks away.

"Instead of voting your own personal preference, I'm asking you to vote what's best for the constituents you represent." He narrows his eyes at me. "Let's do an off-the-record vote so we'll know where we stand. Everyone in favor of the name change and the advancement of our town, raise your hand."

John Stone quickly thrusts his hand up.

"Dottie?" Uncle Gus ducks his head and looks at Dottie from under his eyebrows. "You do want what's best for the people of our town, right? Think of the books."

Dottie lifts her hand a little way, then looks at me and drops it back to her lap. I'm angry, but at Uncle Gus, not at her.

"Scott?"

Scott shakes his head.

Uncle Gus doesn't even bother asking me.

After the meeting breaks up, he sidles up to me. Okay, he probably just walks, but to me it feels like he sidles. "Kristianna."

"What?"

"This name change is going to happen. If we hurry it along, the town would be able to do without things like your parking ticket money. I'm sure Summer Valley would give you a free spot in front of your store."

I snort. "Is that your idea of a bribe? A free parking place?"

He holds up his hands as if he's warding me off.

"Because if it is, you need to go back to sleazy con artist school." I leave him with his mouth open and hurry out to the street.

No sudden heat wave came while we were in the meeting, so I pull my coat around me and walk down the deserted sidewalk until I come to the gazebo in the middle of the town square. I slip into the dome and sit on a bench along the side.

Everything is changing. Deep in my heart, I'm afraid Uncle Gus is right. The name change probably will happen. And our heritage will be lost. My grandmother's years of work to make Jingle Bells a great place to live and raise kids will be for nothing.

I glance up at the sky. When I was little, I'd wish on the first star of the evening. But now, I pour out my heart in prayer to the Creator of the stars.

My life is so mixed up right now, and I don't know what to do. I'm thankful for the blessings I have, but am I about to lose them all? Lord, please help me get control of things. The twinkling stars are blurry through my tears. *On second thought, Lord, help me let go of control and leave that for You. What I need is wisdom. If I'm being selfish about the town name change, please allow me to see that. Because otherwise, I'm going to keep on fighting.*

I pray for a while longer, then get up and walk across the street to my shop. My nose is frozen, but my heart has thawed considerably.

CHAPTER 17

The next day, an hour before the shop closes, the door chime rings and Ami walks in. "Hey, girl." She still has that radiant new-bride look. "What's going on?"

"After-Christmas sales weren't so hot." Should be the busiest time of year for me except the two weeks before Christmas. But surprise, surprise, this year is a disappointment. "I'm marking things down." I pitch her a red marker. "Make yourself useful."

She catches it deftly and grins. "Oh, fun. This is just like playing store when we were kids. Are you finally going to let me decide on my own how much to charge for things?"

"Not a chance. Here's a list with the new prices." I pass her the paper and go back to writing on the tiny tags. "How's it going at school? The kids get used to calling you Mrs. Andrews?"

She looks up from her table of items with a grimace. "Most of them have gotten used to it faster than I have. I keep forgetting to answer to that name. So now they say, 'Mrs. Andrews. Mrs. Andrews?

Miss Manchester!' Then I look up. Sad, really."

I laugh. "I'd hate to have to start calling you something different just because you're married."

"It's weird. You'll see when you get married."

Yeah, well. . . "I'll just take your word for it. How was bowling last night?" Even though I complain about being no good, I didn't realize how much I would hate to miss it. Maybe because it was the last night until April. Or maybe it's just the fact that I was replaced by Lila. "Did Lila show?"

"Oh yes. And she's obviously crazy about Garrett." Ami shrugs. "But I'm not sure he feels the same."

"What makes you say that?" I try for a blend of interest and friendly concern. Hard when my claws just popped out involuntarily.

"Oh, I don't know. You know how shy he is, so it's hard to tell."

Shy? I hadn't noticed really, but I guess with people he doesn't know he is.

"She asked him to go out to dinner and a movie next week, and he told her he had too much going on right now. Does that sound like a guy who is interested?"

My heart leaps. "I don't know." Since the mistletoe incident and the New Year's Eve party, I've figured out I don't know as much about Garrett as I thought I did. Maybe he likes Lila but is playing hard to get.

"I can't imagine why he isn't. Has he said anything to you about her?"

"No, not a word. But other than at church, I haven't seen him much since New Year's." Which isn't unusual. What is unusual is now I find myself watching for him every time I walk to the post office or go out to get a bite to eat.

"Well, you have to help me."

"Help you what?"

She rolls her eyes. "Honestly, I think you don't listen to me sometimes. I've been telling you. We have to fix Garrett and Lila up."

I pause in the middle of marking down a set of nesting dolls. "Do you like Lila?"

She shrugs. "I don't know. But Mark says he's pretty sure she's a Christian, and Garrett needs someone."

I have one thing to thank Shawn for. Even though the earth doesn't move when I'm with him, at least his presence in town has saved me from the newly married Ami and her matchmaking craze.

She grabs the nesting dolls.

I raise an eyebrow. "What are you doing?"

"I've been wanting this, and now the price is right."

"You can have it."

"No way. It's enough to get first dibs on your sale items." She tucks it next to her. "I'll just start myself a pile and pay at the end."

I know better than to argue. "Whatever."

She marks another tag. "So what can we do?"

"Do about what?"

"Focus, girl. Garrett's happiness is at stake. How can we fix them up?"

I shrug. A reply forms in my mind, but before I say it, I'm already doubting my sincerity. Am I about to offer this only because I know she'll refuse? So I'll seem like I'm in the spirit? "Maybe I should quit the bowling team when we start back up in the spring."

"No! Don't be silly. Garrett would have a fit if you quit. And I love our bowling nights. So does Mark." She bounces up and down. "Oh, I know! Maybe we could get Shawn and Lila to join our team."

I can't imagine a worse scenario.

After a minute of silence, she looks over at me. "What do you think?"

I open my mouth to make another suggestion, but instead, I say, "He kissed me." As soon as the words are out, I cringe.

She drops her marker and grabs my arm. "When?"

"Hey! You messed up my tag."

"Forget your tag. When did he kiss you?"

"Christmas Day."

"And you're just now telling me?"

I smile. I didn't mean to blurt it out, but it's a relief that she knows. "You were on your honeymoon. It probably wasn't anything. We were under the mistletoe."

"I don't care if you were under a whole tree full of mistletoe; a kiss is a kiss."

"Really?"

"Of course, really. Take my word for it. Why are you not happy?

Is it still because he's a lawyer?"

Huh? She's rattling on about most lawyers being honest, but I put my hand on her arm. "Ami. Stop."

She shuts her mouth and looks at me. "What?"

"Shawn didn't kiss me."

Her eyebrows draw together. "But you said—"

"Garrett kissed me."

Her eyes widen, and she gasps, "Garrett?"

I nod, my heart pounding, waiting for her reaction. Ami's a little scatterbrained, but she has a good grasp on reality most of the time.

She smiles. "And?"

"And what?"

"And how do you feel about it? About him?"

"That's the question of the year. Right up there with, has he even given it a second thought and is he avoiding me?"

"I guarantee you he's given it a second thought. And yes, he may be avoiding you."

"Thanks a lot."

She shrugs. "I'm just being honest. Garrett would never ever kiss someone just because of mistletoe." She bounces and claps her hands lightly. "I've been right all along. He's crazy about you. And knowing him, he's scared to find out how you feel."

I shake my head. "He's not crazy about me. He called me 'sport' after the kiss and challenged me to a race."

She throws back her head and laughs, then looks at me. "He's called you 'sport' since you were eight years old. Sometimes I wonder if he thinks that's your name. And the challenge was just to give you a chance to act normal in case you don't like him in that way. So do you? Like him in that way?"

"I'm scared." My voice trembles. I've barely admitted this even to myself.

"Oh, Kristianna, scared of what?" Sympathy blends with puzzlement in her tone.

I sigh. So many things. "What if I let myself love him? And he loves me? But then something happens like. . .you and I both know it can when I start trying to make a permanent commitment?"

"This is Garrett. You've always loved him." I open my mouth, and she holds her hand up. "I know, as a friend. But the point is, you trust him completely. If things end up getting serious between you two, nothing bad is going to happen. Maybe it's like you told me on my wedding day. Maybe he's God's man for you."

That thought makes it hard for me to breathe. In a good way. "But the two of you are the constants in my life since Gran died. I'm not sure anything is worth risking that."

She beams at me. "Finding the love of your life is worth the risk."

I frown. "I can't even decide whether to call him to come work on my computer. Much less take that kind of chance."

She snorts and grabs a little snow village church building I just marked down. "Call him. He'll kill you if you let anyone else touch your computer, so you have no choice about that." She places the building in her pile. "And I'll kill you if you don't call me every time you're doing markdowns."

"Is it my imagination, or are we getting fewer positive responses than we did the past two weeks?" Ami leans against a signpost and slips her shoe off for a second.

I nod. "It does seem like it. I guess Shawn has probably covered this ground already this week."

"That last man was downright belligerent. Why couldn't he have just taken the flyer and thanked us?"

I glare over at the whiteboard house. "I don't mind hearing what people think, but I could have done without him siccing his dog on us."

She snickers and puts her shoe back on. "Yeah, I was really scared of the mini-Pom. She couldn't have gotten my little toe in her mouth; she was so tiny."

I grin. "I think it was the principle."

"I guess you're right." She puts her hand on my shoulder. "Onward and upward. And let's pray we don't run into any full-sized dogs."

"Amen."

But by the end of the morning, when we all meet back at the North Pole Café to report in, I'm fighting discouragement. From the looks on their faces, my troops feel the same way.

And to make matters worse, Shawn is sitting in a booth in the corner, his attaché case on the table. Of all the cafés in all the world, he had to wander into mine. He looks up and smiles. If my feet didn't hurt so badly, I'd walk over and tell him again how much he and his petition irritate me, but it's all I can do to plunk down at Scott's table near the door.

Shawn saves me the trouble, though, when he walks over as soon as I sit down. "Hi," he says softly.

The chatter at our group of tables dies immediately.

I nod. "Shawn."

"Can I talk to you for a minute. . .outside?" he asks, giving a nervous glance to the hostile-looking group I'm with.

I don't like scenes all that much, so I stand and follow him out the door. "What's this about?"

"Would you like to go out tonight? Maybe drive into Little Rock and eat?"

I look toward the window of the café, where twenty faces are peering out at us. "Fraternizing with the enemy? I don't think so."

He runs his hand through his hair. "What about when I finish getting the signatures and my job's over? Can we go out then?"

I don't know what to say. I've never mentioned the gifts and notes because that's one of those things that feels like if you talk about it the appeal will be gone. But I've stopped thinking that the anonymous gifts are a Summer Valley Outdoors plan. I'm sure they're all Shawn. "I don't know. Maybe. Can we talk about it again at that time?"

He nods. "That sounds fair." He glances over my shoulder

and flashes me a grin. "I'll let you go. Looks like the natives are restless."

I turn and go back into the café.

"Is he trying to convince you to change sides?" Ruby asks.

I shake my head. "That was personal. So how did it go today?"

"People would tell me they signed the petition already," Ruby says. "Then I would explain to them. . .like you said. . ."—she nods at me—"that they don't have to vote that way just because they signed the petition." Her shoulders fall. "But while no one acted happy about the name change, everyone seems resigned to it."

Echoes of the same came from around the tables.

After everyone else leaves, I linger to talk to Scott. "Where was Dottie today?"

"She said something about getting her hair done." He tugs at his collar. "But I think she's about to switch sides on us, Kristianna."

Ouch. "The idea of a children's wing in the library is too much for her to withstand." I frown. "Just like Uncle Gus knew it would be."

"Yeah, he made it seem mighty tempting, I admit."

I look at him sharply. "Are you tempted to switch sides?"

"No. Call me an idiot, but my daddy always told me that sometimes you gotta draw a line and not cross it. Changing the name of Jingle Bells is my line."

"Me, too." We sit in silence for a minute. I play with the salt and pepper shakers and finally look him in the eye. "Scott, do you think we're representing the people, though? Our constituents? That's the only thing Uncle Gus has said this whole time that bothered me. I don't want to be a public servant who uses her office to further her own agenda."

Scott takes his glasses off and cleans them with his napkin. He pins me with his slightly myopic gaze. "I ask every local who comes into my bookstore which they would prefer. Without fail, all of them say they want to keep the name."

I feel my shoulders relax in places I didn't even know they were tight. "So we are doing what the people want."

"Except." He slips his glasses back on and regards me sadly.

How did I know there'd be a "but" in there somewhere?

"They all want to make a living. And they think the only way to do that is to change the name and embrace Summer Valley."

I slam the saltshaker down harder than I mean to. "I hate to see them bullied into giving up their heritage."

He nods. "Me, too."

"I wish I could know what Gran would think about it." She loved Christmas and Jingle Bells as much as I do. But would she give up the town name in order to save the citizens?

Scott taps his notebook with his hand. "One thing's for sure. Sally Harrington never could abide bullies."

"Well, then, maybe that's our answer. Stand firm."

"Maybe so." Scott pushes to his feet and holds up his folder containing the flyers. "Same place, same time, next week."

"I'll be here."

CHAPTER 18

I frown at my reflection in the mirror. Khaki pants and a blue blouse that everyone always tells me brings out the color of my eyes.

Earth to Kristianna. This is just Garrett coming over to work on my computer. Not someone I need to try and impress. What am I doing, changing clothes in the middle of the afternoon? Wouldn't Gran laugh if she could see me in such a snit about the boy who spent as much time here as he did at his house when we were growing up?

I quickly change again, slipping back into my work clothes—jeans and a Santa T-shirt. As I pull my hair back in a red scrunchie, I grimace. Just another good thing about living in Jingle Bells and owning Forever Christmas. I can get away with Christmas clothes year-round. But for how much longer?

Thanks to changing not once, but twice, I get back downstairs just as Garrett comes in, looking normal but nice in his jeans and a polo shirt. I bet he didn't think about his clothes.

"Hey, Garrett. I hated to bother you." On the phone, I'd offered to bring my computer to him, but he insisted he didn't mind coming here.

"No problem, sport." He stops short of ruffling my hair. I feel foolish. Ami's pretty intuitive, and every few years since junior high, she's accused me of being in love with Garrett. Even if I could ever bring myself to admit she's right, it's definitely one-sided. Garrett will always think of me as a buddy and nothing more. Which, considering my record for broken engagements, is probably pretty smart of him.

Then why kiss a buddy? That's a question that's kept me awake a few nights. I glance at his brown curls bent over my computer. Maybe he felt sorry for me because it was Christmas and I was feeling down? Surely if that was the case, he would have just bought me a cup of hot chocolate. A little peck on the lips I might attribute to his living in California for so long where they seem to kiss on the lips as often as we hug in the South. But that kiss. . . It was no little peck on the lips. It was the stuff memories are made of. . . unfortunately. "Do you see the problem?" I ask.

He looks up, his green eyes sparkling. "It seems to be working."

Yeah, for you maybe. Casual kisses may be something you don't give a second thought to, but— I rein in my crazy thought process and remind myself we're talking about the computer. "It takes forever to boot up."

He rolls his chair back and motions toward the monitor. "I

deleted your temporary files and cleaned things up a little. It comes up pretty fast now."

"Okay, great then." Just in case he's under the illusion that I called him over for a repeat of Christmas Day, I add, "Thanks for coming."

He picks up my new price list from the desk. "I thought I'd go ahead and update your Web site, add in your clearance prices."

"You can take the list and do that from your own computer, right?"

"In a hurry to get rid of me?"

"No, not at all." I'd like for him to stay and talk with me about this elephant in the room, but the only thing worse than ignoring the beast is worrying that I'm the only one who can see it.

He pats the chair beside him. "Then sit down and help me do the Web site. We'll knock it out in no time."

I sit beside him and call out prices as he makes the changes. After we finish, he leans back and looks up. I follow his gaze to the place where the mistletoe used to be.

"Hmm. . . . ," he says, smiling, "so much for Christmas all year-round."

I take a deep breath. Garrett and I have always shot straight with each other. I'm tired of playing games. "I guess I decided that if someone was going to kiss me, I'd rather know it was because of who I am and not because of what's over my head."

He looks into my eyes. "I can't imagine anyone ever kissing you for any reason besides who you are."

"I don't have all that good a track record with reading people's true emotions."

He puts his hand on mine. "I'm sorry you had to go through what you did with those guys. Sorry I wasn't around to pick you up and dust you off. At least the second time."

I shrug, the warmth of his hand burning into my skin. "What can I say? I have trust issues. But with Nathan, I brought it on myself. I could see early on it was a rebound relationship, but I told myself I could make it work."

"Remember how uncomplicated life was when we were kids?" he says. "When we knew what we needed and could easily get it if we tried?"

I blink at the apparent subject change and pull my hand from his to push my hair back. "Vaguely."

"Sometimes I wish it could be that way again."

His eyes are haunted. My heart physically hurts for him. "What do you need, Garrett?"

"If I knew, I guess that would help, huh?" He half laughs, but it sounds hollow.

"You and God doing okay?" He hasn't missed a church service since he got back from California, but I'm not naive enough to believe that means he's automatically doing fine spiritually.

He nods. "I'm pretty sure He understands me."

"Then everything else is just gravy, isn't it?" That's what he used to tell me when we were in youth group together, "If you've got God, everything else is just gravy."

His slow smile spreads across his face. "That's right, sport. Maybe I just need to spend a little more time on my knees."

"Maybe we all do," I say softly, keenly aware of my own tendency to try to handle things on my own.

"The Web site sales still holding steady?" he asks.

"They keep my lights on."

"I'm glad about that. Wish you could have the success you deserve."

"I'll settle for paying the bills."

He pushes to his feet, so I stand, too. "I'd better go."

"Okay, thanks again."

He leans toward me and brushes my hair back from my face. His gaze is locked on mine, and my heart races. But he drops a chaste kiss on my forehead. "See you later, sport."

"Yep. Or sooner."

"Even better." He walks out the door, and I collapse onto my chair. We didn't exactly discuss the elephant, but maybe we at least made it to the jungle.

The next afternoon, the door chimes and several women come in. "Welcome to Forever Christmas, ladies," I call from behind the counter.

"Ami told us you had a clearance sale too good to resist," a stocky redheaded woman says.

"So we decided to be fair to each other and all come at once," the older woman behind her adds. She lifts her glasses that are hanging around her neck and looks at a price tag.

I recognize a couple of the others as Ami's fellow teachers and smile. Apparently, my sweet friend went on a business-finding mission on my behalf. The ladies swarm the clearance tables, some of them wandering off into the full-price sections. This is what the store should be like all the time. How it was before the town began to die.

"What will you do if the name change goes through?" a slender blond asks me casually.

Such a simple question. But it stumps me. I glance at the calendar. Today's my parents' deadline, so it won't be law school, unless I want to pay for it myself. Which I wouldn't mind if I wanted to go, but I don't. I shrug. "I'm not sure, actually."

Starbucks, as I'd told my mom? Not a bad job, but not my dream of running this store, either. Of course, I could keep the store and hope the novelty of a Christmas store in a summer-themed town would be enough. Except I'd have to lose my bitterness. I can see myself at sixty, running Forever Christmas in Summer Valley, grumbling about how it used to be when the town went by its proper name of Jingle Bells. Not a pretty picture.

"It sure would be weird not to live in Jingle Bells, wouldn't it?" the woman with the reading glasses says softly, while she's examining a nativity scene.

My phone rings and keeps me from having to respond to her rhetorical question. I pick it up and paste on a smile. "Forever Christmas."

"Hello, Kristianna."

My heart sinks as I hear my dad's voice. I was hoping today would pass unmentioned. Surely they hadn't really held out any hope that I would respond to their ultimatum favorably. Not after I was so blunt.

"Hi, Dad."

"I'm assuming since we haven't heard otherwise that you decided against law school."

"Yes. Sorry."

He sighs. "Me, too. This is really hard on us, but especially on your mother. She had to fight to get to where she is. And she doesn't want to see you waste your talent. Neither of us does."

"I know. But it's the things we work hard for that we value. And if I ever"—*have a brain transplant and*—"decide I want to go to law school, it will be better if I have to fight for it myself. Right now, I'm working hard for what's important to me."

"Even though I don't really understand your motivation, I'm proud of you for that."

Tears edge my eyes. "Thanks, Dad. That means a lot to me."

"Since I have to give your mother the bad news about law school, how about letting me have some consolation good news for her?"

"What do you mean?" I glance out at the store, where the teachers are still shopping hard. Go, Ami!

"I know it would please her if you'd come to the Valentine's dinner at the Peabody. It's a benefit for that new museum, and she's on the fundraising committee."

Too bad I don't have a dentist appointment so I could have a good excuse not to go. But it's for a good cause, and after Dad said he was proud of me, how can I say no? And as an added bonus, it will fill in the night that unattached singles everywhere dread. "Sure, I'll come."

"Wonderful. We'll see you then." He hangs up the phone without a good-bye, same as always.

I turn back to help the teachers finalize their selections. Twenty minutes later, they've all left with their purchases and I'm staring at my cash register. Who knew seven teachers could pick business up that much? I owe Ami, big-time.

The door chime rings again, and the by-now-familiar teenage delivery boy comes in carrying a large box. The wrapping paper is printed with sand dollars and seashells. He plunks it down on the counter in front of me and runs out the door.

I lean toward the box. It's not ticking. So I'm guessing he was afraid of me, not the package. Probably thought I might torture him to tell who hired him. If I'd been prepared, I might have tried to bribe him with cookies and milk. But since I'm pretty sure who the sender is, that might be a waste of a good snack.

I pluck the note from the small envelope on top and open it.

Kristianna,
Dreams are the glue that hold sand castles together. You can hold on to your dreams no matter how much your world ends up being changed by the tide.

I read it over again. And again.

How does he go right to the core of my soul every time? This one's a little different. More about helping me accept the inevitable than trying to convince me. On one level, that comforts me. On the other, it makes me more determined than ever to fight.

I open the large box carefully and pull out a shimmering sand castle. Amazed, I stand back to absorb the beauty, but the detail draws me in closer. I spend a good ten minutes examining each turret and flag, every set of stairs. What a fascinating work of art.

I pick up the note and reread it. "You can hold on to your dreams."

Is it true? Can I? Could I have a store called Forever Christmas in a town named Summer Valley? Maybe. But what about my neighbors and fellow shopkeepers? What about their dreams?

Regardless of the poetic nature of the note, anybody knows the best way to keep a sand castle together is to keep the tide from reaching it.

The phone rings, and I grab it. "Forever Christmas."

"Kristianna, it's your mother."

Mother always starts our conversations that way, like I wouldn't recognize her voice. "Hi."

"Your father tells me you aren't going to law school. You'll be lucky if he doesn't end up having a heart attack over this decision of yours."

Typical. They both try to make me feel guilty for displeasing the other. "I'll be praying he doesn't."

She pauses like she always does when I mention prayer or God. I think she doesn't know what to do with that part of my life.

"Well, speaking of decisions, he also said that you'd be attending the Valentine's dinner with us."

Before I can confirm, she rushes on, "So I wanted to remind you that when you're with us, you represent us. Please buy something new to wear. You can go to GiGi's or Ferdinand's, either one, and put it on my account."

I open my mouth to say I'll buy my own dress, but then I think of my bank account balance. Plus, if she's demanding I wear something new when I have perfectly good dresses in my closet, then why shouldn't she pay for it? "Fine. Thank you."

"Also, I'm sure your father told you that we bought a table for four, so you'll be expected to bring a date."

Inward groan. Part of the reason I'd agreed to go was to avoid sitting home dateless on Valentine's Day. "No. He didn't mention that."

She huffs. "Men. The details always escape them. Why don't you ask that nice young lawyer?"

I run my hand over the sand castle. "I might."

"Well, make sure whoever you bring wears a tux. And has good table manners."

"I think I can handle that, Mother."

"Good. Then we'll see you on the fourteenth at a quarter to seven."

"Okay, see you then." I say the words to dead air. Something my parents have in common. Too busy to waste time on trivial things like good-byes.

CHAPTER 19

So which one are you going to ask?" Ami pulls a long blue gown from the rack. "This matches your eyes."

I nod, and the saleslady takes it back to the dressing room to put with the others. "I don't know. My parents would rather I ask Shawn. But. . ."

"But you'd rather be with Garrett?"

I shrug. "Probably just because we've been best friends so long."

She rolls her eyes. "Honey, you and Garrett have always had more chemistry than a high school science lab. No worries on that front."

Maybe on my part. But not his. Ami's rewriting history to suit herself. I nudge her. "You're crazy."

"Why do you think I've brought it up through the years? Sometimes the sparks beneath the surface of your friendship are just too bright to ignore."

"Oh, that sounds like a country-and-western song. If you ever get tired of teaching, you might have a second career there," I say, as I look at a cute little red dress.

She raises her eyebrows. "That's fine. Make fun of me. But I'm right, and you know it."

"So what? I should just call Garrett up and ask him to go with me to the Valentine's dinner?"

"Well, first ask him if he has a tux." She reaches over and plucks my cell phone from the outside pocket of my purse.

"You mean right now?"

She flips it open. "It's considered premature to buy the dress before you line up a date."

"Thank you, Emily Post."

"Anytime." She motions to the phone.

I shift from foot to foot, then turn my back to her and punch in Garrett's number.

"Hello?" His deep voice calms my nerves, so I turn back around.

"Hey. How's it going today?"

Ami rolls her eyes again, and I glare at her. I never claimed to be a brilliant conversationalist. Especially under pressure.

"Pretty good. You doing okay?"

"Yes, fine. I wanted to ask you something. But if you'd rather not, it's perfectly okay. . .really."

Ami makes a "move on" motion with her hand.

"What?"

"My parents want me to go to a Valentine's dinner, and I thought you might go with me. It's a benefit for that new museum, and my parents already have the tickets. But you'd have to wear a tux. And like I said, if you'd rather not go. . ." I stop talking—not because I have sense enough to quit rambling but because I'm completely out of breath.

"Sounds good."

"It does?"

"Sure, sport, I'd love to go. What time should I pick you up?"

We arrange the details, and I hang up quickly.

"So?" Ami says.

"So he said he wants to go. He thanked me for asking him. Do you think he heard me when I said he needed to wear a tux?"

She nods. "I don't think he'll have a problem with it. He wore one for my wedding."

"True. Do you think he felt cornered?"

"He's thrilled to go. Trust me." She pushes me toward another rack of dresses. "Now that you have a date, let's find you the dress of your dreams."

"You said you'd try on some, too," I remind her. "For your first married Valentine's date with Mark."

She shoots me a saucy grin. "Going to Buon Natale doesn't require quite as nice a dress as a museum benefit."

"Hey, I love Italian food." *Buon Natale* means "Merry Christmas" in Italian, and it's one of my very favorite restaurants in Jingle Bells.

"Me, too, actually. So maybe a new dress is in order." She lowers her voice to a whisper. "But we'll have to look on the clearance rack for me since my mother's not footing the bill."

"Oh yes. Lucky me. Of course, she is the one who demanded I get a new dress."

"Then c'mon, missy, time to mind your mama."

Two hours pass, and we're on a first-name basis with Barbara, our saleslady. She neatly tucks a clear plastic bag over my new blue dress. "I can't get over how this brings out your eyes. You look so beautiful in it."

"Thanks. I appreciate your help."

"I enjoyed visiting with you girls. Makes me wish my daughters weren't so far away." She shakes out the little pink number Ami found on the clearance rack. "This is a good deal."

Ami's eyes sparkle. "My husband will like it twice as much that way. He's an accountant."

Barbara turns around to bag it, and I nudge Ami. "You just like to say 'my husband,' don't you?"

She nods and grins. "Yep."

Barbara hands us our dresses, and we leave happy.

"So you're going to call and make our appointments at Angel Hair and Nails?" Ami asks as we walk out to the car.

"I feel silly making a big deal out of this. And you know it'll be packed on Valentine's Day."

"Angel was your gran's best friend. Pull some strings and get us into the back room."

The back room is usually reserved for wedding parties and celebrities like Miss Jingle Bells or the May Queen. "I'll do my best."

"Tell her Garrett is your date. That'll do it."

I laugh, but I know it's true. Everyone loves Garrett. "No, I think we'll keep that little fact to ourselves."

"I won't tell a soul, but never underestimate the Jingle Bells grapevine. It's almost scary how quickly news gets around."

"You're right. But as much as the whole town likes Garrett, I'm afraid they'll be upset to hear he's going out with the 'runaway bride.'"

She rolls her eyes. "I oughtta break Jack Feeney's pencil over my knee next time I see him. People don't think of you as a 'runaway bride.'"

I shrug. "The truth is, Ames, my biggest fear is they might have reason to worry."

Brenda twirls her chair around and hooks the red vinyl cape around my neck. "So what do you want to do today?" she asks as she brushes out my hair.

"I don't know. What do you think? Short and spiked with red tips?"

She stops brushing and raises an eyebrow at me in the mirror. "Are you serious?"

Ami giggles from the chair beside me. "Don't let her kid you. Me, maybe. Her, never."

Brenda clutches the front of her smock. "Goodness, girl, you about gave me a heart attack."

"I'm sorry. I really don't know what I want." I used to think that was true of everything in my life, but I'm narrowing the list down. I want to serve God and run the store, and as far as anything else, I sure am excited about going out with Garrett tonight, even if I did have to ask him.

Brenda lifts my hair to the top of my head and purses her lips. "Well, since tonight's the most romantic night of the year, how about a soft updo with some ringlets hanging down the back?"

"Oh yeah," Ami pipes up. "Perfect."

Ami's stylist, Renee, nods. "I agree." She and Ami head to the sink.

"Okay." That should be quite a switch from my signature ponytail. "You know how thick my hair is, though. Do you think it will work?"

"Trust me, honey. Your hair is perfect for this. Now let's go get you washed and rinsed."

"How'd you two rate the back room?" Renee asks as she rinses Ami's hair in the sink next to us.

"I asked Angel." I feel kind of bad, but the commotion in the front is unbelievable with everyone from high school girls to retirement home residents getting ready for the big night.

"She sure does miss your gran." Brenda towels the water out of my hair.

"Yeah, I know. Me, too."

"We all do." She pats my head and puts my hand on the towel to hold it in place. "Wouldn't she just turn over in her grave if she knew what was going on now?"

I nod. I know that's not the most sensitive phrase, but in the South, you get used to it. No disrespect is meant. "We're going to keep fighting this, though. Maybe nothing will come of it."

Brenda laughs. "You should have seen Angel send that boy packing the other day when he came by with his petition."

"Did I hear someone say my name?" Angel sticks her bleached-blond, short-spiked hairdo around the doorway. I'm not so sure about the 'bleached' part. I have a sneaking suspicion she'd be white-headed if she didn't add blond tones.

"I was just telling Kristianna and Ami how you ran that lawyer off," Brenda says.

Angel throws her head back and gives a throaty laugh. "He didn't stay around for a manicure, I'll say that." She hugs me, her tanned skin like leather under my hands. "Good to see you, child."

"You, too. Are you worried about the town name change?"

She shrugs. "Not for myself. Won't nobody make me change my name. My sweet mama, God rest her soul, named me Angel when I was born, and that'll be what's on my tombstone. So why shouldn't my business be Angel Hair and Nails?"

"Will it hurt our tourist business much?" Renee asks as she picks out Ami's curls.

"Tourists." Angel leans against the doorway. "You know, the tourists don't usually come in to get their hair done. Ah, a few do. But they don't worry about the name. Remember when that lady tripped over on Santa Claus Lane and fell in the ditch headfirst?

She didn't care what our shop was named, did she?"

Brenda and Renee both shake their heads.

Renee is giving Ami a trim, and she wields the scissors like a samurai using his swords. But without pausing, she says, "And then there was the time that guy spilled paint in his hair over at the hardware store. Never could figure that one out."

"Me either," Angel agrees, "but we liked to never got it out."

Brenda runs the comb through my hair and keeps her hand on her blow-dryer, obviously ready for the conversation to end. I don't blame her. It takes awhile to dry my hair.

"An-gel!" a voice hollers from the front.

"Oops. Gotta go." She turns to Brenda. "You fix Miss Kristianna up real nice for her date tonight. He deserves the best." She winks at me and sashays out.

"Who are you going out with?" Brenda demands, as she blow-dries my hair.

I pretend not to hear her over the dryer, and in a few seconds, she and Renee are comparing their kids' latest antics.

Ami grins and gives me a thumbs-up behind the magazine in her lap.

Garrett knows where I hide the key to the front door, but like a modern-day gentleman, he calls me from his cell phone when he arrives.

"Let yourself in. I'll be right down." I grab my clutch bag and give myself a quick once-over in the mirror. The dress does bring out the color of my eyes. And my hair—I reach up to my neck and put my finger in one wispy ringlet—my hair makes me feel like a princess. But thankfully, I still look like me. Just a little more polished.

I stop at my door and murmur a prayer. I admit I'm nervous. I've never asked a man out before. And I've never gone out with someone I know so well. Or who knows me so well.

Suddenly I can't wait to see what the night holds. I yank open the door and step to the top of the stairs.

I hear an indrawn breath and look down to see Garrett staring up at me. "You look amazing."

My heart slams against my ribs as I walk down to meet him. "You don't look so bad yourself."

He brings his hand around from behind his back and presents the most exquisite bouquet of yellow roses I've ever seen. "Happy Valentine's Day."

"They're beautiful. You didn't have to—"

He touches his finger to my lips. "Shh. I didn't *have* to do anything." He grins. "Except maybe wear this tux. If you hadn't called me, I was going to invite you to go to Buon Natale. And I'm pretty sure I could have gotten away with a coat and tie there."

As I grab a vase and step in the store restroom to get water for the roses, I smile. I didn't misread his cues. He does intend to take our friendship a step further.

Outside, I lock the door behind us, then slip the key back in its hiding place.

He gives me a hand up into his SUV. "Sorry. I left the Jag at home tonight."

"That's okay. I'm allergic to cats."

When he climbs in and starts the motor, he glances over at me. "I'm glad we're together tonight. It's nice."

I smile. "And a little weird?"

"Way nicer than it is weird."

Good answer.

We ride in awkward silence for a while. What kind of conversation do you make with a date you've known forever?

"Speaking of weird," Garrett's voice booms out in the quiet vehicle, and he looks startled, "did I ever tell you about the precocious seven-year-old I met on the beach, who thought his parents had kidnapped him at birth from his real parents?"

"I don't think so."

"His basis for this theory was that both of his parents loved ice cream, but he hated it. And since he couldn't get them to admit he was adopted, he knew there must have been criminal activity involved."

"Oh, bless his heart."

Garrett nods. "For a week, every day, up and down the beach he'd go, watching to see who walked by the ice cream carts without stopping."

"And that's why he chose to talk to you. Because you didn't stop at the ice cream cart?"

"Yep. I had to buy a triple-dipped Rocky Road cone and scarf it down just to prove to him that I wasn't his long-lost brother."

I laugh. "What a great sacrifice you made for a stranger."

"Yep, that's me."

"So what happened? Don't leave me hanging."

"His parents convinced him that since they all three loved the beach they had to be related."

"Aww, how sweet."

He grins. "The ice cream was sweet; the kid was mildly annoying."

I slap at his shoulder. "Don't try to act like a man of steel. I know how tenderhearted you are."

"You only think that because I could never say no to you. You're my kryptonite."

I can feel the heat creeping up my cheeks. That might be the sweetest thing anyone's ever said to me. I'm speechless.

He saves me from having to reply. "Why did Mark tell me to tell the ducks hello when I told him we were going out tonight?"

"You know. The Peabody ducks."

"Is that a musical group?"

I flip the lighted visor mirror down and look at my makeup. "I can't believe you live forty-five minutes from Little Rock and have never heard of the Peabody ducks. You live a sheltered life."

"Don't rub it in. Just tell me what they are."

I snicker. "They're real live ducks. Every morning at eleven o'clock, with music and fanfare, they waddle from the elevator down the red carpet into the fountain in the lobby. They splash and play in the water all day, then march back out at five o'clock to retire to their 'palace.'"

He taps the steering wheel. "Oh man, somebody get me an application. I finally figured out what I want to be when I grow up."

"Um, I'm sorry to be the one to break it to you, but you don't fit the bill," I quip.

He snickers. "Oh well, the job probably isn't all it's quacked up to be, anyway. Guess I'll just stick with mine."

I know he's joking, but I feel a twinge of sympathy for him. He does a good business in computer consulting, but in the world we're about to enter, where people are defined by their occupations or at least their bank accounts, he and I will be near the bottom of the ranks.

At the Peabody, Garrett tosses the key to the valet and signs the card. "Do your parents know I'm coming?"

Gulp.

CHAPTER 20

I intended to call and tell my parents I was bringing Garrett, even though Mother had mentioned inviting Shawn.

But I didn't.

He gives me a bittersweet smile. "I'll take that stricken look on your face to be a no. They expecting a lawyer, by any chance?"

"Maybe. But I can choose my own dates." And the sooner my parents realize that, the better off we'll be.

"Why didn't you ask him?"

I consider my answer, but I'm not ready to give away too much. So I settle for light. "My mother told me to bring someone with good table manners, and I didn't want her to think she could boss me around, so I brought you."

He winks at me. "Good choice."

When we enter the gala, my dad waves from across the room. Garrett takes my hand, and I hold on for dear life as we walk to meet him.

"Kristianna, glad you could make it." Dad shakes my hand. When he gets in his public persona, it would take a natural disaster to bump him out of it. "Garrett." He shakes Garrett's hand, too, but I notice he doesn't say he's glad to see him. He points us to our table, where Mother sits chatting with a blond standing in front of her.

As we're walking toward her from the side, I watch my mother's animated face with something close to envy. She never talks that much when she's with me. Unless she has a point to make or an ultimatum to issue.

As we draw nearer, I hear her say, "Oh yes, our daughter's coming tonight. She's terribly busy, quite the entrepreneur in a little tourist town not far from here. And the demand for her paintings makes it hard to balance everything. But charitable events are important to her."

I'm stunned by her proud tone, not to mention her grandiose description of my job.

"Who's her date?" the blond asks.

Mother says, "Her date? He's—" The smile on her face freezes, and her eyes glitter with anger as she sees me with Garrett. "Here they are now." She introduces us, drawing an obvious blank at Garrett's name even though we've been friends for twenty years. He graciously covers for her, and when she tells the woman he's "in computers," he nods.

We slide into our seats as the woman moves on to speak to someone else. "Hi, Mother."

201

"Kristianna." Her lips are pursed so tightly that it's a wonder she can get the one word out. No doubt she wants to rail at me for not bringing Shawn, but good manners won't allow it. What a battle must be going on inside her.

During the delicious meal, my parents are polite, if not warm, to Garrett and make no references to law school. When people start mingling while we're waiting for the entertainment act to get set up, my parents excuse themselves to circulate, but we stay put.

I smile at Garrett. "Well, well, not only do you have impeccable table manners, you're quite a charmer, too."

His green eyes twinkle. "Oh, sorry. I should have spilled something or wiped my mouth on my sleeve. Did I mess up your plan to show your mother who's boss?"

I laugh. "Only a little." I sit back in my chair. "Don't look now, but I think the worst is over."

Before he can respond, my mother's best friend, Mitzi, scurries over to us. "So good to see you, Kristianna."

She pats my cheek and turns to Garrett. "And this must be the lawyer."

I open my mouth to say no and think I actually get the word out, but she goes on without stopping, "Your mother is so proud that you've found someone. . ." She pauses for a second, to consider her words maybe, but I'm too stunned by now to speak. "Well, let's just say you've given her more than one gray hair with your taste in friends. But now you've come to your senses, and from what I hear, the law office will stay in the family." She winks at Garrett. "Not a bad deal for you, either, eh?"

We just look at her.

"Welcome to the family," she calls as she bustles on to her next unsuspecting victim.

I put my head in my hands and rub my temples. So much for the worst being over. I have no idea what to say to Garrett. He's not talking, either. Probably too horrified by the dysfunctional mess he's stumbled into. I finally look up, and he's not here. I don't blame him, but I'm startled. They don't come any steadier than Garrett. I glance over toward my parents, and there he is, talking to my dad.

A few seconds later, he comes back to the table. "Unless you're just dying to hear the opera singer, I got us out of the rest of this."

"I take back what I said earlier. You *are* Superman." I grab my clutch purse and follow him out of the room. When the big double doors clank shut behind us, I turn to him. "What did you say to them?"

"Your mother was busy talking to someone, so I just told your dad I thought you were getting a headache and we were going to go. Then I thanked him for a lovely evening. I didn't mention that your mother *was* the headache."

I smile. "Thanks." I might as well brace myself for a nasty phone call from Mother tomorrow about leaving early. But it'll be worth it.

"Anytime."

"I'm sorry about what Mitzi said. She doesn't have good sense."

He laughs. "She was just repeating what she'd been told."

I look at him, so distinguished looking in his tux, and feel a new surge of anger at my mother. "I'm even sorrier about that."

He pulls me into a one-armed hug as we walk down the carpeted hallway to the glass elevator. "Kristianna, some people can't see past the surface. We should feel sorry for her."

I nod. "I tell myself that, but sometimes it's hard."

"I bet if I had a job as a Peabody duck she'd look at me differently."

"Oh, that's for sure." We walk up to the elevator, but I grab his hand before he can punch the button on the wall. "I've got an idea. Follow me."

"Back to the benefit?" he asks as we pass the double doors we just exited.

I shake my head. The crystal clear tones of the opera singer warming up waft out to us. Not bad, but not what I'm looking for right now. "Nope. Just passing by."

He follows me to the wall of glass doors at the end. Like a gentleman, albeit a clueless one, he pushes open the door and stands back to let me go out.

The night breeze cools my hot face. I put one hand to my hair. Thankfully, Brenda used enough hairspray to withstand a tornado.

I lead Garrett over to the glass-and-redbrick enclosure where the famous Peabody ducks are happily napping. "Welcome to the duck palace," I whisper. "Not exactly what I expected when I first heard they lived in a palace, but it works."

We watch the ducks for a bit, then wander over to the waist-high brick wall overlooking the Arkansas River. I lean on it in silence, watching the moon glisten on the water, peaceful in the presence of the man beside me.

"So many things in life aren't what they seem once you scratch the surface," he finally says.

"No, I guess not." I shoot him a puzzled look. He's more enigmatic than James Dean these days.

"Still, you know the ducks are much more comfortable here than they would be in our idea of a palace. So sometimes, it's just semantics."

I glance over at him sharply. That sounded like more than a casual comment. "What are you really talking about?"

"If you lose the Jingle Bells name, will you lose the town you love?"

I groan. I should have known. He's never said which side of the issue he's on since I stopped him in the bowling alley that night. But considering he's always busy when we're door-knocking or having committee meetings, I was pretty sure where he stood. I just didn't want to face it. I take a step away from him and shiver. "How can it be the town I love if it's not 'Jingle Bells'?"

"If the name changes, will Scott still put a table of books on the sidewalk on sunny days?"

I shrug. "I guess."

"Will Joe down at the coffee shop still brew coffee strong enough to force you into facing the morning whether you want to or not?"

"I suppose."

"I know you love the town, Kristianna, but the town is the people, not the name."

"If someone changed my name to 'Mary' tomorrow, would you like that?" He'd probably just call me "sport" anyway, so it's a silly question.

"No, I'd hate it." He moves toward me, but I take another step away. "But I'd accept it if that's what it took to keep from losing you."

I look up at him. "Have you signed the petition?"

He shakes his head.

"But you agree with it?"

Moonlight makes his eyes hard to read. "Do I want the name change? No. Do I think it's inevitable if we're going to survive as a town? Yes."

Deep down, I knew that was how he felt.

He takes my hand. "I need to explain—"

I don't pull away, but I tug him toward the doors leading back inside. "You know what? Let's not talk about this anymore tonight. I think I just need a break. And right now, I'm freezing."

We ride almost all the way home in silence, though not an uncomfortable one. I guess both of us are thinking about the night. I glance over at him. At least I'm thinking about the night. He could be thinking about the ducks in their glass palace for all I know. Wish I could figure out exactly what's standing between us.

"Thank you for going with me," I say softly. "I feel like I should apologize again for my mother."

"You don't owe me an apology. She's a strong woman with strong opinions."

"If you say, 'Just like her daughter,' I'm getting out of the car. Without waiting for you to stop."

He laughs. "You're not like her in many ways, but you both have a determination and grit that shouldn't be underestimated."

I can't argue with that. "How're your mom and sister?"

"Mom's happy. Tim's been good for her, and he treats Beth just like she's his own. She's as content as a sixteen-year-old can be, I think."

"Oh, I remember those years. You feel like you're completely grown, but the rules say you're still not."

He raises an eyebrow. "It never sat well with you for someone to tell you what to do, did it?"

"I guess not. I respected Gran enough that I minded her no matter what I thought, though."

"We all did. She was the wisest woman I knew."

I swallow against the lump in my throat. "Me, too."

He pulls his SUV into a spot behind my car and kills the motor.

My knees shake as we walk to the front door. Makes it hard to walk in these spindly heels. A siren wails in the distance as I find my keys in my bag and turn to face him. "This was really fun."

He nods. "I enjoyed it."

Okay, I think we've talked that to death. "Well, I'm tired. I'd better go up."

"Your hair is beautiful like that."

I put my hand up to it. "After the wind on the roof of the Peabody, it probably looks like a rat's nest."

He shakes his head. "Makes you look like a princess."

"Princess of Power, that's me."

He laughs. "I remember that." He reaches out to wrap a ringlet around his finger, then releases it. "Sorry. I've been wanting to do that all night."

"No problem."

"Good." His voice is husky. He puts his arm around my waist and leans closer. Before our lips can touch, a fire truck roars around the corner, sirens wailing, horns blaring. I jump back against the door as the red truck screeches to a stop beside us.

"Busted," Garrett whispers.

I never giggle unless I'm nervous, but I do now. "I guess Mr. Pletka smelled smoke."

Two firemen jump out. One goes into the laundry, but the other one stays out on the sidewalk and sniffs.

Garrett nods toward the man, then turns back to me. "Happy Valentine's Day, sport."

"You, too."

He watches from his vehicle while I let myself in the door. I give him a feeble wave, close the door behind me, and take the yellow roses up to my apartment.

Ami's a Google expert. Thanks to the popular search engine, she knows everything in the world. The drawback to that is, when you're in the middle of a phone conversation and she's at home on her computer, she'll start googling things you're saying.

So I'm telling her about my date with Garrett, but I haven't gotten very far when she interrupts. "According to this, yellow roses mean 'I love you, but I'm unworthy of your love.'"

"Really?" That makes no sense.

"Yeah, or they could mean 'My love for you is waning.'"

"Great."

She ignores my sarcasm. "Or indicate jealousy."

I snort. "Or they could indicate the Stewarts were out of everything else." Or that he didn't want me to get the wrong idea by giving me red roses, which no one would ever have to look up the meaning of.

"Fine." She fakes an injured tone. "If you don't want me to share my knowledge with you, I won't."

"Too late. You already did."

"Oh yeah. So tell me about the rest of the date."

"He handled my parents very well." I tell her how he got us out of the banquet early without lying. "And even when my mother called to read me the riot act for leaving early, she couldn't really find anything bad to say about him."

"That gives him bonus points."

I gasp. "Are you scoring him?" We used to do that in high school—score our dates on things like whether they picked us up at the door or honked for us to come out. Bonus points for every time they acted like they really cared what we thought.

"Just in my mind. No worries. He's scoring high."

I laugh. "He'd be so glad to know."

"Actually, as many times as he heard us do it back then, he probably has an unfair advantage."

"Is this too weird? Me dating Garrett?"

"Not at all. Mark and I are best friends, too. We just didn't know it until after we started dating. What difference does it make what order you do it in?"

"Thanks." I hang up relieved.

But when two weeks pass and Garrett hasn't called to ask me out again, I'm kicking myself for my assumptions. I've seen him at church and at the town meeting, but always with a group. Since bowling hasn't started back yet, it's not too hard for him to avoid me.

"He's just shy," Ami assures me.

"Oh? Did you google that?" I ask sarcastically.

Her sympathetic understanding just makes me feel worse.

CHAPTER 21

As February melts into March, I throw myself into the "Save the Town" campaign. The committee tries to ignore the rumors that are blooming out faster than the trees, even though Ruby got it from "a good source" that Shawn has almost all the signatures he needs to put the name change on the ballot.

At the March town meeting, I'm tired of playing ostrich, so I ask Uncle Gus if this is true.

His smug smile makes my stomach churn. "When the petition is full, I'll notify the town council members. Unless"—he gives Scott and me a pointed look—"you think we can have a unanimous vote right now and save time and money."

I shrug. "Not unless John and Dottie have changed their minds."

I glance over at them, but they don't look my way. Dottie is another one who avoids me these days. I sent her a little card telling her I didn't blame her, but I guess she feels guilty. I try to catch her on the way out the door, but she's gone before I reach her.

Another week passes, and I know I need to start preparations for the Spring Festival. I pick up the phone and call Dottie.

"Jingle Bells Library."

"Dottie, hi. It's Kristianna."

"Oh. Kristianna." I hate the fear in her voice. Am I so fanatical that she thinks I'm going to yell at her? Probably.

"I'm planning my basket for the box auction. Are you putting some together?"

She laughs, a little halfheartedly but at least she laughs. "I've been making baskets for this thing for as long as I can remember. I think everyone would faint if I didn't."

"They probably would. Your baskets always go for the highest."

"Well, maybe so, but we both know it's not because those men are craving my company. More like they've had a taste of my fried chicken and are willing to put up with me to have it."

I laugh. "Don't sell yourself short."

"Usually I do several and let the married ones share with their wives. Then if there's a widower or two in the bunch, I'll split my time among them."

"That sounds fair. But I need to ask you something. What could I put in mine that would make it stand out?" Years ago, the baskets were closed, to make it more of a game, but now they're open, with cellophane over the top.

"Hmm. . .let me see. Homemade lemonade is always a big hit. And like I said, fried chicken. But honey, as young and pretty as you are, you could put bread and water in yours and it would sell."

I smile. I want it to sell high enough to help me show people that we can raise money for the things we need in Jingle Bells without selling out to Summer Valley. I don't think my charm's going to work for that.

"Thanks, Dottie."

"Oh, your gran always made those chicken Florentine sandwiches for the auction. They melt in your mouth and smell mighty good, too."

"That sounds perfect." And easy. "I think that's what I'll do."

"Okay, see you there. And Kristianna?"

"Yes?"

"I'm sorry about switching sides. And I'm afraid I've handled it poorly."

I glance at the flyer she made the night we had the first meeting, secured to my refrigerator door with a magnet. "I'll admit it kind of surprised me."

"I know. That's why I haven't wanted to face you. I'm ashamed, I guess. But I just feel like I have to vote what I think is best for the people."

"That's what each one of us has to do, Dottie. Don't be ashamed of that."

"Thanks, sweetie, for letting an old lady off the hook so easy. Friends?"

"Yes, ma'am. Always."

As we hang up, I smile and look over at the wilted yellow rose

I saved when I threw out the Valentine's bouquet. If only all my relationship problems were so easily resolved.

"While they're getting ready to start the auction, let's go hit Uncle Gus in the face with a pie," Ami says as we weave through the booths.

Mark laughs. "You sound entirely too enthusiastic."

If he only knew how much I'd like to smack the mayor—with more than a pie. Especially after the way he's manipulated people like Dottie. "Hey, that's a great idea. Plus it's for a good cause. Let's go." I turn my face toward the sky, soaking in the glorious warm sunshine. Arkansas's March weather is iffy, but today is beautiful. Maybe things are looking up.

"You girls are bad influences on each other. Where's Garrett?" Mark looks around. "I'm feeling outnumbered."

He would have to bring Garrett into it, just when I'm relaxing a little.

Ami shoots him a warning look that he doesn't see at all, but I intercept.

I force a smile. "He's been really busy lately, Mark. So you'll just have to learn to stand up to us on your own."

"In that case, I'd better forget feeding pie to the mayor and save my money to buy Ami's basket. I'd hate to have to watch her eat lunch with someone else."

Ami tucks her arm in his. "We're a package deal, big guy. If someone else wins my basket, he'll have to take you, too."

"I'm not worried about that. But there's just enough food for two, and I know who'd have to do without."

She slaps him playfully on the shoulder.

I snatch a yellow daisy from the nearest lamppost and sniff it. Oops. Silk. I carefully put it back. It looks real, at least. No tacky plastic flowers here. "Nobody else does a spring festival like Jingle Bells."

Mark shakes his head. "Nope. They sure don't. No one else would be crazy enough to put candy canes and daisies in the same decorative scheme."

Ami snorts. "Decorative scheme? I thought I told you to stop watching *Trading Spaces*."

Mark sticks his bottom lip out in a mock pout. "Hey, if it's good enough for Frank and Doug, it's good enough for me."

Ami raises her eyebrows at me. "See? He knows them by name. All of them. It's an addiction, I tell you."

I shrug. "He's ready for you to buy a fixer-upper."

"Maybe we can if—"

Uh-oh. When people stop in midsentence, it usually means they just remembered their audience. I spear Ami with a look that says, "I'm getting to the bottom of this." No need to try to get out of telling me. "If? If what?" Like I don't already know.

She waves away my question with her hand. "If nothing."

"If the name change goes through." I say the words flatly because I can't say them any other way. I feel like a little girl who built a fortress only to discover that the walls are trick props that close in on her when she least expects it.

"Hey." Ami grabs my hand. "We're against the name change. On general principles. But if it goes through, we'll probably be better off financially. That's just a consolation prize. It's not something we want to happen. You understand that, don't you?"

I pull my hand away. Not really. I don't understand. Not one little bit. What is wrong with these people? Jingle Bells is my childhood sanctuary. My shelter in a rough storm, my. . . You know, it's mine! And they can't change the name at all. They just can't. Not while I have breath in my body. Suddenly I feel like Scarlett O'Hara. I want to throw my fist in the air and declare, "As God is my witness!" And we know how that story ends.

The clang of a bell ends the conversation and my inner drama.

"Folks, come on over for the Forty-Eighth Annual Jingle Bells Box Auction." The auctioneer's voice booms out over the loud-speaker. "We'll begin the bidding in five minutes."

We walk, without talking, to the rows of folding chairs arranged in front of the stage. I just don't know what to say, and I guess Ami feels the same way. I realize she hasn't changed sides. But if she can accept it, and even profit from it, will she still fight as hard?

I don't know where he comes from, but as soon as we sit down, Garrett slides in next to Mark.

"Long time no see." Mark gives him a quick handclasp.

"Sorry, man." Garrett leans around and waves to Ami and me. "Been real busy."

Yeah. Right. Busy avoiding me.

Albert, the local auctioneer, rings the bell again. "Let the bidding begin. First basket up is. . ." His descriptions are poetical and long. And the first basket still starts out at just five dollars.

Behind me, I hear someone call, "Couldn't get a bag of KFC for that!"

Spurred on by the heckler, I guess, bidders jump in right and left, and soon the first basket is gone for nine dollars.

"Oh, mine's next," Ami whispers and elbows Mark.

He opens the bid at ten dollars, and she frowns at him.

"What?" he hisses.

"Do you know how far I drove to get that?"

"Yes, and now I'm having to pay for it twice." He raises his hand. "Fifteen," he hollers.

Albert stops and looks at him, then shakes his head. "The newlywed over there just raised himself."

Everyone laughs, and Ami and Mark both have sheepish grins.

"Fifteen, do I hear twenty?"

Garrett raises his hand. "Twenty."

Mark whips his head around to look at him.

Garrett shrugs. "I like takeout. And I don't mind eating with the two of you."

I give him an incredulous look. Hello? Newlyweds on a picnic? Third wheel? You know what? Maybe he's just dense. Probably I'm just somebody for him to kill time with and I'm blowing everything out of proportion.

"Twenty-five!" Mark yells, with a mock glare at Garrett.

When no one else bids, Albert congratulates Mark and moves on to the next basket.

"So, I guess I'll have to share this with you?" Mark grumbles to Garrett.

I can't hear Garrett's reply, but Mark laughs.

My basket ends up being one of the last ones. I'm not worried about who buys it. Unlike a lot of the single girls, I gave no hints to a certain someone about the identity of my basket. It will sell strictly on its contents and my presentation, and if I have to eat lunch with toothless Mr. Rivers, I will. I'm just hoping it brings in a decent amount for the town.

Albert holds it up for the group to see. "Oh my, what a delicious-smelling lunch here. We've got some fancy chicken sandwiches, homemade lemonade, and a freshly baked apple pie." He shakes his head. "It's a wonderful thing—no matter how much things change, they stay the same. I've seen many a basket come through with this exact meal over the years. And I was afraid it would be missing this year." He gives me a broad wink. "It's enough to make you believe in Christmas forever."

Oh great. Every head turns to look at me, and I scrunch down in my chair.

"Wonder whose basket that is?" Mark whispers facetiously.

I shrug. But I know my red face and the fact that I'm half as tall as I was a minute before confirms Albert's hints.

"Do I hear an opening bid?" Albert goes into his auctioneer rattle.

Garrett raises his hand. "Twenty dollars."

Same as he bid for Ami's. But he'd better be careful. He might end up having to eat lunch with me.

"I've got twenty—"

"Thirty," a voice yells from the opposite aisle.

Shawn.

"Forty," Garrett shoots back.

"Fifty."

"Sixty."

My face is burning so badly that it feels like I fell asleep in the sun. This is not what I had in mind, but on the bidding goes.

"One hundred fifty," Shawn calls.

"Two hundred," Garrett says, not even glancing my way.

CHAPTER 22

What is Garrett thinking? I know he can't possibly afford this. Plus, if he wanted to eat with me so badly, why hasn't he called me?

"Two hundred," Albert echoes, but before he can go into his auctioneer call, Shawn raises his bid to two hundred fifty.

Garrett raises his hand. "Three hundred." Does he think this grand gesture—spending money he doesn't have—is going to make me forget that he blows hot and then cold?

I whip out my cell phone and quickly type in a text message—PLEASE STOP—and send it to Garrett.

I watch him and begin to think that either his phone is set to vibrate and he doesn't notice it above the commotion or he's going to ignore it in light of the tense bidding war. The bid is up to four fifty by the time I see him pull his phone from his belt and read the screen.

"Five hundred," Shawn says.

The fascinated onlookers swivel their heads to look at Garrett.

He slips his phone back in his pocket and folds his arms across his chest, his face stony.

Albert looks flustered for a second but quickly recovers. "Five hundred dollars. . . Going once. . . Going twice. . . Sold! to the highest bidder!"

The crowd breaks into applause, and Albert motions to me. I wiggle my fingers in an embarrassed wave.

A few minutes later, when it's over, I step past Mark and Ami to speak to Garrett, but he's gone. I look around, but he's nowhere. I guess I hurt his feelings, but he should be thanking me for saving his money. I'd have promised him sandwiches later, but I only had time for a very short message.

"Kristianna?" I spin around to see Shawn smiling at me. He holds up my basket. "Ready to eat?"

I'm bemused and uncertain how to handle this. By putting the basket together, technically I did agree to eat with him. But isn't five hundred dollars a steep price to pay for a date?

Still, he did pay it. "Sure. There are picnic tables set up under the pavilion."

"I know a better place." He guides me to his tiny sports car.

"Your car?"

He lowers his eyebrows. "Very funny. We're going to ride in the car to get there, okay?"

"Of course. I knew that." I just wasn't thinking. Actually I was thinking. But about Garrett's bidding so high on my lunch basket, too. And his leaving so quickly.

Shawn puts the food in the minuscule trunk, and I fold myself into the passenger seat. When we take the paved road on the outskirts of town, I glance over at him. "We going to picnic at Crystal Lake, or are you just taking me out to show me where Summer Valley Outdoors is going to be when y'all finish bullying the whole town into going along with your plan?"

He clears his throat. "Actually, you'll officially find out next week at the town meeting, but my job is done."

My stomach rolls. "You got a thousand signatures?"

He pulls into the lake picnic area and kills the engine. "Yes, just yesterday. But I wanted to tell you before you found out from someone else." He opens his door.

"Bad news is bad news, no matter who the bearer is." I glance over at the huge empty building next to the lake. It's a waste, I admit. But the cost is too high. "But I guess I'd rather hear it from you than from Uncle Gus." And I'm clinging to the fact that it took them this long to get a thousand signatures. How long will it take them to win the majority vote?

"That's what I was hoping. Sorry if I forced you into eating with me." He comes around, opens my door, and offers his hand.

I put my hand in his and let him help me climb out of the tiny car. "You didn't force me into anything. Except maybe into the car."

He pats the shiny red fiberglass. "It's more for speed than comfort, I admit."

I nod. "Guess I'm all about comfort."

He retrieves the basket from the trunk. "Here's one comfort I'd hate to do without. I'm starving."

"I feel bad, though, that you spent so much on lunch." I kind of laugh and nod out toward Crystal Lake, spotted with boats. "Entering the festival bass-fishing tournament would have cost a tenth as much and probably been a much better investment."

"You haven't seen me fish, obviously." He gives me a wry grin. "Okay, I admit I wasn't planning on dropping five hundred dollars today. I guess I'm a little competitive."

That's an understatement. "I think both of you must be."

His eyebrows draw together. "Speaking of both of *us*, I got the impression you and Garrett were just friends. Was I wrong?"

"No." I think back to that first night at the bowling alley when the four of us were bowling and Shawn came in. Garrett hadn't jumped in to stop me from showing Shawn around town. So why waste his life savings on a lunch basket to keep us from eating together? "We're friends." I think.

I take the tablecloth from the basket and spread it on the table closest to Crystal Lake. I purposely put my back to the Benning Building. I want to forget everything today. "We're lucky to have such a beautiful day in late March."

He nods, accepting my obvious subject change graciously. "I love winter, but I'm always glad to see spring." He places the plate of sandwiches on the table.

I pour a glass of lemonade for him and one for me. "Me, too. Spring is a season full of promise."

"Every season is full of promise in Jingle Bells," Shawn says.

I set the bowl of potato salad on the table and look at him openmouthed. "That sounds like something straight off a postcard. This from a man who wants to change the name of the town?"

He shrugs. "The name is nice, but this town will always be special."

I grin. "I'm glad you like it. I do, too."

"Just one more thing we have in common."

I look over at his deep blue eyes and the movie star cleft in his chin. Why doesn't being with him make my heart race? "One more thing?"

"Well, this is probably stretching it, but your parents are lawyers and so am I."

"And, as I'm sure you've noticed, I have a deep and abiding distrust for lawyers," I say teasingly. "We *do* have a lot in common."

He smiles. "Especially since I actually have a license to practice law now."

"You're—Oh, you passed the bar. Congratulations. The world could probably use more lawyers like you." I realize as I say it that I'm getting over my aversion to lawyers. No two are alike. No more than all artists are the same. I offer him a high five.

He slaps my palm. "I was hoping for a hug, but I guess a high five is better than a handshake."

Heat flares up my cheeks. "Shawn, as crazy as it may seem, I've grown kind of used to having you around."

He rolls his eyes. "Oh boy. Here it comes. The great brush-off."

I feel awful. I wish I'd never even put a basket together. Although

I guess this conversation is inevitable. "I think if you stay in town, we'll probably end up friends." I busy myself filling our plates.

"And if I move back to Little Rock, does that mean we might be more than friends?"

"You *are* a lawyer, aren't you?" I'm stalling.

"Just answer the question." He grins. But I can tell he's really asking me.

I shake my head. "I'm sorry. Friendship is all I have to offer, Shawn."

"I may have won the auction, but he won in the long run, didn't he?"

I don't pretend not to know who he's talking about. But his question is ridiculous. Things couldn't be more unsettled between Garrett and me. "No. It's not Garrett. . . ."

"Don't kid yourself, Kristianna. When he's around, your whole face lights up. I noticed it the first time I saw y'all together at the bowling alley, but I thought that if neither of you realized it yet, maybe I still had a chance."

I want to deny it, but even more, I want to ask him if he thinks Garrett's face lights up when he sees me, too, or if it seems one-sided. But I can't ask that.

"He obviously feels the same about you." Shawn obligingly answers my unasked question.

"I think you're mistaken, but it's not worth arguing about. Would you say the blessing for the food?"

He proves what a great guy he is by accepting my subject change

CHRISTINE LYNXWILER

once again and thanking God for the five-hundred-dollar meal we're about to eat.

After we finish eating, he looks over at me. "Worth every penny. It was delicious."

"Shawn. . ."

"What?"

I consider my words. They're a long time coming, and they need to be just right. "I owe you a big apology for how I've treated you since you came to Jingle Bells. I understand about your job, but when I put that together with your profession, I just let it get to me. But you're all right in my book."

"Thanks, Kristianna. I have to admit you did kind of give me a complex for a while." He shrugs. "Who knows? Maybe the fact that you couldn't stand me was partly why I was so determined to get you to go out with me."

I laugh. "Yeah, I bet rejection's a new experience for you."

A sheepish grin spreads across his face. "I don't like to lose."

I toss our trash in the nearby can. "That's a trait my parents value highly. Why don't you call and set up an appointment to interview with them if you're still interested in a position with their firm?" I smile over at him. "Just between us, I think it would do them good to work with a Christian every day."

He places the leftovers in the basket. "Think they'd want me even if their daughter didn't?"

"I can't guarantee anything, but I know they'd be blessed to get you. And I'll be glad to be a reference for you." I half snort. "For what it's worth. You might do better without my referral as far as my mother's concerned."

"Thanks. I think I'll take my chances with the referral if you're willing." Which proves he doesn't come close to understanding my relationship with my parents, but that's okay.

"No problem."

We walk slowly back to the car without speaking. I have a feeling he's thinking about job possibilities. To my embarrassment, I'm replaying his earlier words concerning Garrett and me. As the gentle breeze from the lake flits across my face, my heart does a dance of its own.

"So you really haven't talked to Garrett since the auction?" Ami murmurs to me as we lace up our bowling shoes Saturday night.

I shake my head. "I've called his phone several times, but it always goes straight to voice mail. I even sent him text messages saying we need to talk. But he ignored them, too."

"You saw him at church, didn't you? I noticed him sitting on the opposite end of your pew."

I grimace. "Yeah, I noticed that, too, but he slipped in at the last second; then when it was over, he was out the door before I could get to him." It's not like our church has a huge attendance. You have to really want to steer clear of people not to run into them there.

"Maybe you'll get to the bottom of this tonight. It's almost like he's avoiding you."

I glance at the door just as Lila walks in, clutching her bowling bag, her red hair caught up in a no-nonsense ponytail. "Don't look now, but it's *exactly* like he's avoiding me."

Ami, of course, looks immediately. "Oh no. What is he thinking?"

"That our agreement is if we can't be here, we'll make sure a replacement bowler shows up?"

Lila approaches us before Ami can respond. "Hi. Garrett asked me to fill in for him. Okay?"

I bristle like a tough chick whose turf has just been invaded. Maybe I should be popping my gum and slapping my fist in my palm. In my mind I flip up my collar. "Fine by me."

Ami gives me a puzzled look. "Sure, Lila. Glad you came."

"Garrett sick?" I ask. Besides sick of me?

She shakes her head. "Sore, maybe. He helped me move yesterday."

So while I've been text messaging and calling, he's been man-handling Lila's furniture. I feel so much better knowing he hasn't been sitting home moping. Not.

"Move?" Ami pipes up. "Move where?"

"To Jingle Bells." Lila flips her ponytail over her shoulder and unzips her bowling bag. "Soon to be Summer Valley."

Listen here, chickie, we're going to have to take this outside if you're not careful. "The election's not for a few weeks. We won't know the future town name until then," I say through tight lips.

"Oh, sorry." She chuckles. "I keep forgetting there are people against it."

I try to smile. "Last I heard, at least half the town is against it. Hopefully more."

"Yes, well, I guess we can bowl together without agreeing on it."

I guess.

"So where exactly in Jingle Bells are you living, Lila?" Ami asks politely.

For the next few minutes, we listen to her rave about the great deal she got on a house because the father lost his job and the family had to move.

Mark comes in just as she finishes talking, and he kisses Ami. "Sorry I'm late. We got a new account right before closing time. Hey, Kristianna." Puzzlement flashes across his face when he sees his coworker. "Lila."

"Lila's here to take Garrett's place," Ami says, her arm still hooked in her husband's.

"Oh, is he sick?"

"No, just busy, I guess," Lila answers.

"And sore from helping Lila move," I offer. "Thanks to the buyer's market around here, she's our newest Jingle Bells resident."

Mark nods. "I knew that."

Ami gives him a measured look. I know she's probably remembering how he'd not told her about Shawn working for Summer Valley.

Lila turns her back to open her bag.

Mark shrugs toward us and mouths, "Sorry, I forgot."

Ami flashes him an "all is forgiven" smile.

CHRISTINE LYNXWILER

We get through the bowling, but when it's over, none of us mentions the snack bar.

On the way home, I call Garrett. But once again, no answer. I hang up without leaving a message. Why add to the ten I've already left? If he can't at least give me a chance to explain about the auction, then maybe he's not who I thought he was.

CHAPTER 23

I smooth down my white dress and stare at myself in the mirror. My eyes are huge. Am I ready?

"Are you ready?"

I spin around, and my dad, looking quite dashing in his black tux, is holding out his arm.

"My knees are knocking—does that count?"

"Having cold feet is natural, honey." He tucks my hand in his and pats it.

"Especially as many times as you've tried this," Mother says from behind him as she walks by on an usher's arm and through the double doors.

"Ignore her," Dad whispers. "This is your day."

Ami, wearing a gorgeous green velvet dress, looks back at me and gives me a thumbs-up, then disappears through the same doors Mother did.

Dad squeezes my arm. "It's our turn."

We rustle up to the doorway, and I look out into the auditorium of our church building. It's packed to overflowing. Everyone I've ever known is here. Gran waves at me from one of the front pews, and I resist the urge to run to her.

The wedding march begins to play, but my heart pounding in my ears drowns out the music. My hands are clammy, and my throat closes. I can't go through with this. Dad guides me down the aisle, and I keep my eyes fixed on my bouquet, mentally forcing myself to take another step. And another.

We're halfway, and I freeze. I can't do it.

"Look up," Dad whispers.

And I do.

There at the front of the church is Garrett, his green eyes twinkling. His smile calms me, as it always does. As it always has. Peace washes over me.

I start walking again. Instead of screaming, "Stop!" my heart is hurrying me along. I'm almost there. Garrett holds out his hand. I reach toward him, but my phone rings. My gaze flies to my bouquet. Where is it? Who is it?

It rings again. I jerk upright and blink. The Dream. As usual, I'm sweating. I grab my phone, no longer ringing but still lit up, and look at the caller ID.

Ami. I'll call her back. Right now I'm too disoriented to talk.

The clock on the bedside table says 9:00 a.m. I never sleep this late, even on Saturdays. But Sarah offered to fill in for me today, so I didn't set the alarm. It's been a week since the auction, and

I haven't been sleeping well.

I pad into the bathroom and dress, the whole time running through the Dream in my mind. Would I have gone through with marrying Garrett if Ami hadn't called? And does it really matter what happens in a dream?

Maybe not, but I know one thing for sure. I'm not going to let that irritating man ignore me another second. Just as I stomp into the kitchen and grab my picnic basket from the top of the pantry, Ami calls again.

"Hey."

"Hey, what are you doing today?" Her voice still has that newlywed perkiness.

I consider telling her she ruined my dream earlier. But maybe it was better I woke up before it was over. "Cooking."

"What's wrong with you?"

I grunt. "Sorry. I'm going to give Garrett what he wanted."

"Baseball season year-round?"

"Ha-Ha. Chicken Florentine sandwiches. And all the rest."

"Why?"

"To show him what a big baby he's being not taking my calls."

"Because he thinks you like Shawn."

I snort. "If I like Shawn, why does he think I keep calling and messaging him?"

"So let me get this straight. Garrett's been ignoring your calls, so you're making him a meal?"

"Don't sound so shocked." I balance the phone with my shoulder and grab a mixing bowl from the cabinet. "It's not like I'm proclaiming my undying love or anything. It's just a nice gesture."

"When are you going to perform this meaningless nice gesture?"

Isn't she quite the comedian for Saturday morning? "Very funny." I snag the ingredients from the fridge. "Today. If I can find him."

"Actually, he and Mark are fishing today."

"At Crystal Lake?"

"Yep."

"Perfect. Come over and help me, and we'll surprise them with lunch." Maybe it'll be less awkward with Mark and Ami as a buffer.

Two hours later, she shows up and I give her an exasperated look. "I'm almost done cooking."

She shrugs. "Why else did you think I was dragging my feet getting over here? I didn't want to ruin your meal."

Right. She hates to cook. And that's the truth. But I thought she'd probably figured it out since she's married. "You're not that bad. I haven't heard Mark complain."

"That's just because he has all the takeout numbers memorized. But I'm trying to do better. We're eating out of our own kitchen at least one night a week."

"That's great." I pull the apple pie from the oven and set it on the counter. "What did you cook this week?"

She breaks off a loose corner of crust. "Cereal and milk."

I slap at her hand. "That's not a real meal."

She shrugs. "It's not takeout."

"Help me pack these sandwiches in the basket."

She picks one up and inhales. "They smell delicious."

"If Mark likes them, next week I'll teach you how to make them."

"Better yet, you can teach him how to make them, too."

A newlywed cooking class. Why didn't I think of that? "Did you call Mark and tell him we were coming?"

"Yes, but I told him not to tell Garrett. So at noon they're going to be at dock two."

I glance up at the clock. Eleven forty. Perfect. "Help me get this stuff in the car. We'll have to hurry."

On the way, I tell her about the Dream. "But don't overanalyze it," I add.

She purses her lips. "How did green velvet look on me? Did it clash with my eyes?"

I laugh at her "shallow girl" impression. "Horribly. People shrieked when you walked in."

She grins. "So you made it to the front of the church, and it was still a nightmare."

I don't say anything. But the part of the Dream where I saw Garrett waiting for me was anything but a nightmare.

We pull into the Crystal Lake parking lot exactly three minutes before noon. Just time enough to grab the things and set up at the picnic table closest to dock two.

When the boys putter up in Mark's bass boat, I see the surprise on Garrett's face.

Ami and I walk to the dock to meet them. I'm just glad Garrett doesn't cut and run. He looks like he might want to.

"Did y'all catch anything?" Ami asks.

"Nothing worth cooking," Mark answers and tucks her into a hug.

I wave at Garrett on Mark's other side and smile, maybe a tad facetiously. "Hi." *Avoid this, buddy.*

He nods. "Hi."

Now there's a promising start. I glance over at Ami and Mark, who have their heads together and have forgotten we exist. I pull my phone and type in a message: "I said, 'Please stop', to save you money." I hit SEND. Then I walk on over to the picnic table and sit down.

A moment later, he sits down beside me with his phone in front of him. I get a new message icon and hit READ. "I got your message. Loud and clear."

I type in, "No I don't think you did. But if you'd returned my calls, maybe you would have."

I don't look at him but just hit SEND.

In a second a new message comes back. "It was obvious that you wanted to eat lunch with Shawn."

I type, "I don't think that was obvious at all. I made you the same lunch today. For free." Oops. Too much. I backspace and start over. "You're mistaken." I send it to him before I change my mind and delete that, too.

He gives me a measured look and types in, "I don't think so."

As I read his words, I growl under my breath and notice that the table is really quiet. I look up to see Ami and Mark watching us with bemused expressions on their faces. "Did you bring your cell?" Mark whispers to Ami.

She shakes her head. "It's in the car."

"Then I guess we don't get to have secret conversations."

"Don't kid yourself," Garrett drawls. "You two have secret conversations all the time, with us right here."

I nod. "Definitely."

Ami grins. "You've got a point."

"You hungry?" Garrett asks me.

"Not really." Extremely irritated? Yes. Slightly happy that he's jealous? Yes. Hungry? Last thing on my mind.

He looks over at Mark and Ami. "You honeymooners go ahead and eat. We're going to go for a walk."

"Have fun," Mark calls as we start down the tree-lined path.

When we're out of sight, Garrett pulls me to a bench.

"I thought we were walking," I blurt out.

"We walked. Now we sit. And talk." His face is grim. Maybe I was wrong about his feelings for me. Wouldn't it be ironic if he gave me the "let's be friends" talk in the same park I broke the news to Shawn? Ironic, maybe. Incredibly painful, definitely.

The water laps against the shore. A bird chirps in the tree above us, and another one answers. I stare at my hands clenched nervously in my lap.

"Why did you tell me to stop bidding unless you wanted to be with Shawn?" Garrett blurts.

I sigh. "It had to be pretty obvious I wanted to save you money. Why did you ignore my calls and messages when I tried to explain?"

His face reddens. "I didn't want to hear pity in your voice."

Pity? This man who has driven me crazy the past few months thinks I love him out of pity.

He's looking at the water. Is he saying what I think he is? Or is he just repeating what I know—that he loves me as a friend? "What do you mean?" I ask quietly.

"Mean?" He looks at me now, his eyes wide. "What do you think I mean? Don't you know the whole town pitied me when you came home from law school with that huge rock on your hand? Everyone but you knew how I felt."

"Garrett—"

"I had to leave. I knew better than to think I could stand by and watch you breeze in here on holidays with your husband and kids, expecting us to hang out together." He gives a bitter laugh. "A man has to know his limits."

The pain in his voice is palpable. I open my mouth to speak, but he holds up his hand. "Just for the record, we didn't 'lose touch.' I lost touch. I even gave up my friendship with Ami so I wouldn't have to hear about you."

The scenery around me is blurry, and I realize my eyes are filled with tears.

"Then Mom told me she read in the paper about your broken engagement."

I'd have to be blind not to see what comes next. "Then you found out I was engaged to Nathan." Why did I allow that to happen? In my heart, I knew that engagement was a mistake from the beginning. And look at the heartache it caused me.

"Happy again. Without me."

His words chill me. Everything I've feared is true. I *am* a runaway bride. Hearing him spell it out like this makes me know. Dream or no dream, I'll never walk happily down the aisle to meet the man I love. "It was a mistake."

He shrugs. "I'm not one to cast stones. I've made my own share of mistakes, just trying to do what I thought was right."

"So where does this leave us?"

He doesn't speak, and my cell phone, still in my hand, blares through the silence.

I glance down at the screen. "It's the shop," I murmur. Of all the times. But Sarah *never* calls.

"You'd better answer it," Garrett says softly.

"Hello?"

"Kristianna," Sarah says, "did your dad get in touch with you?"

"My dad?" I repeat dumbly. "No. Why?"

"He called here about twenty minutes ago. Said he'd tried your cell phone and it went to voice mail."

"Okay. I'll call him."

"I hated to bother you."

"No, Sarah, thanks for calling. Something must be wrong."

I hang up and look helplessly at Garrett. "I have to call my dad."

I punch in his number, but it goes to voice mail. I hang up without leaving a message and call my own voice mail. No messages. "I need to go home," I say. "Maybe he left me a message on my home phone. Or maybe I'll get in touch with him on the way." I force a laugh. "I'll feel silly if he just wants to plan a surprise birthday party for Mother or something, but it isn't like him to call at all, much less persistently."

"I understand. Go," he says. "Mark and Ami can ride home with me."

"Are you sure? I know we were in the middle—"

"Go. We'll finish this later."

That sounds ominous. But I give him a weak smile and hurry down the path to my car.

CHAPTER 24

I barely get out of the lake parking lot when my dad answers his phone. "Hi, Dad, what's up?"

"First, let me tell you. She's going to be fine."

She? "Mother?" I can't even imagine anything wrong with my mother. She's always seemed indestructible. "What happened?"

"Her appendix ruptured. They did surgery."

"Surgery? When?" I'm praying silently even while I'm waiting for his answer.

"Last night."

"And you're just now telling me?" I know I'm yelling. And I know I shouldn't be. But real families don't wait to tell until afternoon the next day if someone has emergency surgery the night before.

"She didn't want you to worry."

I can't imagine why. I figured she'd be glad if I was worried. But I don't say this. Instead I say, "She's conscious?" I head the car toward Little Rock.

"Yes. But she's in CCU. We can only see her every four hours."

"She's in Critical Care." I feel like a parrot, but this is so sudden.

"Yes." He gives me the hospital details, then repeats, "But she's going to be fine."

"I'll be there in forty minutes."

"You don't have to come."

Just try and stop me. I'm part of a family even if my parents don't want to think so.

When I walk into the CCU waiting room, I look twice at the man sitting in the chair in the corner, a rumpled blanket half across him. A half-empty cup of coffee is beside him on the table. His face is drawn, and he looks like he's been doing without sleep for weeks. It takes my brain a minute to process the fact that this is my dad.

I hug him, and he pats my arm. "Were you up all night?"

He nods.

I plunk down into the chair next to him. "You should have called me," I murmur.

"Probably. But when I was afraid she wouldn't make it, I couldn't bear to tell you. Then when I found out she would, we hated to bother you."

"You're my parents. How could it bother me to know one of you was fighting for your life?" Well, that didn't come out right. "I mean, you could never bother me by calling to tell me."

He draws his brows together. "You're here now. That's what matters."

He's obviously been worried sick, and he didn't call me. Because she didn't want me to worry? Or because he didn't think I'd care?

For a few minutes, he tells me about the symptoms leading up to her attack; then he grows silent. His eyelids look heavy.

I touch his shoulder.

"After we see her at five, you're going to go home and get some sleep. I can stay with her tonight."

He agrees without protest, and I know he must be exhausted. He dozes for a few minutes while I stare at the big white clock on the wall. Is it my imagination, or do the hands on this clock move much slower than most? I'm sure I'm not the first person to think that.

I call Sarah and tell her what has happened so she knows to close up for me, then use the quiet time to pray earnestly. For my mom's health. But also for our battered relationship.

Finally, the hands swing around to five o'clock. I shake Dad gently. "We can go see Mother now."

He's instantly alert. "Okay. Let's go."

When we enter the unit, the beds are separated just by curtains, and many patients have nurses sitting at the ends of their beds. Dad holds back one panel for me to go in.

Mother looks up, her blue eyes sunken in her face. "Kristianna." Her voice is stronger than I expect, but slightly slurred.

I hug her gently and drop an actual kiss on her cheek. I have no patience for elbow hugs and air kisses just now. And she's too weak to protest. I even smooth her hair down. "How you doing?"

She shrugs and rolls her eyes. "I've been better."

I force a smile. "I can see that. But by tomorrow, you'll be trying to figure out how Dad can smuggle some work in here to you."

The barest hint of a smile tilts her lips. "You know me too well."

Not really. But I just look up at Dad. "You heard that. So don't let her talk you into any contraband briefs."

He chuckles. "I'll keep that in mind."

He moves over to Mother's other side and drops a kiss on her forehead. "We're going to go and let you rest before they kick us out."

She grabs his hand. "You look awful. Go home and relax before you end up in here beside me." Her words are slow and measured.

"I'm here to make sure he does. Hope you can put up with me coming in every four hours to see you, instead of him."

"I guess I can if I have to." Another little smile.

She's almost cheerful. Must be the lingering effects of the sedative.

"You don't either one have to stay."

I shake my head. "You're not getting rid of me that easily."

She relaxes, seeming satisfied that she asserted her independence, but I think she's glad I'm here. And that fact makes me feel better than it should, probably.

I touch her arm. "I'll be praying for you." It always feels awkward when I say that to either of them—but it's true, and she might as well know it. What's she going to do? Demand I not pray for her?

Her gaze meets mine. "You do that."

Dad slips his arm in mine and pats my hand as we walk back into the empty CCU waiting room. "I hate to leave you here alone."

I slide my other hand over his. "I'll be fine."

The doorknob wiggles, and we both look up. No one has been in here since we got here, but the waiting room is for all family and friends of CCU patients. "I'll be fine," I reiterate, because I'm sure Dad's wondering about leaving me with strangers.

The door opens, and Garrett walks in, clutching a white paper bag and two drinks.

"Hey," he says and pulls me into a loose hug.

"Hey," I whisper. "Thanks for coming."

"Sarah told me you were here. How's your mother?" Although Ami calls my mother "my mom," Garrett never does. I think he understands that our relationship is more formal, more rigid. Semantics, I know, but it makes a difference.

"She's better, but they'll keep her in CCU overnight."

He sets the food down, reaches behind me, and shakes my dad's hand. "Mr. Harrington."

"Garrett. Good to see you."

"Dad's going home to get some sleep." I give Dad a kiss on the cheek. "See you in the morning."

He nods and looks at Garrett. "You going to stay with her for a while?"

"I'm here for the duration unless she kicks me out."

"You be sure and behave so she doesn't have to."

Garrett chuckles. "Yes, sir."

I cringe. Does Dad think we're going to make out in the CCU waiting room? I guess he's just being fatherly.

When he's gone, Garrett holds up the sack. "Did you ever eat?"

"No." I haven't even thought of food. But something smells delicious.

A few minutes later, we're chowing down on chicken Florentine sandwiches.

"After I heard about your mother, I was going to try to make you the sandwiches you missed out on at lunch and bring them to you." He grins. "I asked Ami to help me."

I smile. "Talk about the blind leading the blind."

"Yep, you got it. Thankfully, Mark mentioned that San Francisco Bread Company had them. So I just picked some up before I came over."

"Thanks. They're delicious."

We eat in silence for a few minutes. When we're almost done, Garrett looks at me. "Pretty scary situation with your mother?"

I nod. "It's still touch and go, really. They think the infection is under control now, but it was bad."

"I'm sorry."

"Me, too. But I'm thankful she's doing as well as she is." I wad up my wrapper. "I'm thankful you're here, too."

He takes my wrapper and makes two points in the trash can, then follows with his own two points. "I'm glad I could come."

"You don't have to stay all night, though."

"You did hear me promise your dad I'd behave, right?"

I feel my face redden. "I know my virtue is safe with you. But these couches aren't the softest beds in the world. And at nine, I'm going in to see Mother. And again at one and five. So it won't be a restful night."

He crosses his arms in front of his chest. "You'll have to do better than that if you're going to scare me off."

He's so stubborn. I know better than to argue. I shrug and stare up at the tiny TV in the corner.

"You gonna pout?" he teases. "You look like you used to when I got tired of playing Masters of the Universe."

I blow my straw wrapper at him. "Your He-Man always ran out of energy before my She-Ra."

"You've always been impossible to keep up with." He picks up the wrapper and shoots it into the garbage can.

"Maybe you just haven't tried hard enough."

He shrugs. "That's a possibility, I guess, but not very likely."

I tuck my foot up under me, unsure what to say to that.

He squeezes the cushion. "These couches shouldn't be bad to sleep on."

I guess he really is here for the duration. The thought should irritate me. But it comforts me instead.

When the six o'clock news comes on, I use the remote to turn the volume up. The anchorwoman runs through the news headlines quickly and then says, "And now live from Jingle Bells, Jason Ragsdale reporting on the division in the little town where, according to the sign, the spirit of Christmas lives in their hearts all year long."

I sit up straight and give Garrett a wide-eyed look.

Most of the time, the television stations act like Jingle Bells doesn't exist. But there is Jason Ragsdale standing right in front of Jingle Bells Elementary School. "Teachers report an increased level of tension even among the young children here in Jingle Bells as the moment of reckoning approaches. Now that the name-change decision is on the ballot, tempers are even higher."

"No kidding," I mutter.

"Several citizens have speculated whether things will ever be back to normal in this little town, no matter which way the vote goes."

I glance over at Garrett. "What do you bet Uncle Gus will be on?"

He nods.

"With us now is the mayor of Jingle Bells, Augustus Harding, affectionately known to his constituents as Uncle Gus."

I snort. "Affectionately?"

"Sir, normally you'd think a mayor would be against changing the name of his town, but you're actually for the name change, aren't you?"

"I'm for the people of Jingle Bells. And it makes no difference what the town is—"

I punch the power button on the remote and toss it over beside Garrett. "Sorry. If you want to watch the rest of it, I'll go out."

He shakes his head. "I've seen enough."

I lay my head back and look up at the ceiling. "Why do people act like it's nothing to change the name?"

"Maybe they've just considered what will happen to Jingle Bells if new business doesn't come to town."

I tap the back of my head gently against the wall, then sit up and meet his gaze. "Jingle Bells is about more than just a name. It's about the spirit of Christmas living in our hearts all year long." I wave my hand in the air as if outlining the welcome sign. "You don't have to tell me that sounds corny. I know it. But it's not. When a man and a woman and a little girl can come together for a week in a place so magical that it turns them into a family for that brief time once a year, the sign is true."

"Your gran—"

Tears swim in my eyes. "I know Gran had a lot to do with it. But so did Jingle Bells. Gran's gone. I can't stand it if I lose Jingle Bells, too." I guess the strain of our confrontation at the lake, finding out about Mother's surgery, and seeing the TV segment all add up to too much.

I rush into the restroom and lock the door behind me. Harringtons don't cry. Especially in public. So why are tears streaming down my cheeks?

CHAPTER 25

I lean against the wall for a few minutes, then wash my face and come out. Garrett's gone. I can't blame him. I sit on the couch to wait the three hours until it's time to visit Mother again.

But before I can pick up a magazine, Garrett comes in, arms loaded with pillows and blankets. "Just in case you want to take a nap or anything before bedtime," he says, like my outburst before didn't happen.

"Thanks."

He sets them down on the couch across the room and comes back over to sit beside me. "Here, sport, thought you could use a pick-me-up." He slaps a Heath candy bar gently across my arm. My all-time favorite.

"What would I do without you?" I say the words without thinking about their meaning.

He stares at me, his eyes unreadable. But I can't take the question back. It's too true.

For a split second, we just look at each other, saying so much without speaking.

"Starve?" He gives me a crooked grin.

I release the breath I didn't know I was holding and nod. "Probably so."

We talk about nothing for a while. He entertains me with anecdotes of computer-illiterate people, then laughs when he has to explain the punch lines to me half the time.

I nudge him. "Hey, I know how computers work. I just prefer people over machines."

"I don't know," he drawls. "With computers, if you always put in the same thing, you get the same thing. People are more un-predictable." He half smiles at me. "Some more than others."

"Do you mean me?" My voice squeaks with mock indignation.

"I admit sometimes you react to things differently than I think you will."

"For example?"

He shrugs. "Not to bring up a sore subject, but take this whole name-change thing. I never realized it was the name of the town you loved so much. I thought it was the people. So I figured you'd be for anything that would save the people."

"It's not the name. I mean, it is, partly. But just because of what it represents. Did you remember that Jingle Bells was named over a hundred years ago because a little girl was lost in the snow?" I peel the wrapper off my Heath bar.

"Didn't her mama suggest that the rescue party spread out

and sing 'Jingle Bells'?"

I nod. "It was her favorite. They'd sing a verse, then wait. Finally someone heard a tiny little voice answer with the chorus."

The door opens, and a woman and man walk in. She has an overnight bag on her arm and looks like she's been crying. They glance at us and make their way to the opposite side of the waiting room to a group of couches.

Garrett and I exchange sympathetic looks.

In a minute, he says quietly, "Don't you figure that was just a legend about the little girl? I never thought it really happened."

"I don't know." I keep my voice low, too. "But I do know she's not the only little girl that Jingle Bells saved."

"You?"

"Because of Jingle Bells, Christmas came to represent more to me than a day the world set aside to celebrate Christ's birth. It was a time I felt like my parents loved me and knew I was alive. To me, it means love and family."

His eyes are dark and hooded.

I'm an insensitive clod. "I'm sorry, Garrett. I know Christmas isn't the best time for you."

He looks away from the pity I'm sure is in my eyes. "It was more than just that first Christmas he left. Every year after that, Dad would call and say he'd be there Christmas Day with presents. Beth always got so excited."

I reach over and slip my hand into his. He still doesn't look at me, but he doesn't pull away. "He never came. Sometimes he'd make an appearance a week or two later, with some excuse about how he'd forgotten our gifts and would mail them to us. Most of the time he never showed at all."

"I'm sorry."

He squeezes my hand. "It's okay." He nods toward the man and woman across the room who have their backs to us but are sitting apart from each other, staring straight ahead without talking. "Most people have been through worse than that."

Maybe so. But hurt is hurt. I have a hard time understanding people like Mr. Mitchell. "Do you still hate him?"

He shakes his head. "He did what he did out of weakness."

"So you've forgiven him?" I don't know why I'm pushing it, but I have to know.

"Yeah. I have. When you feel that sorry for someone, it's hard to hold a grudge against him."

I think of my mother, lying in a hospital bed, fighting for her life. Of course I love her. She's my mother. But do I forgive her? I know I should.

We spend the next half hour reading in companionable silence. I look up when the waiting room phone rings. The woman on the couch jumps to grab it. She speaks into the phone, then turns to me. "Harrington?"

My stomach lurches, but I stand and take the phone from her.

"This is Jeanine, your mother's nurse. I was just calling to give you an update."

"Yes?" I keep my voice level.

"Everything's about the same. Based on her latest blood work, the antibiotics seem to be working. She's resting comfortably. You'll be able to see her for a few minutes at nine."

"Okay. Thank you." My knees are weak as I hang up.

"Something wrong?" Garrett asks.

I relax back against the couch cushion. "No. Everything's fine. But they need to seriously reconsider that policy. I mean, it's nice to call, but it would have been nicer if I'd known they were going to."

"Yeah. They probably told your dad."

I slap my forehead lightly and run my hand across my face. "Of course. I'm sorry. I'm not thinking clearly."

"You've been under a lot of stress."

I put my hand on his. "You've always made excuses for me. I remember I used to get in trouble with Gran and you'd take the blame."

He gives me a rueful grin. "Your memory of me is distorted. I wasn't perfect. And I'm sure not, now." He says the last under his breath.

"Don't you go getting the bighead. I never said you were perfect." Even as I say it in my best teasing tone, my heart slams against my rib cage. Because in my book, he's pretty close.

My phone rings. It's Ami, checking on Mother. We chat for a while, and Garrett gets up to stretch his legs. While we're talking, I notice him in conversation with the couple across the room. He sits down with them, apparently at their invitation. Dad beeps in, and I hang up with Ami to take his call. While I fill him in on what the nurse said, Garrett walks back over. The man and woman are sitting closer together, talking quietly.

"Bye, Dad. Sleep well."

"Thanks, Kristianna. I'll try."

"I love you," I say softly. If he doesn't say it back, that's okay. But I'm not going to take a chance that he doesn't know.

"Yes, um. . .you, too. Good night."

I smile as I hang up.

"Maybe this will be good for you and your parents," Garrett says.

"Maybe."

At nine, he offers to go in with me to see Mother. I let him off the hook.

"Yeah, no use straining her to be polite to me." His lopsided grin lets me know he isn't too offended.

She's asleep when I get in there, but I sit by her bed for a few minutes. Her face looks so peaceful. I pick up the thread of prayer I've had going silently ever since Dad told me she was sick. She shifts and grimaces. I wince. My prayer changes.

Lord, please help me to forgive her. Help me to love her like You do.

I'm still praying when Jeanine sticks her head in. "You can wake her if you want to. She's been asleep for a while."

I shake my head. Actually we get along better like this. "She needs her rest. I'll be back at one."

When I get back to the CCU waiting room, Garrett has food waiting.

"Grilled chicken salad with ranch."

"Thanks." I glance over at the couple across the room. Their food is from the same drive-through as ours. Not a coincidence, I'm sure. But I don't mention it. I remember when we were about fourteen and Ami and I found out Garrett was giving the money he got from selling aluminum cans to old Mrs. Wheeler. When we asked him about it, he stammered some excuse about her making pies for him. After that, we pegged him as a secret do-gooder.

He hasn't changed much.

While I clean up from our meal, he spreads the blankets and pillows on two couches in our area. "You go to bed this early?" I ask jokingly.

"No, but I thought you might want to rest before the one o'clock visit. I'll wake you if you do."

"Thanks. I might stretch out for a while. But you don't have to stay up. I can set my phone alarm."

"Shush, sport, and go to sleep. I've got your back."

Truer words were never spoken, I think as I drift off to sleep.

Sometime later, I wake, and Garrett's sitting on his couch, looking at a sports magazine. "Go back to sleep, sport."

He'll make a good dad. I roll over and don't wake again until Garrett shakes me gently. "It's time."

I slip into the restroom and wash my face. When I come back out, Garrett's standing there waiting. He gives me a quick hug and drops a kiss on the top of my head. "My offer's still open if you want me to go with you."

"No, thanks. Now it's your turn to sleep."

Inside Mother's cubicle, she's wide awake. Her face is pinker, and she looks more like herself.

"I thought you were never coming." Her words are still a little slurred.

I glance at the clock at the foot of her bed. It's 1:05.

Sigh. Sometimes I mess up without even meaning to. "Sorry. I had to wash my face."

Her expression softens. "You were asleep, of course. I'm sorry."

I really can't remember her ever apologizing to me for anything. "No problem."

"You're so much like your gran."

From anyone else, I'd take that as a high compliment, but from her, I know it's not. "Maybe that's because I was with her so much."

I flinch after I say it. Now is not the time to open this Pandora's box.

"She did a good job of raising you."

"Mom," I say softly, "let's not do this here." I glance at the wires running from her. "I'd hate to get kicked out for making your blood pressure go up."

She shakes her head, and it rustles against the crisp white pillowcase. "I meant it."

"Okay."

"Your dad and I didn't realize you'd grow up so fast. We thought we'd just leave you with your grandmother for a while so we could establish our practice." She grimaces. I'm not sure if the pain's physical or emotional. For all I know, this could be the meds talking. "If you ever have kids, don't blink or they'll be grown before you know it, visiting you in the hospital. Or in the old folks' home."

Okay, definitely the meds are making her maudlin. Still, I can't stop the peace that washes over me. Maybe she didn't leave me with Gran all the time because she couldn't stand to be around me. "You're a far cry from a nursing home, Mother."

"She always made me feel less."

"What?" As soon as I ask, I realize what she means.

"Your grandmother. She always made me feel like I was less than enough. Less than worthy."

I can't even imagine. To me, Gran was the most loving woman who ever walked the earth. But that does explain a lot of Mother's resentment toward her. And I'm finally realizing that, as unbelievable as it sounds, she was jealous of my and Gran's relationship. "Not worthy? Of Dad?"

"Just in general."

I can't remember the last time she opened up to me. Maybe I should see if she can take this drug at home. . . .

"You're so much like her."

Maybe not. I was kidding anyway, of course. "*I* make you feel less than worthy?" This from a woman who tells me constantly in every way that I'm not good enough to be her daughter?

"Is Jared here?"

I sit for a second, without speaking. I'm glad she changed the subject, because now is not the time; I know she's not herself, but I'm flabbergasted. "He's at home resting, remember? I stayed here."

"Alone?"

Why didn't I just sleep through this visit? "Garrett Mitchell's staying in the waiting room with me."

"All night?"

"Yes. There are other people in there, too."

She nods. "Well, at least you're with someone you know."

Jeanine sticks her head in the door. "Time's up."

I lean in and kiss Mother's forehead. She grabs my wrist. "Thank you for being here."

"I wouldn't be anywhere else."

She releases me. "Get some rest."

"You, too."

I stop at the nurses' station and wait for Jeanine. "She was talking oddly. Is that normal?"

"Perfectly normal. She's just disoriented. By morning, she'll be back to herself."

"Okay." With that reassurance—and I use the term loosely—I make my way back to the waiting room.

The lights are as low as they'll go but are still plenty bright enough to see by. The couple is asleep, and Garrett is stretched out on his couch, eyes closed and mouth slightly open. He sleeps cute.

I pull the blanket up over him, even though he's completely dressed. It's chilly in here.

His eyes pop open. "Hmm?"

"Nothing. Go back to sleep."

He obeys instantly.

I snag a Gideons Bible from the end table, sit on the other couch, and pull the blanket up over my legs. I'm reading through the Psalms this spring, so I flip over and read for a while, then close the cover and stretch out.

Oops. Forgot to set my phone alarm for five. I sit up and do that quickly, then snuggle down again and say a silent prayer.

I lie in the dim light, listening to Garrett's even breathing, and stare at the ceiling. I can't quit thinking about what my mother said about Gran—and consequently me—making her feel unworthy. I may be overly optimistic, but what if her own sinful life is causing her to feel that way? When I remember things she said about Gran after her funeral, I realize that every one of them could have come from this same root emotion.

My alarm wakes me, and I shut it off before Garrett wakes. I glance over to see if I woke the couple, but they're walking out the door, apparently to visit their own CCU patient. I wash my face hurriedly and rush to Mother's bedside, just in case she's watching the clock. But no, this morning, she's sleeping peacefully.

I sit by her bed and pray some, but mostly I think. Things between us will probably never be what you would call normal. And I don't even expect her to stop making my life miserable. But

I understand her better than I did before this. And that makes her easier to take. At least for now.

Before I leave, I lean over and kiss her cheek. She barely stirs. I stand for a minute and look down on her, so calm and relaxed. "I forgive you," I whisper. And I really do.

I leave and bump into Dad right outside the curtains, looking rested and ready to take on the world in his crisp suit and red tie.

"Hey, kiddo." How many years has it been since he called me that? I can't remember the last time.

"Good morning, Dad."

His eyes widen. "Everything okay?"

"Sure. Why?"

He reaches his hand up and touches my cheek.

I realize my face is damp with tears. "Yeah, just putting some old hurts to rest."

He nods. "You're a good girl."

I shrug. "God's a good God."

He opens his mouth, then shuts it, then opens it again. "I'd better get in here to see her. Even if she's asleep, I can tell her I'm here."

"Yeah. I'll see you in the waiting room."

CHAPTER 26

I'm getting in my car after church when Garrett waves me down. I lower my window as he lopes across the parking lot. He leans on my open window frame and peers in. "Hey, glad I caught you. How's your mother? Have you talked to your dad since five?"

"No, I'm heading back over there now." I glance at my dashboard clock. "I should make it for the one o'clock visit. Or even better, they may have her in a room."

"The reason I stopped you is"—he shifts from one foot to the other—"I'm flying out to California for a while."

"Today?"

He nods. "Unless you think you'll need me."

"No, I don't need you. Do you want Shadow to stay with me?" I like the dog, and right now, I'd probably welcome the company—but going back and forth to the hospital might make it difficult.

"Nah, you've got your hands full. Mark and Ami said they'd keep him. But thanks."

"You're welcome." Gran always said I needed to learn to wait on the Lord. And I try. I really do. But I'm not so great at it. "When are we going to finish the conversation we started yesterday at the lake?"

His eyebrows draw together. "I need to take care of a couple of things before we have that conversation."

"In California?"

"Yep."

Okay, now I'm nervous. Is some leggy beach babe waiting, just looking for one more chance?

He leans in and loops his arm around my neck. "See you, sport. Take care."

"You, too," I say as he jogs back over to his truck.

The next Saturday, I'm working in the shop when Mother calls me. Since she's home and not back to work yet, she calls frequently to tell me exactly how I need to fix my life. Too much time on her hands, if you ask me.

She jumps right in without a hello. "You know, you'd think if I wanted to know things about my own daughter that I wouldn't have to read them in the newspaper."

"What are you talking about?"

"*The Jingle Bells Journal.* Your dad insisted we subscribe to it so we could keep up with what goes on in that little town of yours. And it's a good thing."

"Really?" I'm flipping through a catalog from one of my suppliers.

"Yes. If we hadn't, I don't suppose you would have ever told us about your friend."

What is she rambling about? I brought the paper in but haven't opened it yet.

"Now I'm glad you finally got together with him."

"Got together with who?"

"Garrett, of course. Do you have any idea what he's worth?"

I frown. "Are you taking more medicine than you're supposed to?"

"Very funny. Trying to distract me."

I lean over and snag the paper from the far side of the counter and flip open the front page. My eyes scan the headlines, looking for anything she could be talking about. I don't have to look far. Front and center in big bold letters: LOCAL MAN OWNER OF SUMMER VALLEY CORPORATION. I quickly read the article:

> In a surprise twist to the ongoing hostilities regarding the name change in Jingle Bells, Arkansas, our investigation revealed that the owner of the Summer Valley Outdoors Corporation is none other than Jingle Bells resident, Garrett Mitchell. Mitchell founded the e-company three years ago in Lakeland, California.

The paper falls from my hand, and I slide to the floor, still sitting. "Mother, I've got to go." She's still talking when I hang up, but I can't talk another second. My stomach clenches, and I pull my knees up toward me. "Stay calm," I mutter. Jack Feeney gets things so messed up. This is the same man who called me a runaway bride. And I know Garrett. He wouldn't hurt me for anything, much less do something to destroy me. This has to be a mistake.

I grab my cell phone from my pocket and hit his number. He'll laugh, but I have to hear him tell me how wrong this is.

"Hello?" His voice is like it always is—like it always has been—reassuring.

"Garrett." I swallow, my throat suddenly sore and achy. "It's me."

"Kristianna, what's wrong?"

"The paper—it says. . ." I can't even get the words out because they're so ridiculous. I half laugh, half sob. "It claims that you. . .you own Summer Valley Outdoors."

"Oh no."

"I know!" My voice squeaks, but I can't help it. "Crazy, huh?"

"You have no idea."

Relief eases the knot in my stomach.

"Oh sport, I wish I were there. I'm in the middle of meetings I can't leave."

"I'm okay. It's okay. They'll print a retraction."

He continues as if I didn't speak. "If I were there, I could make you understand. When I started my online business, it was tiny. Then it grew. And I wanted to expand, but I had to have invest—"

Most of his words form an indistinct blur, except the first ones. "What business?"

265

He clears his throat. "In order to open a—"

"What business?" I repeat, squeaking again.

When he speaks, I can barely hear him, but I do. "Summer Valley Outdoors."

Struggling to breathe, I hit the red END button and set the phone on the floor. I hear it ringing again, but it sounds very far away.

I wrap my arms around my knees and struggle to think, but every time I get to my conversation with Garrett, I stop. I don't know how long I sit there. The ringing quits for a while, but then starts again and seems to go on forever.

Finally, the doorbell chimes over the ringing phone. I don't move. If they're customers, maybe they'll wander back to Sarah's Quilting Corner and visit with her. Or leave. I don't really care what they do as long as they don't bother me. I put my head down on my knees and try to be invisible.

But the footsteps *click-clack* on the hardwood floor and make an unerring path around the counter to me.

"Hey, sweetie," Ami says in the tone she'd use for a hurt child on the playground. "Let's get you upstairs."

I look up at her. Tears are wet on her cheeks.

"You know?"

She nods and tugs me gently to my feet. "C'mon, we'll talk upstairs."

I allow her to guide me up to my apartment. When we get through the door, she hands me my still-ringing phone. Anger surges through me. I throw it across the room with all my might.

It lands on the sofa, harmlessly. Ineffectually. Just like my puny efforts to save the town. A sob catches in my throat. "I won't let him do this."

"He already has," Ami says quietly.

I spin around. "The election isn't for another three days. It's not over until then."

"I meant what he's done to your heart."

I take a deep breath and shake my head. "I'm not going to think about that. I can't."

She snorts. "Like you can keep from doing it."

Too true. "My best friend, the only man I've ever really loved, is the enemy, prepared to destroy the town I cherish. When did my life become a B movie?"

"Your life's not a B movie. It's a blockbuster. Maybe even an Oscar winner. And I want a young Meg Ryan to play me."

"How are we going to de-age Meg Ryan?"

She shrugs. "Don't try to confuse me with reality." She guides me into the kitchen and puts me in a chair. "I'm going to fix some coffee. Then we'll figure this mess out."

I raise my hand. "And after that we'll banish world hunger and do away with war."

She looks back over her shoulder. "That's the spirit."

"That was sarcasm."

"I know. See? You're almost back to normal."

I don't say it, but the truth is, normal has never seemed further away.

The gifts and the notes. I sit straight up in the bed and peer at the bedside clock. It's only 2:00 a.m. The anonymous gifts and notes were from Garrett, not Shawn. I'm sure of it.

I throw back the quilt and snatch my robe from the bedpost. I wrap it around me as I take the stairs two at a time. I saved all the "Summer Valley" gifts and notes behind the counter. I flip on the overhead light and squat down to pull them out. First the basket with the beach towel, flip-flops, suntan lotion, and of course the books. Books that Garrett would know I wanted to read, since I'm sure I mentioned the titles in front of him numerous times. I pick up the note.

> *Kristianna,*
>
> *If Jingle Bells dies with its name intact, is that a victory? Sometimes our hearts can't see clearly what is right before us. If you could open your mind to change, you might be amazed by the view.*

I plop all the way down on the floor, cross-legged. "Hearts can't see clearly. . . ." I thought my heart finally was seeing clearly. But apparently I missed the part where he stabbed me in the back.

Tears fill my eyes as I pull out the beach bag with my name woven on the front in red. I pull out the snorkel mask, the pearl-and-diamond earrings, and then the mother-of-pearl jewelry box. "Love Me Tender." I flip open the note.

*Praying for you to have a Jingle Bells Christmas filled
with love, happiness, and especially peace. Relax. The battle
can wait.*

The battle waited, all right. And I waited until I'd almost lost
before I realized who my enemy was. Filled with righteous indignation,
I shove the beach bag items over to the side and stare at the big box
I know holds that gorgeous sand castle. I have that note memorized.

*Dreams are the glue that hold sand castles together. You
can hold on to your dreams no matter how much your world
ends up being changed by the tide.*

That arrogant man. I'll show him that he's not nearly as strong
as the tide.

I sit on the floor for a while, then slowly trudge up the stairs
and to bed. Anger doesn't do much for inducing sleep.

"Are you sleeping any?" Ami asks as she ladles soup into a bowl and
plops it in front of me. Her mother is a huge believer in the healing
properties of chicken noodle soup, but since Ami can't cook, she
showed up at my door with two red-and-white-labeled cans.

"Some."

"Some. How long will you keep going like this? By election
time, you won't even be able to vote."

"I have a few days to get rested up."

"You know, maybe if you would answer your phone, Garrett could ex—"

"Ames,"—I take a sip of my soup, because I know she won't be satisfied until I do—"I'm glad you made peace with Garrett." *In spite of his backstabbing, two-faced, lily-livered behavior.* "And I promise I'll never put you in the middle or try to make you choose sides. But in return, you agreed. . . We—cannot—talk—about—him. Okay?"

She sighs. "Okay. Did you know your parents are hiring Shawn? We can still talk about Shawn, can't we?"

"I did not know that. But I'm glad. And yes, we can talk about everything. Except Garrett."

"Gotcha." She hugs me. "Well, in that case, I've got to get home and feed He-Who-Shall-Not-Be-Named's dog."

"You *are* going to take that act on the stage, aren't you, funny girl?"

"Only if you'll be my straight man." She gives me a quick hug and lets herself out.

After she leaves, I run my finger down the Scotch-taped list on the workshop wall and punch in Uncle Gus's cell phone number. He answers on the first ring.

"This is Kristianna. I understand the latest polls show the town is dead-even split on the name-change issue."

"Yes, ma'am, that's what I hear, too."

"You'd probably like to change that just as much as I would."

Only in the opposite direction. "What if we have a town meeting Monday night and give everyone a chance to share his or her views? Sort of an open forum."

"Well, now. We've never done anything like that."

"Look at it this way. If you're as good as you think you are at speaking, you might convince Scott and me. Then we can have a unanimous council vote and not have to mess with that part of the ballot Tuesday."

"Now that you mention it, this open forum might be a good idea."

"You can give a talk, and I'll speak for Jingle Bells."

"For the name, you mean."

"That's right. For Jingle Bells." I know it sticks in his craw for me to say that since he's the mayor, but hey, the truth hurts. "I'll go first, then you. Then whoever wants to can follow."

"We'll have it at the high school auditorium. The last town council meeting, we barely fit everyone into the city hall."

"Sounds good. See you there."

CHAPTER 27

The next night, I enter the high school auditorium with Mark and Ami. They slide into seats near the back, while I head toward the front. Someone, probably Uncle Gus, has set up microphones on a long table in front of the council members' chairs. I'll say this, he was right to move it to the auditorium. We're way beyond the maximum capacity for city hall. Looks like half the town is here. At least he put us on floor level and not up on the stage.

My stomach swirls. I'm not a speech maker. I'd rather get a root canal. But someone needs to remind these people that there are other businesses in the world that won't make us change the town name. And other ways to bring in tourists. We just need to find them. And we will.

Uncle Gus and Dottie are talking at the end of the table, and John Stone and Scott are already seated.

"Hi, Kristianna," Mrs. Stewart calls. "We're voting for Jingle Bells." She holds up a sign that says JINGLE ALL THE WAY, with the word BELLS inserted with an arrow between the JINGLE and the ALL.

Mr. Stewart gives me a thumbs-up.

I smile at them, and they kiss each other, then smile back.

I see Shawn a little farther over, and oh my goodness, Lila is sitting with him. I raise my hand, and they both wave.

Birdie calls to me. "Count me undecided, sweetie. But I love you anyway."

Beside her, Sergeant Montrose nods, so I guess he's undecided, too. Or he loves me anyway, too. Either way, I need to talk to them after the meeting if my speech doesn't change their minds.

Jack Feeney flips through his notebook as I pass by. He did me a favor, I guess, by exposing Garrett, but sometimes it's hard not to fall back into that old "shoot the messenger" mentality.

I'm almost to the front when an unnatural hush falls over the crowd. I glance up to see if Uncle Gus is getting ready to call the meeting to order, but everyone is looking toward me. No, they're looking past me.

I turn around, and Garrett is right behind me. "I need to talk to you privately." He looks like he hasn't slept in a week.

I force down the sympathy that automatically comes. No rest for the wicked, I guess. I step back and glare at him. "I have nothing to say to someone who would betray not just me, but the whole town." I don't yell exactly, but I don't whisper, either. After all, isn't it better for Summer Valley supporters to know what he's like, before they vote?

"Betray you? I was trying to save you."

"Save me?" I glance over at Brenda and Renee, our Valentine's Day hairstylists, who happen to be sitting right beside where Garrett and I are standing. "Beware of a man who wants to save you. Usually there's an ulterior motive."

Garrett frowns. "My ulterior motive was keeping this town from going the way of a thousand other towns across the country."

"Oh my goodness. Stand here in front of me and act like a martyr, why don't you? And the fact that you stood to make megabucks never crossed your mind?"

"You tell him, sister," Elva Campbell hollers from behind me.

His face flushes. "I didn't have to open the business here. I still don't have to. I could have gone thirty minutes down the road and found a town that'd change its name in a heartbeat. Without this hassle."

He's right. Which makes it worse. "Why didn't you?"

"Because you're not the only person who cares about this town and these people. I was born and raised here. When I had a chance at success, it only seemed right to share it with the town."

"And we're grateful," says Billy Farmer from behind Garrett.

"You got that right," someone else calls.

"Go mess with somebody else's town," a voice pipes up from the back.

"Excuse me." Uncle Gus's voice echoes over the loudspeaker. "We need to call this meeting to order."

I spin around and bump into Jack Feeney, who must have

274

sneaked around behind me to hear better. He's writing frantically in his notebook. I brush past him and make my way to my seat.

Garrett approaches the table and whispers something to Uncle Gus, then takes a seat in the front row in my direct line of vision.

I narrow my eyes and look over his head.

The mayor pulls the mike toward him. "Because the town seems to be squarely split on the name-change issue and we're going to the polls tomorrow, it was our intention to allow people to speak their minds tonight. However—"

There is no way he's going to get out of this.

"However, as many of you know, one of our own, Garrett Mitchell, is the owner of Summer Valley Outdoors."

The crowd goes wild in an alarming mix of boos and cheers. Uncle Gus slams his hand on the table three times. The sound reverberates through the sound system, and the noise dies down.

"Garrett has, just minutes ago, returned from a trip to California, where he's been meeting with his investors. He's going to report on that now. I feel positive there will be no need for speeches after he's done. So with no further ado, I'd like to turn the floor over to Garrett Mitchell."

Garrett stands with his chart.

I jump up. "If I'd known this was just another chance for you to shove your propaganda down our throats, I wouldn't have come." I point at Uncle Gus. "You promised that we'd all have a chance to talk."

He rolls his eyes. "When do you ever wait for a chance to talk?"

Garrett stops in front of me. "Kristianna, let me do this. Then you can talk if you want to."

"Why should you go first?" I can hear my words booming through the auditorium, but I don't care. If I set aside my anger, then nothing is left but the hurt. And I won't go there.

"You're not being logical."

"I have a right to stand up for what I believe whether it's logical to you or not."

"You're just saying that because she's a woman," calls Angel from the front row. "You wouldn't call a man illogical."

"Let him talk," a man calls out. "Find out what he has to say."

"Yeah, let's hear him." The cries for hearing Garrett out come from all corners of the room. I even see Sam, looking sober and interested, watching from the front row.

I put my hands on my hips. "Fine. But when you finish, I'm going to tell you what I think."

He smiles at me. Smiles. Not a smarmy, smirky smile. But the regular old everything's-going-to-be-okay smile. The one I've trusted my whole life. "I'm counting on it."

I take a deep breath and purse my lips. "Go ahead."

Still carrying his chart or whatever, he walks up the steps behind us to the stage microphone. The other town council members turn their chairs toward him. I consider not moving, but as bad as I hate to admit it, I want to see his face.

He clears his throat. "As the paper reported"—he nods to Jack Feeney—"a few months after I moved to California, I started a small online sporting goods business called Summer Valley Outdoors. After a couple of years, I was ready to find investors and open my first store."

"Spare us the history lesson," I mutter.

Uncle Gus glares my way, but Garrett ignores me.

"I'd heard that Jingle Bells was suffering after the distribution center left. Bringing the store here seemed like the perfect idea. But then, one of my two investors had a market survey done, and as you know, it showed that if the town around the store was called Summer Valley, the store would be more popular." He shrugs. "Something about a village feel. It wasn't what I wanted, but I felt it was the lesser of two evils for Jingle Bells. The other option being not putting the store here."

A few murmurs come from the crowd. At least one "Oh no." And a "Good option." So they're still split, but the yelling doesn't resume. He definitely has control of his audience. Beneath my fury and the hurt, a twinge of pride lurks. He's come a long way from humble beginnings. If only he hadn't turned into a rat fink.

"However, last week, someone pointed out to me that Jingle Bells is more than just a name. Just like all of you, I've read the sign. I knew it was the town where the spirit of Christmas lives in our hearts all year long. But I'd forgotten how the name came to be. How a little girl was lost, but an entire town banded together to find her, willing to sing a nonsensical song in the cold, all night long, if that's what it took to do it. That same attitude is here today. You're willing to do whatever it takes to help one another."

He holds up his chart, or whatever it is, and removes a blank sheet of poster board from the front of it. He lifts up the remaining board for everyone to see. It's a rough sketch of our welcome sign. Only it says WELCOME TO THE TWIN CITIES—JINGLE BELLS AND SUMMER VALLEY—WHERE THE SPIRIT OF CHRISTMAS WARMS OUR HEARTS ALL YEAR LONG.

Oh boy. I remember what Woody Feezor told us at our first committee meeting when this idea came up. I raise my hand. "How is that going to help Jingle Bells? If you incorporate the area around the lake as the town of Summer Valley, we won't get any of the taxes from the new business," I say into the mike. People need to think this through before they get their hopes up.

"Good question," Garrett says, beaming at me like I just congratulated him on his plan. "Normally, that's right. However, if the town council votes on it, Summer Valley can be an annex of Jingle Bells with all taxes and revenue to remain under Jingle Bells' authority. Our investors are willing to agree with this, if your town council is."

Oh. Well, then. Scott nudges me. "That would work."

"Are you sure?" I whisper.

He nods.

Call me suspicious. I'm still looking for the catch. "Why didn't you do this in the first place?"

He gives a self-deprecatory laugh. "I don't know. I guess I didn't think of it until I was properly motivated."

What does he mean? Is he getting some extra kickback? "What motivated you now?"

"You."

Driven by anger and a sense of injustice, I've had no qualms about speaking out, but now that he's talking to me personally and not the audience as a whole, I'm suddenly aware that we're having a private conversation in front of half the town. "Me?" I squeak.

He nods. "I didn't mean to 'betray you.' I'm sorry. In the beginning, the fact that I owned Summer Valley was going to be a surprise. A pleasant one, I thought. Then I realized how strongly you felt about the name change, and I couldn't figure out how to tell you. Will you forgive me?"

All the anger washes away like pollen after a spring rain. I can see how this whole crazy mess happened. If I'd listened to him earlier and not been so close minded, maybe we wouldn't be having a public showdown. "Yes."

"Good." Garrett sets the sign down and again turns his attention to the audience. "Since I was old enough to notice there was an opposite sex, I've loved one girl. Most of you know she's led me on a merry chase. But I've let her get away twice because I was too slow to speak. I hope you'll all forgive me for making a public spectacle of myself, but I don't want to make the same mistake again."

Still on the stage, he gets down on one knee.

In front of me.

I can't breathe.

"Kristianna Harrington, whether we live in Jingle Bells or Timbuktu, I love you with all my heart. Will you marry me?"

I stare, mesmerized, at his twinkling green eyes. All I can do is nod.

"Now's no time to go speechless, girl," Dottie yells from the end of the table.

Uncle Gus sticks the mike in front of my face.

"Yes," I croak.

Garrett jumps down off the stage and takes me in his arms. With no mistletoe above us, he seals our deal with a tender kiss that's impossible to misunderstand.

The crowd goes wild.

EPILOGUE

In honor of my upcoming nuptials, I close the store at noon. As I flip over the CLOSED sign, I glance out at Jingle Bells. My town, safe and sound. I sit down with a hot cup of coffee and flip absently through a Chadwick's catalog. When I turn the last page, I glance around the shop. What will I do with the rest of the day? Maybe I'll take Ami's advice and have a short nap, followed by a nice long bubble bath.

As I head upstairs for some prewedding pampering, my phone rings. I snatch it from my pocket. "Hello."

"Hi, Miss Bride-to-be!" I'm not at all surprised to hear Ami's voice on the other end. "How's your wedding day so far?"

I grin at the excitement in her voice. "Silly. It's just like any other day. You know we're not making a big deal of it."

"It doesn't matter if you're just getting married in the preacher's office. It's still your wedding day. Is it okay if I bring lunch over? A girl has to eat, even a soon-to-be-married one."

"How about in a couple of hours? I just ate a late breakfast. So-o. . .I'm heading upstairs for the power nap and bubble bath *someone* recommended."

She giggles. "See you at two thirty or three."

I don't know if everyone showers after a bubble bath, but I do. Otherwise, I feel like a soapy mess. I'm barely out of the shower and dressed when Ami knocks. "Come in."

She pops in, sets a duffel bag down, and waves a takeout container from Buon Natale.

"Mmm. . .my favorite."

She grins. "I know. It's your day."

While we're eating, Garrett text messages me. We decided to go one step further and not even talk to each other today, but apparently he decided text messages are exempt. I'm glad.

I hit the READ button on my cell phone and frown.

"What's wrong?" Ami asks.

"Something's come up. The preacher isn't going to be able to do the ceremony until eight."

"Bummer. You'll have to wait an extra hour to be united with your true love." She puts on her best Billy Crystal voice. "Love. Twoo love."

I laugh and swat at her with my napkin. "You've watched *The Princess Bride* too many times."

She shakes her head. "Not possible."

"Twoo, I mean true."

When we finish eating, she grabs her duffel bag. "Since you guys decided you didn't want to take the time to plan a real wedding, I wanted to do a few traditional things." She begins pulling makeup and hair products from her bag.

I smile. "I love your enthusiasm. But you don't have to feel sorry for me. Garrett wanted to wait and give me a big Christmas wedding."

"I know," Ami says. "And after you teased me about not being able to wait to marry Mark, you're the one who wanted to elope."

I shrug. "It's amazing how being in love shifts priorities. I'd rather have today with Garrett than a thousand Christmas weddings with someone else. We've waited long enough to be together. Simple is the name of the game today."

"And that has nothing to do with you being scared to walk down the aisle, right?"

I motion with my finger across the left side of my chest. "Cross my heart." No fear.

"I believe you."

After I clean up from lunch, I give in and allow Ami to be my stylist for the day. She won't let me look until she's finished. Much later, she spins my desk chair around to let me see the results in the mirror.

I'm stunned. I look very bridelike. "Don't you think this might be a little overboard for the preacher's office?" I stick a finger in one of the cascading curls coming down from a not too "done" updo. "It's gorgeous, but I'm just going to be wearing that off-white dress we found on clearance, nothing fancy."

"Garrett will love it." She grins at me in the mirror.

"He did say he liked my hair up when we went to the Peabody on Valentine's."

She's too busy "making me up" to respond. She sweeps my cheek one last time with the blush brush. "Perfect. Now I've got to go get ready. You don't want your witness wearing yoga pants and a ponytail, do you?"

She slips out the door, and while I'm trying to decide whether to keep the new look and take a chance on looking really foolish, I hear a knock downstairs. "We're closed," I mutter, but I go anyway.

I make it to the door, and the teenage delivery boy who brought all the Summer Valley gifts is standing patiently waiting. I open the door, and he holds out a beautifully wrapped box. I laugh aloud at the candy-cane paper. I don't even have to ask who this is from. He disappears quickly just like he always does.

I rush inside, tear open the paper, and lift the lid. What in the world? A gorgeous white wedding gown. In my size. With shoes to match. Again in my size. I open the card.

Can't wait to see you in this. Someone will pick you up at 7:30 sharp.

I look at the clock in disbelief. Forty-five minutes. I have forty-five minutes to get completely ready. My hair, done. My makeup, done. I murmur a prayer of thanks for Ami.

I slip the dress on, amazed. It looks exactly like something I

284

would have picked out—but nothing like the two I sold on eBay—and it fits like it was made for me. The shoes are perfect. In the bottom of the box is a smaller box. A diamond-and-pearl necklace that will go beautifully with the earrings I already have.

A few minutes later, I feel like Cinderella as I turn in front of my full-length mirror. The updo completes the look. Ami must have known about this surprise. I try to picture the look on Brother Tom's face when I walk into his office looking like this. Can you say overdressed? But happy.

I make my way carefully down the stairs to wait for my ride. I'm turning out the lights when I hear a jingling noise in the distance. At first I think I'm imagining it, but there it is again. *Jingle, jingle.* Curiosity nudges me out the door. My eyes widen as two beautiful white horses *clip-clop* to a stop. Behind them is a sleigh. Eighty degrees in the shade and I'm pretty sure there are wheels at the bottom, but it's definitely a sleigh.

Tears edge the corners of my eyes. Garrett has given me a little piece of my dream Christmas wedding. And even though I was happy with wearing my clearance dress and driving to the preacher's office, I love him for it.

"Miss Kristianna, you've never looked lovelier," Sam says as he takes my hand and helps me into the carriage.

"Thank you, Sam. You look nice, too." He looks sober and happy. Just one more thing to make the day perfect.

Once I'm seated, he slowly eases away from the curb. We're going slowly enough that my hair doesn't blow. As we jingle our way through the streets, there are hardly any people out. Here I am, in a gorgeous dress and a horse-drawn sleigh, and there's no one to see, no one to wave to. Oh well, they probably all ran to hide from the crazy woman on a sleigh ride in June.

I lean up. "Sam, the church is the other way."

He just laughs. "Just sit tight and enjoy the ride."

Before I can say anything else, he turns. The daylight is just beginning to fade away, and I can see a glow coming from up ahead. From. . .the mayor's house. As we get closer, I see them. Strings and strings of Christmas lights. We pull up in front of the beautiful mansion, and my dad is waiting. In a tux. And Ami's beside him. In a beautiful green bridesmaid's dress, clutching two red rose bouquets.

I've died and gone to Christmas wedding heaven.

I blink the tears away and allow Dad to help me out of the carriage.

Ami smiles at me. "Welcome to your dream wedding." She hugs me tightly and hands me the bigger bouquet.

I turn around and try to take it all in. Christmas lights on all the trees and candy canes all along the sidewalk leading up to the house. Everyone in town, it seems like, is in a folding chair on Uncle Gus's lawn. I bet Mrs. Harding loves that. Behind the house, I can just make out the edge of a tent, all lit up. Even a reception.

Before I can say anything, the music begins to play. Ami starts slowly down the sidewalk toward the porch. The front door of the house opens, and Brother Tom walks out, followed by Mark.

Last, but certainly not least, comes Garrett. My precious, amazing Garrett.

"Are you ready?" Dad asks, holding out his arm.

The music changes to the wedding march, and everyone stands. I glance toward the front, and there's Mother. She's clutching a tissue, and though she may try to claim it, I don't believe she's suffering from allergies. Garrett's mom is standing by her, and even though I haven't seen her in years, I can't wait to hug her.

I tuck my hand in Dad's arm and walk slowly down the aisle. But not too slowly. My knees aren't shaking, and I have *no* desire to run anywhere but forward.

Finally, we stop where Garrett waits.

"Who gives this woman to be married?"

"Her mother and I do," Dad says proudly and places my hand in my groom's.

A drop of moisture hits my bare arm. Oh no. Surely it's not going to rain. I look up and gasp. It's snowing.

Garrett smiles at me. "It's a snow machine," he whispers. "Merry Christmas."

I laugh as I gaze into his dancing eyes. Suddenly I remember that Christmas afternoon, sixteen years ago on Snowy Mountain, when a green-eyed boy gave me a pop-top ring and I gave him my heart.

Who knew he'd never let it go?

ABOUT THE AUTHOR

Award-winning novelist Christine Lynxwiler lives with her husband and daughters in a small town nestled in the north Arkansas Ozarks. She has written many books including *Arkansas* and *Promise Me Always*.

When writing *Forever Christmas*, Christine used her own love for both the hometown of her childhood and her current hometown as a pattern for Kristianna's passion for Jingle Bells, but the quirky townspeople are strictly figments of her imagination. When she's not working on her next deadline, you might find Christine kayaking on the nearby river with family, poking around auctions and estate sales with friends, or curled up alone in a quiet corner with a great book.

Besides being a child of the King, her list of blessings include a wonderful husband and two amazing daughters, a large family (including in-laws) who love God and each other, a close group of writer friends, a loving congregation of believers at Ward Street Church of Christ, and readers like you who encourage and support her dream of being a writer. Please visit her Web site at www.christinelynxwiler.com and sign the guestbook to let her know you stopped by!